I0738558

THE ORACLES OF ZION

UNDER
THE
PURPLE SKY

V. C. CHENEY

Signs & Wonders Books

Copyright © 2020 by V. C. Cheney. All rights reserved.
No part of this book may be reproduced, stored in a retrieval system,
or transmitted in any form or by other means--electronic, mechanical, photocopy,
recording, scanning, or otherwise, without the prior written permission of the
publisher.

All inquiries should be addressed to: administrator@vccheney.com

Published by Signs & Wonders Books
PO Box 19737 , 2875 Ashton Road
Sarasota, FL 34276
www.vccheney.com

Printed in the USA
Paperback ISBN 978-1-7353903-2-1
Ebook ISBN 978-1-7353903-0-7

Cover art and illustrations by V. C. Cheney
Lyric, *All of Creation* by V. C. Cheney

This book is dedicated
to my other half
who encouraged me to write this book,
to my son
who aspires to be a writer,
and to my daughter,
who once told me she desired wisdom.

☞ CONTENTS ☜

☞ PREFACE ☞

In the past, my ideas for writing a novel weren't original. The idea for this book came to me when I was studying the Holy Scriptures to prepare for teaching. I knew right away that the *Ruach Kodesh* (Holy Spirit) had inspired my idea. Five years later, I rewrote the last draft of this book. I didn't realize until later that I had created a fictional universe. From my imagination, I offer a futuristic epic tale set when the Old Earth has passed away, and the New Earth has become a reality.

These are the premises of the story: If Adam and Eve had not rebelled against their Creator, what would the world be like? Or imagine a world like the Messianic Millennium on a larger scale, its boundaries extended throughout the galaxy. It is a world in which the Jewish sages likened to *HaOlam HaBa*, "The world to come." In the story, the Adamic race has seeded the galaxy and established many worlds.

I consider the novel as an extended, embellished parable written in the form of today's modern literature. The Jews were the first people to use analogy as a story form. They had a way of illuminating Scriptures by using parables with common themes: Rabbis and students, royal personages and their loyal subjects, owners and servants, farmer and seeds, and the Kingdom of Heaven.

I wrote this story to uplift us and give us hope for the future. The Scriptures are not all gloom and doom. We should do as the prophets of old, who often gave people warnings balanced with hope for the future.

This book includes a glossary at the end of the book for those of you unfamiliar with the transliterated Hebrew words and a few invented words.

~The author, V. C. Cheney

ECHOES OF TIME

*I observed the task that Elohim gave
to His people to keep them busy.
Elohim makes everything flow perfect in its own time,
But He has also planted eternity in the human heart.
Even then, people cannot discover
what Elohim has planned for them.
He has given people the desire to know about their future,
But they cannot fully comprehend the past and the future.
No one can see the full extent of His work from beginning to end.
~A Treasury of Elder Solomon's Wisdom*

19,309 YEARS AFTER NEW EARTH, THE PLANET KRISTALIS

The halls of the Academy were alive with the excited chatter and throng of students. It was the last day of the semester. The youthful Elders, in their white garments and mantles, watched the students like shepherds over their flocks, as they flocked to their last classes.

In another quieter part of the Academy, a solitary Elder stepped outside of the Academy to walk under the colonnades, holding a long staff mounted with a white stone. He wore a white traveling outfit. He carried his luggage with ease, as if it weighed nothing. As he walked, the long fringes of his gold-striped mantle flapped against his legs. A soft wind swept through his snow-white hair. His staff tapped lightly on the deck of the colonnade as he gazed at the azure sky and the sparkling ring of the planet. He set down his luggage to take one last look at the beauty of the place. The building shone of iridescent opals mined from the planet Kristalis, so named because of its bountiful resource of opalescent stones, diamonds, and crystals.

He took a deep breath to remember the smell of the place, to carry within him the fragrance of the Edenic garden. He looked at the large pearly double doors of the Academy, which were always open. The Kristalians had imported the huge pearls from the raging ocean of a planet that produced giant mollusks.

He touched the smooth column, looking at its opalescent stone surface. The rainbow colors on the surface reminded him of the diverse students who came here.

He had imprinted everything about the place in his mind, by sight, by hearing, by smell, and by touch. He had fulfilled everything he set out to accomplish when he first came. He prayed silently, *Abba Father, it is time to move on. I have passed on my mantle to the next generation of Elders. It was not so long ago that some of these new professors used to be my students. They now possess the knowledge about the Ancient of Days, about the origin of the Adamic race, the history of the thousands of millennia since New Earth. They have grown in wisdom. Abba, I thank you for the opportunity you have given me here. I am blessed. I am ready for the next endeavor.*

He stepped down from the colonnade. He needed to do one last thing. He mentally called for his longtime companion. *It is time for me to go. Let's say goodbye.* He waited until a large, white, fleecy, winged horse came toward him. He reached out toward the winged creature.

They stood head-to-head as the Elder touched the head of the creature with his forehead. *I will miss you, old friend. I told you this day would come. I must go far away.* The Elder stroked the horse's neck as he spoke mentally.

The horse whinnied softly. *I will miss you, too. Why can't you take me with you?*

The Elder sighed. *You know why. If I take you with me, you will be the only one of your kind there. You will miss your family. They will miss you.*

The horse whinnied softly again. *Will you come and visit us?*

The Elder replied. *When I can.*

The horse snorted. *You better!*

The Elder. *Farewell.*

The horse. *Farewell.* The horse bowed to his longtime companion as an honor to their friendship. Then he trotted back the way he came.

It was time to move on. An unknown world was waiting for the Elder. Suddenly, he disappeared in a brilliant flash of light. The Spirit had carried him away to his destination, along with his luggage. The place where he stood was empty.

Another brilliant flash appeared and a different Elder stood in its place, similarly dressed, carrying a staff mounted with a white stone. He dropped his luggage as he surveyed the Edenic garden for the first time. He came to the Academy to accomplish a mission of utmost importance, for the destiny of one world was at stake. His name was Elizon. And he was an Oracle of Zion.

CHAPTER ONE

ENDURING LEGACIES

*How wonderful it is to see the Lord of Hosts fulfilling the very
promises He gave to our people millennia ago.
These are the days when harmony reigns everywhere.
Truly, yesterday I saw a wolf frolicking with a lamb.
Today, I see a little child leading the wild animals to the brook.
Tomorrow, I will see a leopard lying down with a goat.
The holy mountain of Adonai has become a place of serenity.
They do no harm in His holy places.
The whole realm is filled with the knowledge of the Lord, as the
waters cover the sea. Gone are the days of violence and wars.
~Reflections of Elder and Prophet Isaiah*

THE PLANET KRISTALIS, FIVE YEARS LATER

Daleah Inara Joyce opened the window of her
bedroom. It was another balmy day on Kristalis. The
fourteen-year-old girl sniffed the fragrant smell of the vast
pine forest that surrounded her family estate. Her ears
perked at the songs of various birds that had awakened

her earlier. The sound of barking interrupted the songs. Daleah opened the double doors and stepped out onto the patio. A large white wolf had been waiting for her, his tail wagging excitedly.

A colorful garden with an abundant variety of fruit-bearing trees surrounded the house. Enormous fruits glistened like jewels, their branches strong enough to bear their weight. Ripe vegetables dangled in the bushes. Lush vines entwined the arched trellises along the paths. Tufts of root vegetables covered the rich, moist soil in meandering rows.

The estate nestled atop a gentle hill that provided an unobstructed view of the sky above the tall pine forest. Daleah's hazel eyes gazed upward at the clear azure sky and the graceful white arch, the ring of Kristalis that encircled the planet like a halo.

Daleah skipped on the garden path toward the mailbox, her curly dark-blond hair bouncing. The white wolf hopped after her. The mailbox nestled inside a bush, held sturdily by its branches and profusely entwined with leaves. Two white squirrels with thick, fluffy tails leaped down and landed on the mailbox to greet Daleah, holding their paws toward her.

Daleah shook their tiny paws with her fingers while greeting them, "A good morning to you both!" She looked inside the mailbox and saw the two letters the postal doves had dropped. She reached for them and a viper came out from underneath the bush, wrapping itself around her arm. It didn't startle her.

"Oh, it's you, Mister Twisty!" She said to the snake, "I didn't see you!" It stuck out its forked tongue at her, uncoiled itself from her, and went away. Holding the envelopes in her hand, her heart skipped a beat as she saw the return addresses. They were from the Academy. The letters were the reason she had been going to the mailbox daily for the past two weeks.

"Lupel! Look!" She announced to the white wolf, who was playfully poking the white rabbits with his nose. She waved the letters in her hand, "The letters I've been waiting for! Finally!" The wolf grinned at her with his sharp teeth, lifted his paw, and tilted his head. He understood her. He was happy for the little human.

She rushed back excitedly to her bedroom, Lupel following her. At her desk, she removed the wax seal carefully, keeping it intact, and opened the letters with the sharp edge of the letter opener. She saved the seal in a box with other seals. Lupel squatted next to her, watching her face. He knew how to read facial expressions and understood the various human emotions. Daleah read the first letter, from the headmistress of the Youth Academy of Aliyah, with the fancy logo and esteemed title of the Galactic Commonwealth of Zion, Ministry of Education.

19314.7.5

Dear Ms. Daleah Inara Joyce,

Our faculty is delighted to inform you that we have admitted you to the Youth Academy of Aliyah. We selected you for admission from among thousands of applicants from all over the Galactic Commonwealth of Zion. We are excited about the prospect of having you at our Academy. The semester will begin on the fifteenth day of the ninth month of this year. Enclosed, you will find the information to prepare you before the semester begins.

Blessings in Messiah, Headmistress Mariel of Emmaus

Daleah squealed with joy at the news and rushed to the kitchen to tell her parents, who were tending her little quadruplet brothers. Lupel followed, his tail wagging.

"Mama! Papa! Finally, some good news!" She burst out excitedly, waving the letter in her hand, "I have been accepted to the Academy!"

"Naturally!" her father answered, grinning, "My little sunshine! We knew you would be!"

"Congratulations, dear!" Her mother was smiling, "Today is a special day for you!"

"Can we drive into town to get my school stuff soon?" Daleah entreated her parents, "I need to be ready!"

"It's too soon for that," replied her father. "We have two months until the semester begins. Please relax, we will get your things." He walked toward the greenhouse that adjoined the kitchen.

"But look, it's a long list!" Daleah exclaimed as she waved the list of school clothes, supplies, and books.

"Don't be dramatic! It's not that long," replied her mother, "I will look at the list when I'm done here." She was wiping the toddlers' squirming faces and lifting them from their chairs.

"Thank you so much, Mama!" She replied, overjoyed. She walked back bedroom to read her letters, unaware that her little brothers followed her. Lupel perked up, for he knew the rule about the little ones not being allowed in her room. They wanted to see what made her so excited. Lupel ran ahead of them and barked softly to warn Daleah. She was about to sit down and turned to see them stumble into her room. Lupel tried to block them, but he wasn't enough.

"No, no, no! I cannot allow you into my room. Go back!" Daleah ordered and dragged them away from her room, back to her parents. She could only grab two at a time. "Mama! I want to read my letters in peace. Please, please keep them out of my hair for a while!"

"I swear, the minute I turn my back, they run off!" declared her mother. "I can't keep up with them. Come, let's go play outside!" She clapped her hands to get their attention.

"Playtime!" Her father announced as he came into the kitchen, "Who wants to go see the rabbits?" Daleah's parents led the little ones outside, while they squealed excitedly about the rabbits.

Daleah went back to her room, flopped down to finish reading her letters, and sighed. Lupel followed her again and laid down, instinctively knowing Daleah needed to feel relaxed. Daleah savored the opportunity to be alone, even briefly, for quiet moments like these were few. She opened the other letter from her twenty-thousand-something-year-old ancestress, Elder Shanielle, whom she affectionally called Ancie Shanielle. The letter reflected her personality with its exquisite cursive penmanship.

19314.7.5

My dear sweet Descie,

You should have received the letter of acceptance from the Academy by now. I am happy for you, knowing how much you wanted to come here. I missed your visits to our Academy, and I especially missed the excitement and enthusiasm you bring in learning about life. Having lived for over twenty millennia, I have seen all there is to be excited about. Seeking wisdom is desirable, rewarding, and never tiring. Our awesome Creator is the One who keeps us in a constant state of delight about life. He is a deity who does unfathomable wonders and who performs countless miracles. He continues to amaze us.

Time will pass swiftly, and before you realize it, you will be at the Academy sooner than you expect. You will have the best time of your life, making memories you will cherish forever. And hopefully, you will pass on an enduring legacy to your future children, as I have done.

Your loving Ancie, Shanielle

Daleah smiled as she finished reading. She had truly missed her dear Ancie Shanielle and her cherished wisdom. Daleah gazed at the letter awhile, examining how beautifully it flowed. So different from the plain straight text on her electronic tablet. She was going to count the days until she arrived at the Academy. She read the attached page that came with the first.

Dear Ms. Daleah Inara Joyce,

The faculty of the Youth Academy of Aliyah congratulates you on being accepted to our excellent school. Enclosed you will find a list of required items for you to bring to your first day at our Academy: Your dorm room number, information about the classes and professors, a class schedule, maps of the campus and the village. The twelve-week semester will be split into two six-week sessions, with a one-week break in between. Throughout the two sessions, you will be attending one class in the morning and one in the afternoon every day of the week, except for the Shabbat day of rest.

To ease the transition of your first academic experience, we offer two days of absorption, with an introduction to life on Aliyah, complete with a comprehensive tour of the campus and village before the semester begins. Absorption will be a time to meet the people of Aliyah and make new friends. We wish to make you feel welcome, well-settled, prepared, and eager to begin your classes. The third day is an orientation day to encourage you to focus on your academic potential, to get to know your professors, to meet your counselor, and to select the classes for the next semester.

After you check into your room, we invite you to join us in the assembly hall for the opening ceremony.

We hope your stay at the Academy will surpass all your expectations. Until then, we await with pleasure for your arrival in two months.

Sincerely Yours, The Faculty

Daleah smiled widely in delight at the prospect of meeting people from other worlds and learning at a place other than home. She eyed the neatly stacked homeschool books on her desk. She loved learning, but lately, her little brothers had become a distraction, and her homeschool assignments had lost their appeal.

Daleah read her list of courses and squealed a "Yes!" when she saw Shanielle's course in Penmanship, Calligraphy, and Bookbinding. Since visiting Aliyah, she had dreamed of becoming a scribe and a historian, of being able to express words of wisdom as beautifully as Ancie Shanielle. Transcribing into her tablet wasn't as exciting as doing things with her hands. She would enjoy feeling the texture of paper and pen, letting her thoughts flow from her mind to her hand and forming beautiful cursive words on paper.

She skimmed the memo about her four other courses. The memo listed her classes—The Foundations of the Faith, with Professor Aaronia; The Life of the Messiah on Old Earth, with Professor Mariel; Introduction to Prayer and Spiritual Warfare, with Professor Elizon; and the last course, The Story of Our Origins, with Professor Bethuel.

There was a knock at the door. Lupel barked. Daleah's mother walked in. "Let's look at that list and see what you need," her mother said. "Your father and I have been discussing our errands, and he will drive you in the hovercar to town tomorrow to get your books and school supplies. The day after tomorrow, you and I will get the white fabric for your new prayer mantles and clothes. We will have fun sewing them together. You'll have the best clothes. How's that?"

Daleah squealed with joy and stood to hug her mother. Lupel sensed the excitement and stood up with his tail wagging. Being a large wolf, he stood taller than Daleah's mother. The three of them hugged together. The rest of day went on blissfully as Daleah daydreamed about her future. She dreamed of her clothes she will wear, of the friends she will make, of the wisdom she will receive, and of the experience she will gain.

In another part of the galaxy, a fourteen-year-old boy lived in a suburb. Haro Lametz Gallant was sitting at an ornate desk in his father's wood-paneled office. He loosened his necktie and gazed at the clutter, illuminated by the soft light of the antique bronze lamp. Behind him, the window revealed a setting sun surrounded by a purple sky. Framed photos of the family were everywhere. The largest was a formal family portrait with all three generations, surrounded by an elaborate frame.

The family photo stirred memories in Haro. He remembered how he had been impatient that day, feeling stiff in the fancy suit, vest, and tie. His wavy brown hair was parted in the middle and groomed to an unnatural glossy black. His dark brown eyes were scowling slightly as he forced himself to smile. He had felt annoyed because his older sister had been so cheerful. She showed up at the photography studio straight from the beauty salon, wearing her favorite long dress, her hair skillfully curled, and her makeup done. She had a way of making him feel less presentable. Haro had always been the opposite, preferring relaxed clothes, not caring if the colors matched —while she was meticulous, her colors harmonious, and not a single hair out of place. He lifted the photo frame, staring closely at his father's countenance. His father looked proud of his family. His glossy hair was also parted in the middle, which was the fashion of the time. His neatly trimmed sideburns were long enough to touch the corners of a long, curled mustache, hiding an amused smile. For the first time, Haro noticed his father's eyes showed a certain sadness. Haro wished that he had paid more attention, but now it was too late.

On the desk were several powered-off-devices: a large thick laptop, two mobile communicators, and a tablet. They were of the same common bronze and copper metals, with display screens shaped like a convex squircle. The desk was void of papers, bills, pens, pencils, paperclips, or staplers. Haro opened a drawer and found more photos of his family, all printed on thin, hard plastic. He shuffled through the photos. His sister on the tire swing in the family backyard. Haro waiting for the bus for his first school day. His parents at a party drinking wine. The dog in the kiddy pool with him and his sister. The kitten sleeping on Haro's shoulder.

Haro's gaze lingered on a particular photo—his grandfather was smiling and pointing his finger at something, and a banner behind him that said, "Happy Birthday Haro." Grandfather died when Haro was eight, but the memories still lingered in Haro's mind. The entire family loved the old man and his tall tales of fascinating adventures. Haro shuffled the photos again. Haro, his father, and grandfather, were standing in front of the log cabin by the river, happily grinning because they caught the biggest fish of their lifetime. Haro would miss them both.

He shuffled the photos again. He halted as he held the photo of his father standing next to a white car with the gleaming chrome of the grille and wheel rims. His father looked proud that day, announcing to everyone within earshot that his new car was a classic. Haro remembered how excited he was to help his father upgrade the car's engine. When washing and waxing the car, his hands glided easily over the smooth rounded edges of the body, the domed shape of the hood, over the fenders of the jutting wheels, and the round headlights. It didn't have any sharp edges. It was curvy and smooth, like his father's easygoing personality.

It was also the same car that his father died in. The past few days, Haro was feeling numb. He had been too busy helping his mother prepare for the funeral to focus on his feelings. The funeral was over. Haro felt the grief beginning to weigh him down. He ran his hand through his hair, sighing. He put the photos back in the drawer and slammed it, his eyes teary. The guests were still in the other room, mourning with the rest of his family. He wasn't too keen on hanging out with them.

He thought to himself, *Mom never uses the office. Maybe I should use it to feel closer to Dad.* He opened the bottom drawer. It was full of electronic gadgets that he recognized because he had repaired them himself. Haro had a unique talent for fixing electronics. When he was four years old, no one noticed at first that he liked to put his older sister's broken doll together, making it walk again. Then a year later, he took apart the communicator and put it back together. His parents had mixed feeling about his talents—first, elation at his genius, then horror when they realized the school authorities might find out and take him away. The local school had a protocol for gifted children, enforcing their transfer to schools where they might never see their families again. They would have turned Haro into one of those BITE officers, known to be ruthless and relentless in their pursuit of technological enforcement.

Haro's parents had shielded him and trained him to hide his genius. As Haro grew up, he appeared as ordinary as every youngster at school. His parents fostered his talent, giving him electronics to repair or upgrade. They would find anything, even the ones from trustworthy neighbors. When Haro got older, his parents became more relaxed about his safety.

Among the gadgets in the drawer was a device that Haro didn't recognize. He lifted it and turned it around. He felt its contour and material, smelled it, and shook it close to his ear. It was a habit ingrained into him after years of repairing many electronics. There was a slight rattling noise. He frowned. He took a screwdriver from the tool drawer and unscrewed the metal box. Lo and behold, inside the metal box was another box, a wood one with some carving on its lid. Curiously, he picked it up gingerly. It smelled odd, like cedar. He opened it, and to his shock, inside was a folded letter and a calligraphy pen.

In Haro's world, papers and pens were things that just didn't exist because they were illegal. Possession of such items meant one year in prison. Haro looked at the doorway to make sure no one had seen him. He slammed the wooden box shut and put everything back quickly. He shut the drawer, his heart beating fast. If that letter had any religious text on it, the punishment was even worse: the death penalty. In Haro's world, owning any religious text was forbidden.

He left the office quickly and went to the kitchen to help himself to the food that the sympathetic neighbors had brought for his family. He munched nervously, hoping the food would calm him down, his mind dwelling on the wooden box and its content.

His older sister Ladya came in. As usual, she looked perfect, the same as she did earlier in the morning, her hair pinned in a chignon, and still not one hair out of place. She was wearing a tasteful black funeral dress with long gossamer sleeves. Facing Haro, she was moving her hands rapidly. Ladya had been deaf since birth, and sign language was her mode of communication. Haro watched her hands move, understanding her. "Where you? Mom asks for you."

Haro scowled at her and responded in kind, moving his hands just as rapidly. Growing up with a deaf sister had challenged him to learn to communicate in sign language. He spoke and signed simultaneously. "Does it matter? I wanted to be alone to breathe! When is everyone going home? Why can't we grieve alone?" He didn't want her to know what had transpired in his father's office.

"Hey! Don't blow top! Mom, her friends, help us much. Look, much food! Mom not need cook, one week! Mom needs support." Ladya was signing fast, her face mimicking Haro's dour expression. "Maybe, if you invite Jamik, you not GROUCHY!" Had it been another time, Haro would have been smiling. Ladya Victoria Gallant had a witty way of expressing many emotions with her face. Her hands flowed like a dancer, sometimes mesmerizing, sometimes hilarious. Despite her deafness, her sense of humor made her popular with her friends.

Haro wasn't in the mood to mingle with people, much

less his best friend Jamik. "You already know, I haven't hung out with Jamik for a year," he replied, still scowling. "He is busy with his sports activities. He does not have time for a nerd like me. Whatever! I am going to bed!" And he stormed out of the kitchen, going straight to his room. He had made up his mind. He would wait until his sister and mother were asleep to look inside the wooden box again. He had nothing better to do.

From his bedroom window, Haro watched impatiently as the guests left the house. Then he paced quietly in his bedroom until his family was asleep, listening to his sister's routine before her bedtime. Being deaf, she made the most noise. Finally, the house became quiet. He tiptoed into his father's office, closing the door quietly. He retrieved the wooden box for the second time. He unfolded the letter gingerly and tried to read the first line of the cursive handwriting. He wasn't used to reading any handwriting, having grown up with the clean text of digital devices all his life. To his surprise, the letter was meant for him. The handwriting was elegant, reminding him of his sister's flowing hands.

19313.3.20

My dear Haro,

No doubt this letter comes as a surprise to you. Your grandfather and I have something of great importance to tell you about our family's legacy. It goes a long way back to the beginning of our world. Just follow the diamond. Please destroy the letter after you read it and keep the pen in a safe place.

Your loving Father, Mardochi

That's it? A perplexed Haro looked carefully into the box for more content, but there was nothing except the letter and pen. As he turned it over, he saw the carving on the lid of the box—a diamond shape around the emblem of a hand that pointed sideways. He remembered all the times he and his father watched detective shows on the television and how his father loved to talk about clues. *The pointing hand is a clue?* He opened the drawers to look at the photos again. He selected the photo of his grandfather using the pointed hand gesture and found more photos. He put them on the floor, in the order of the pointed locations. He followed the directions their fingers were pointing. And when he finished, he found what he was looking for. He smiled, feeling elated. The fingers were all pointing toward the same location. At the top was a photo of himself and his father inside the treehouse. His father was holding him, pointing down at the ground. Whatever it was, his father must have buried it under that tree. *I will have to dig tomorrow.* He put everything back the way he found them.

And that night, Haro slept peacefully, dreaming of the family treasure he hoped to find. Following the clues made him feel closer to his father and grandfather.

Early in the morning, Haro left for school on his high wheeler, not wanting to take the school bus. After school, he hurried home the same way. He quickly changed from his plaid school uniform with its matching vest and ascot cap to more comfortable clothes, a tee shirt and shorts. His sister would not be home for a while, and his mother was still at work. He got the shovel from the garage and hurriedly dug under the treehouse in the fenced backyard. And there it was, another wooden box, wrapped in protective plastic. His fingernails were dirty, but he felt elated. He put the dirt back in the hole and covered the ground with dried leaves.

He went to his room and locked the door. He cut and unwrapped the plastic. It was a similar wooden box, bigger than the first one. He opened it, his heart beating faster. Inside were two rolled scrolls, one sealed and the other unsealed, a bottle of black ink, another calligraphy pen, some broken wax seals, a signet ring, a lighter, and a short stack of blank papers at the bottom. He picked up the unsealed scroll first. The paper was warm and soft, so unlike the cold metal gadgets that he handled all the time. The touch comforted him. He unrolled the scroll and read the beautifully curved handwriting, addressed to Haro's father, Mardochi.

19280.12.28

My dear son Mardochi,

No doubt this letter comes as a surprise to you. I am writing to impart something about our families and our legacies. Our family had a long and unique history that traces its roots to the beginning of Indigor. Our people arrived on Indigor on large spaceships from a planet called Nova Terra and a city called Nova Zion, where the children of the great patriarch Abraham dwell.

Indigor is not the world from where humans originated, as our educational system has indoctrinated us. The good news is—we are not alone. There are others like us, from beyond our world who have visited us regularly, unbeknown to most of us. They do not make their presence known publicly because we have corrupted our world for too long.

I come from a long lineage of men trained in the Brotherhood of Scribes and Keepers, a remnant who have carried on the truth about our origins. At the time of this writing, only enough wax remains that you must use to seal the next letter to one of your future children. Our Brotherhood had been working underground for the last six generations since the persecution. We had no choice but to hide our identities to stay alive. Hopefully, your child will be of the seventh and last generation to remain hidden. Soon the truth will come out, and everyone on Indigor will read the scrolls of the Ancients about our true origins. You must ensure that this family legacy continues.

Please understand, our Brotherhood is the only surviving remnant with a connection to the original homeworld. We call these visitors the Elders, a race of ancient immortals sent as emissaries by the Creator to ensure that we guard His Holy Writings and keep the faith. They are wise and trustworthy. You have much to learn about the Creator and His chosen people. You must prepare for your training in the Brotherhood, as my father, my grandfather, and our ancestors have done. I cannot give you more details because our government is always watching. The clues are in your memories.

Your loving Father, Abisak

Haro remained frozen for what seemed like forever, absorbing what he had just learned. It was beyond anything he had ever imagined. Finally, he moved and counted the broken seals in the box. There were six seals. He knew the unopened scroll with the seventh seal was for him. He broke the seal with great care and opened the seventh scroll.

19313.4.26

My dear son Haro,

If you are reading this, then I have passed from this life. I did not have time to tell you everything. I hope that the wisdom I have imparted to you will be enough for you to carry on our precious legacy.

Your mother does not know the location of the Brotherhood or that I am a part of them. I married your mother because she believed that we are not the only intelligent life in the galaxy. Then I shared with her our family's belief in the Creator and the Savior. She was overjoyed and believed completely. It is our job to protect our families, and I did my best.

These are troubling times. There was a time when the authorities almost caught your grandfather, but he escaped barely alive. His brother sacrificed himself so that your grandfather could live on to carry the family's legacy. Do what you can to find the Brotherhood, and from there, they will help you.

Your loving Father, Mardochi

Haro finished reading the letter with a sigh. Then he read all the letters again, contemplating the loving words, and memorized them, even the numbers at the top of each letter. He didn't know what they meant, but they must be important. Then he put each item back inside the wooden box, including the calligraphy pen from the first smaller box. Then he stopped and changed his mind. He moved the "clued" photos, the ones with the pointing hands, into the larger wooden box. *Better safe than sorry.* Then he looked around his bedroom for a place to hide the box. After pondering awhile, he made up his mind. The grille that was covering the air vent near the ceiling was a good hiding place. He moved his desk chair under the grille and took a screwdriver from his desk drawer. Standing on the chair, he unscrewed the grille and slipped the box inside the vent. Haro smiled as he screwed back the grille, feeling the air coming out. *It should be safe for now.*

Haro hid the first smaller box under the pillow. He thought of his father working as a scribe for the Brotherhood. *Where to begin the search? Where would they hide? What are they like? Are they aware of his existence?* His mind was full of questions.

For the next two months, Haro looked at the box, his mind pondering over the words of the letters, even without having to hold them. He treasured each word in his heart, repeating them to himself silently. He looked at the newly framed photo of the cabin for days. The photo helped him to focus on finding more clues from his memory, from the time he spent with his father.

And knowing more about his legacy had made his grief more bearable.

CHAPTER TWO

OF DREAMS AND ANGELS

This is the fulfilled prophecies of the latter days of Old Earth.
The word of Adonai that came to Joel, Son of Pethuel…
Adonai has poured out His Spirit on all humanity.
His sons and daughters are prophesying.
His old men are dreaming dreams,
And his young men are seeing visions.
~Prophet and Elder Joel,
Book of Fulfilled Prophecies

NOVA ZION, TWO MONTHS LATER

Once upon a universe, there was a place of beauty where every soul longed to go, a place that existed in the nucleus of the cosmos. At night, this Light was visible to the naked eyes, even from the furthest edge of the galaxy. And amidst this magnificent Light stood the sparkling city of Nova Zion. The Light from within this city infused all things and all its people. And below the city was the planet Nova Terra, a place where people dwelt in everlasting peace. There was no night, nor any need of the sun or moon, neither did the city cast any shadow on the planet. The Light was soft and pleasing, the kind that did not make the eyes squint. One could feel being drawn to its warmth in the infinite freezing void of the cosmos. Its warmth was of both temperature and temperament. The city sparkled like a rainbow, its walls built of twelve layers of precious stones, each layer a distinct color. It had twelve pearly gates that were continuously open and welcoming. And beings from all over the galaxy streamed to the city, bringing their wealth, waiting in line to see the One whose name they uttered with reverence, for His name was holy.

From the center of Nova Zion, a group of angels burst forth and went toward the stars. The angels, seen as pinpoints of light, flew past the Moon, Mars, past the asteroids belt, the Sun, Jupiter and Saturn, the comets, the multitudes of stars, and the giant colorful clouds. As they traveled the void at incredible speed, the sky shifted, and the starry heaven rolled like a scroll.

Two angels separated from the others and flew toward a bright white dwarf sun, toward a cloudless blue planet encircled by a white ring. One of them plunged toward the planet, everything came into view—hills, trees, geysers, rivers, lakes, and houses. He veered and flew horizontally toward a shimmering village floating on an oval disk above the land. He flew past winged white horses who were flying at a slower pace. Everything in the floating village, the handsome houses and its streets, gleamed of opalescent stones. Then he zoomed into the village center, toward an imposing building, with a sign that said, "The Academy." In the blink of an eye, he was in a room next to a man praying on his knee.

THE PLANET KRISTALIS

The tall kneeling figure of Elder Elizon was facing the window. He kneeled on one knee, eyes closed, head bowed, one elbow on his other knee, hands intertwined, and pressed on his forehead. For the past three days, he had been praying intensely without ceasing. He wasn't even tired. He felt more energized. As he looked up toward the horizon, the light of the sun revealed a youthful face with handsome features, long hair the color of pure snow, tied at the back of his muscled neck. A long prayer mantle covered his head. He wore a white linen tunic hanging loosely from his lean muscled body, over white pants and a gold sash tied around his waist. His figure glowed brighter as he prayed. His head became engulfed by a fiery halo. The white of his clothes lent a luminescent softness to his fiery aura.

A vision came to him. *He saw himself among the stars. His arms and legs became longer, his body transformed into a bridge that spanned between two different spheres. One sphere was blue and the other purple. A ring of angels encircled the blue sphere with hands held. Underneath himself as the bridge flowed a river of living water coming from a glowing throne. It gushed like a torrent toward the blue sphere. He took some living water in his cupped hands and threw it on the purple sphere, but the water evaporated. Then three other Elders appeared to help him. They took some living water from the river and helped him sprinkle the purple sphere. The water trickled into the sphere slowly. Together they continued until the river of living water split into two rivers. Then the new river flowed from the throne toward the purple sphere in a steady stream.* And the vision ended.

He sighed, knowing the interpretation of the vision. Eyes still closed, he felt a presence and saw it in his mind's eye. It was an angel with four wings, standing before him. He heard the angel in his mind. *I am here.* Elizon was ready. He stood up to look at the angel of the Light. Elizon opened his eyes, which were an intense aquamarine blue, like the water of a shallow sea. Elizon and the angel stood face to face. There was no element of surprise. Elizon greeted the angel with a smile, inclined his head as a sign of respect, to acknowledge his presence. The angel did the same. Elizon waited for his message.

The angel unfolded his wings and placed them lightly over Elizon's frame. His powerful, yet gentle, voice filled the room. "Elder Elizon, the Supreme King has heard you since the beginning of your request. I have come on the wing of a special message from Him who is, was and always will be. Elizon, our Father finds you in high esteem. He is pleased with your work as an Oracle of Zion. You understood the vision. Our Father the King summoned to join the Commonwealth Council of Emissaries as the new emissary of Indigor. We have appointed three new Oracles to join you in your mission. Your work is a blessing to others, you will continue to receive visions and prophesy."

The angel had confirmed what Elizon had sensed all along in the vision. Elizon replied, "Blessed is Adonai Elohenu, Creator and Ruler of the Universe who commanded us to be a light to all people. I am honored Our Creator has chosen me to serve Him for such an important endeavor. I accept my new appointment as the emissary for Indigor." He inclined his head again. And the angel retracted his wings and vanished.

The second angel went forth, halfway around the same blue planet with its sparkling white ring. As he plunged toward Kristalis, he flew over the hills, above the lush carpet over a land of the blue pine forest splattered with red maples. The houses and towns came into view. He zoomed in to a large estate surrounded by the forest and instantly appeared in a girl's room. The girl with curly hair and freckles was sleeping atop of her brightly colored bedcover, clutching a paper and a pink pen. The paper listed the items she had packed, check-marked with her pink pen. The white outfit and mantle, which her mother had sewn with the long fringes, hung on her closet door. Daleah had proudly embroidered the silver crown and stripes on the mantle. On the floor next to her bed, her pink suitcase laid open, clothes neatly folded and carefully packed.

Earlier that day, Daleah Inara Joyce had been struggling with decisions, what to bring and what not to bring. Preparing for her first important trip away from home was not her forte. The sun was setting when she fell asleep, not even bothering to change into her pajamas.

A vision came to her. She flew on wings and landed in an unfamiliar wilderness. She looked around. It was devoid of life, like a desert, as far as the eyes can see. She shielded her eyes with her hand, looking. Finally, she spotted other people at the horizon and walked toward them. She didn't know any of them, but they were all young like herself. They walked toward each other. One of them was different in form, for he had the face of a young lion and stood upright like a man. She glimpsed the wings on his back. She walked with him and the others in the unknown country, toward the East, until they arrived together in a place that was teaming with life. Then the dream ended.

The angel spread his wings over her bed and spoke softly, "Daleah, Our Father, the King has blessed you," but she didn't hear him. "For you will be the first of many to walk a path no one has trodden on before." She awoke with a start, for she had immediately felt a presence in the room, but didn't see anyone. She got up and walked past him, blind to his presence. She went down the hall to the family room. Her parents were resting, sitting in their favorite armchairs, reading the Holy Writings on their tablets.

"Mama, Papa, did you come into my room recently while I fell asleep?" She asked.

Her parents turned to look at her. "No, dear, we haven't," replied her mother, "We didn't know you were asleep."

"Has my little lamb finished packing for tomorrow's big day?" Asked her father, grinning.

"It's done. I packed everything I need," she answered,

still puzzled, "Where is everyone?"

"Didn't you look at the time?" Her mother replied, "Our guests have gone home except for your sister and your niece. They are putting your brothers to bed."

"Oh, I'm going back to bed," Daleah announced. "Tomorrow will be another long day. Good night, Mama, Papa!" They replied in kind and went back to their reading. She went back to her room, her face still puzzled. The dream had been so vivid. There must have been an angel in the room, she told herself. *That must be it. Ancie told me of dreams and angels. I will find out more later.* Daleah was determined to find answers to the meaning of her dream, for she had always been inquisitive.

THE PLANET REGALOR

The third angel flew toward another planet, one that looked much like Old Earth, a blue sphere with white swirls and two small moons. A tall, beautiful woman was praying intensely. She was an Elder—tall, glowing, and wearing a white garment. A glowing aura surrounded her figure, partly covered by long and thick white hair that ran down the length of her back to her legs and held back by intricate braids. Her face was chubby like a teenager, but with the demeanor of someone wiser and more mature.

A vision came to her as she prayed, troubling her spirit. *She was flying over a land filled with purple flowers with tall spikes that grew toward the sky. They were beautiful, but so thick that they covered the entire land, in every nook and cranny, that they blocked out the light. And the people of that land became trapped in the crushing darkness. They cried out in their imprisonment. Then a lion appeared among the spikes, then an ox, an eagle, and a man with a rugged face. The four of them cut down the tall spikes to create a path and let some light shine through.* And the vision ended, and she felt a soft wind blowing toward her, which was impossible because she was in a closed room. She waited, eyes closed, and heard a still small voice in her being. Elder Moralee, *I am here to give you a message.* She knew the angel was in the room.

She opened her eyes and stood up to look at him, his wings surrounding her. She answered, "I am ready for your message."

"Elder Moralee," the angel spoke, his voice almost like thunder, "Our Father, the King has found you highly esteemed and blessed. You understood the vision. Your mission will begin with meeting Elder Elizon at the Academy on Kristalis. Once there, you will present yourself as a new Oracle of Zion. You will tell him of your vision. This is your mission as ordered by our Supreme King."

She acknowledged his message. "Blessed is Adonai Elohenu, who commanded us to be a light to all people. I have waited, and I accept my new mission as an Oracle of Zion. May you go with blessings." And the angel vanished, hurtling back toward the cosmos to complete his next mission.

THE PLANET EVANGLAR

The fourth angel zoomed toward a jungle planet, a white sphere covered in white clouds. He flew over a land with foliage so dense that he could not see the hidden houses. He slowed down over the misty clouds, searching with his spiritual eyes. Then, in the blink of an eye, he was standing before two identical Elders. The twins were kneeling and praying, surrounded by glowing auras joined as one.

These unique twin Elders received the same dream. *A giant white dragon with wings trampled the beautiful earth, destroying everything in its path with its fiery breath. The One who reigns from the heavenly throne struck it with a lightning bolt, and the lizard lost its whiteness and transformed into a giant snake, its color of the red earth. Its arms, legs, and wings fell off like branches cut down from a tree. It couldn't fly anymore, but slithered everywhere, prowling and devouring whoever crossed its path on the land. One day, the dragon crossed paths with a group of children and chased them.* And the vision ended.

The twin Elders opened their eyes and stood up simultaneously. They knew the moment that they received the vision that the angel had arrived. The angel spoke, his wings surrounding them both, "Greetings, Elders Benzi and Zephan, you are both highly esteemed and blessed. You are to go to Elder Elizon at the Academy on Kristalis and present yourself as new Oracles of Zion. You will tell him of your vision. From there, you will know what to do. This is your mission as ordered by our Sovereign Father."

They both stood up and acknowledged his message, speaking in perfect sync. "Blessed is Adonai Elohenu, benevolent and gracious King, who commanded us to be a light to the universe. We accept our new mission as Oracles of Zion. We are ready. You have our blessings and our thanks, brother."

"I have one more request. Please pray for my brother Alaniel as he goes to the lost people of Indigor. He needs your help to break through the line of defense of the adversary." And he vanished.

THE PLANET INDIGOR

The fifth angel traveled swiftly to another planet far away, to a purple sphere with pale pink clouds rotating around an orange sun. He flew past a communication satellite. When he zoomed in, another angel blocked him. They stopped in mid-air, face to face, their wings fluttering as they hung suspended in the void above the planet. The other angel's countenance was darker, for he had lost much of his light. He looked as if the dark void of space had swallowed him. His wings were barely visible.

His sharp, glowering eyes glowed red as he recognized the angel. "Hello Alaniel," Locitan greeted him, "my old friend. What is your business here?"

"Hello Locitan, long time no see," replied Alaniel, as his whole being glowed brightly, "I have come here on the wings of a message for someone. I respectfully ask that you let me pass." He moved aside to pass Locitan, who blocked him quickly.

"Who is the message for?" Locitan's tone was more of a command than a request.

"I cannot tell you."

"This is MY domain. You might NOT pass unless I say so. You have two choices. Follow me and I will let you pass. Or go back and tell Our Father you have no business being here."

"Do not blaspheme Our Father. He created you and loved you. You owe Him your loyalty and respect." Alaniel continued boldly. "He sent me here, so step aside and let me do my job as His messenger." He tried to move, but Locitan blocked him again.

"No, you will not go down there." Locitan insisted stubbornly, his arms crossed at his chest.

"Do you want to fight me again?"

"Maybe, if you tell me who the message is for, maybe I can relay it myself." If there was something Locitan hated more, it was being kept in the dark, but that was his fault. He got himself stuck in this world for rebelling.

"You are unbelievable. What makes you think I am stupid enough to believe you?"

Locitan shrugged his shoulders and replied, "I never thought you were stupid but misguided. If you don't like it, then go back to your domicile." He shrugged his shoulder, arms still crossed.

Alaniel appeared unruffled. He knew Locitan was goading him into becoming angry. Alaniel commanded calmly, "Enough of this chitchat. Let me pass."

"What happened to our friendship?" Locitan asked, a little more sweetly.

"I didn't come here to talk about us. Our friendship is a thing of the past."

"Oh, come on, do you remember the pleasant times we had when we were young? We played together, chasing each other around the heavens, playing hide and seek in the luminaries?"

Alaniel sighed, as patient as ever, "I remember well, but I am not here to reminisce about our playtime from eons ago." Then Alaniel changed his tone and spoke with power. "Locitan, it's time to face the truth. We are no longer friends. We are in opposite camps. You made your choice when you rebelled. You might be the chief of this world, but our Father still owns this planet, and He still owns you. He is permitting you to remain, but it's only a matter of time before He will remove you. You know the story of our kin, of the first rebellion. You know the final demise of the one who deceived the first world and led a third of our kin into rebelling against our Father. Where are they now? Have you learned nothing?" Alaniel ended his words with finality. He was biding his time, knowing he would pass soon.

Alaniel's sharp, powerful words of truth infuriated Locitan. And this time, Locitan's dark and translucent countenance finally lit up, but his glow wasn't a brilliant, beautiful white like Alaniel's. It was a reddish glow, and out of his mouth came angry words, like fire. It was as if he had transformed himself into a dragon.

"You know exactly why I and the others of our kin have rebelled!" He roared, his eyes a fiery red glow. "Don't bother denying it! Your precious King doesn't care about us! We are nothing more than slaves to His wish, doing this and that, going here and there. Do you recall a time when He had made humans lower than us? And then He had crowned them with glory! First, we were nothing more than glorified babysitters, and now we are their servants? Is that what has become of our kin? We might as well not even exist! We are nothing more than pawns on his universal chessboards! Don't you ever tire of relaying his idiotic messages to these pompous Elders? Have you forgotten that He created us first? We have the right to claim our proper place in the cosmos!" Locitan had finally revealed the true cause of his fury.

Alaniel didn't flinch at Locitan's cutting attack on the

character of their Father. Alaniel braced himself, refusing to yield. Locitan's scathing contempt of the humans and Elders seemed to echo throughout the planet below, as if putting a curse on it.

"You are spouting falsehoods and you know it." Alaniel replied with long-tried patience. "The Elders are our friends. We serve Our Father together. There is no competition between us. Your imagination has run amok. You have deceived yourself. We are still sons of Elohim, and there is no reason to hate the humans and the Elders. I am far from being jealous of our new brothers. I love them as much as I love my Father. And he has always loved all of us. That's who He is."

"It's not jealousy! It's the truth!" Locitan bit back with angry, fiery words, glowing more reddish in appearance, "And it's you who deceive yourself. Your love for Him has made you blind! And I will find the one you are seeking below and destroy him. YOU WILL NOT PASS!" He raised his arm in anger to strike Alaniel, but Alaniel was ready. Alaniel moved swiftly aside as Locitan lifted his arm and attacked the emptiness where Alaniel had been. Locitan turned to see Alaniel become a tiny pinpoint of light, zooming in swiftly toward the purple planet. Locitan roared so loudly that the void of space seemed to reverberate. His minions heard him and came rushing to his aid.

The moment Alaniel arrived on Indigor, he changed his form to hide. He had to act with haste, for he knew Locitan would send his minions after him. These assignments were not a new thing for him. He had done them for many eons. Old Earth had not been the only fallen world.

Alaniel had to arrive further away from his planned destination. He kept looking back, double-checking to make sure he was not being followed. Each time he stopped to hide, he transformed to look like a native. It wasn't difficult, as he was a being made of light. The only thing he minded was having to shrink his form from his normal eight feet to six feet. He wasn't used to being smaller, compacting his molecules of light tighter together. If he stayed too long in this form, he might burst.

Finally, he arrived at his destination as the sun was setting. For a while, he watched a house from across the street, hiding behind a shed where the owner's large guardian dog was sleeping. The dog didn't bark at the stranger, but seemed to know that he was different. The dog gave Alaniel a puzzled look, tilting its head. Alaniel bent down and stroked the dog, who took pleasure at the touch. The house across the street had become quiet, the lights going off as people went to bed. The timing was right. Alaniel transformed to mimic a neighbor walking with his dog. He crept slowly closer to the house, pretending he was a human who looked bored. He had millennia in perfecting the art of mimicking humans. It was the reason the Father had chosen Him specifically for this task.

☞ ☞ ☞

Alaniel appeared suddenly in the room, minus the dog. Haro Lametz Gallant slept peacefully. Alaniel stretched his wings over the boy and whispering words of comfort and blessing. For Alaniel had come came to bring a message to Haro.

A vision came to Haro while he slept. *He was being chased by unsavory characters. He was running, his right fist holding on to something that looked like an ancient scroll. He kept running away from his chasers until he found a hiding place and rested. When he opened his hand, he realized he wasn't holding on to anything. Instead, there was something else—the palm of his hand had one word inscribed on it. It was a word in an unknown language. Then the word dissolved into his hand, and he felt it moving inside his arm, his chest, and his heart, like a warm tingling sensation. It continued to spread through his entire being and made him float. He saw himself being lifted high in the sky, toward the stars, toward a brilliant light that enveloped him.*

The dream was so vivid, he awoke abruptly, sitting up in his bed. He didn't care much for dreams but he knew in his heart that this dream was different. He sat still in his bed, pondering over it. What made this dream so intense tonight? Angel Alaniel was in the room, but Haro could not see or feel his presence.

For the first time in his life, Haro recorded his dream. He couldn't use paper or pen, so he took his dictation device and recorded his dream. The scroll in the dream reminded him of what he had found. He kept the dream alive in his heart. Then Alaniel vanished from the room.

☞ ☞ ☞

Locitan's minions heard his roar. Three of them came to his aid—Woevil, Vexid, and Griop. They looked like smaller and more grotesque versions of Locitan himself.

"Magnificent lord," asked Vexid, "what happened?"

"Are you a moron?" Locitan questioned with a sneer, "A messenger is the only thing that makes me angry! What else do you think happens in this void? It's not an entertainment venue for your pleasure!"

Vexid looked contrite and bowed to him, "My apologies! Who was it, my lord?"

"Does it matter who it was?" Locitan, still fuming red with anger, retorted, "These messengers are all the same! Get back to Indigor and start searching!"

He seethed. His minions wouldn't move, even with their fear of him. They didn't know where to start. Finally, he said, "If you want to know who I confronted, it was my old friend, Angel Alaniel. Get on with it!"

"Honored prince," uttered Woevil, his head bowed, afraid of offending Locitan, "we aim to please you. Do you know who he was looking for?"

Locitan paused and mulled over what had happened. "If I knew, I would tell you! They are all stubborn, refusing to divulge His plan! As it stands, I don't have any clues. There have been no angelic activities around this planet for months. The message must be important. We must find the recipient of this message and we must not fail."

Another minion named Griop asked, "Glorious master, did you see where Alaniel went? His landing location might give us some clues."

Locitan calmed down to think more clearly. He pointed to the location where Alaniel had landed. "Go now! There is no time to waste! The last time we let an angel pass through, things didn't go well. Fail me and suffer the consequences!"

Woevil, Vexid, and Griop went as commanded by their chief, dreading failure. When Locitan used to go into a terrible rage, he shrunk his minions to the size of pebbles he liked to kick around. And while they had shrunk, Locitan had become bigger. Never again would they want to be teensy, insignificant minions!

Alaniel was ready to go back home to Nova Zion, but he knew it would not be easy. At sunrise, he retraced his steps, going back the same way he came, far away from the boy's home. He arrived at the exact place where he had first landed. He knew he would have to confront Locitan again, this time with his minions. Alaniel preferred confronting the latter, who were less cunning. He knew Locitan would not be alone this time. He prayed fervently for the other angels to help him break through the line of defense that Locitan had enabled.

THE PLANET SERFARETZ

The sixth angel flew toward the same solar system where the planet Kristalis was, but went past it. He arrived at another planet filled with thick clouds and a large moon. He flew over the immense rocky mountain ranges, and swiftly zoomed toward a high mountain, finding himself in an enormous cavern. The inside of these mountains were filled with an intricate matrix of thousands of caves. The inhabitants had built exquisite dwellings from the natural substance of their environment, floors upon floors of them, as high as the caves went. The lights from their windows and lampposts lent a festive atmosphere to the normally dark cavern. The dwellers in these caves were the Seraphies of the four races.

The sixth angel zoomed into a spacious and elegant room where a young Seraphi of the feline race was standing. He had the face of a lion with a lustrous grey mane, like silver. He seemed to know immediately that the angel had arrived to visit him. Without even a single prayer or guidance or an appointment, the Seraphi was expecting the angel the minute he left Nova Zion.

The young feline turned immediately to the angel and said to him, "Greetings in the name of the Holy One, blessed is He." They stood face to face, both of equal stature. The feline inclined his head and unfurled his two wings upward.

The angel replied, "Greetings in the name of our Creator, Rory Lionel DeTabor." He also inclined his head and unfurled his wings upward to touch the tip of Rory's wings, a gesture that was the standard form of greeting for all winged beings.

"I am honored the Holy One has deemed me worthy to receive a message."

"Rory, the appointed time you and your family have been waiting for has finally come. You must proceed to your destination with your entourage."

"I hear your message and accept the Holy One's command. May His will be done. Wishing you a speedy journey back to Nova Zion."

"Not yet, I have one more trip to make. We will need your prayer for my brother Alaniel as we break through the line of defense set by Locitan on Indigor."

"It will be done as you asked. Farewell!" They both

retracted their wings, and the angel disappeared the same way he had left.

Moments later, three of Rory's close companions felt compelled to show up at his house. Like Rory, Mona, Soraya, and Nataniel were young Seraphies. Since time immemorial, the Seraphies were always in a group of four, each of a distinct race. Rory was of the feline race, Mona of the bovine race, Soraya of the eagle race, and Nataniel of a human, more rugged and robust in appearance. Even though they were different, their families have coexisted in peace for many millennia. The four of young Seraphies were as close-knit as any family could be. They grew up together, schooled in the same school, and played in the same playground.

Rory told them of the angel's visit. "Our families must be informed. The Holy One has opened a new door, and the time is now. Our parents have planned this for years with the Council of Seraphies. Let us pray and prepare for the voyage and for the Angel Alaniel to break out of Indigor." They were all in agreement, their heads nodding. They prayed with unfurled wings, covering and encircling each other. Toward the end of the prayer, the intensity of their prayer formed an orange glow at the center of their circle that went upward like a pillar of fire. The Holy Presence had blessed them. There was no need to say anything, for they all understood. And the three Seraphies went back to their home to prepare for the journey.

THE PLANET INDIGOR

Alaniel had been right. All the other five angels had fulfilled their task of bringing the good news and were on their way to help him out.

Alaniel bent his knees and zoomed out toward the stars at the fastest speed he could muster. Locitan had been waiting with his many minions, watching for Alaniel, but they didn't expect the five other angels to come from behind them. With the power of their speed, these angels overpowered his minions by crashing into them so hard they hurtled far away. Alaniel easily overpowered Locitan with his speed and flew away with the other angels, back toward Nova Zion.

An angry Locitan did all he could to roar at his minions. Woevil, Vexid, and Griop tried in vain to placate him, but it was no use. He reduced them to the size of tiny pebbles, kicking them around. After a while, his anger was spent, and his reddish glow diminished. He ordered his minions to look again for the one who received the message. The frustrated minions lamented at their failures, but the angelic messengers rejoiced at the success of their missions.

CHAPTER THREE

THE WISE ELDERS

Surrounding the One who sat on the throne
were twenty-four other thrones,
And seated on them were twenty-four Elders.
They were all clothed in white and
had gold crowns on their heads.
~ Elder Yochanan,
Book of Foundation Elders

KRISTALIS, THE NEXT DAY

A certain group of Elders worked as professors at the Youth Academy of Aliyah on the floating village known as Aliyah, high above the land of Kristalis. Floating villages and cities were not uncommon on the planet Kristalis, like the first beautiful city, Nova Zion, that settled on Nova Terra millennia ago.

The new semester was about to begin, and the professors were busy preparing for the big day, when the new students arrive at the Academy. Elder Shanielle was in her elegant office, filled with bookcases full of neatly organized scrolls encased in gold, silver, and copper cylinders, and hundreds of books bound in the same precious metals. Her eyes skimmed the shelves, searching for a book she wrote many eons ago. She picked a heavy book imprinted with an embossed title, *The Chronicles of Kristalis*, and her name. She read the first page where she wrote about the beginning of a new world.

7325.8.27

The first space pilgrims ventured into the galaxy and settled on the beautiful new world of Kristalis with its sparkling white ring. They built beautiful cities with precious stones of opals, crystals, and diamonds. People were thriving…

Kristalis is a world without evil, without the inevitable outcome that comes with corruption. The eons are seemingly endless and filled with multitudes of people untouched by sickness, death, chaos, strife, and sorrow. The Kristalians, being ageless, never experienced the ravages of entropy that come with anything flawed. They don't view themselves as immortal. In their world, immortality is perfectly normal. Evil doesn't exist because the goodness of the Light imbues the fabric of their lives. The Light of the Everliving Creator is everywhere, stretching millions of light-years throughout the cosmos. And yet, that Light connects to the people of Kristalis.

Despite all that goodness, the Kristalians are not naïve. They possess a knowledge of evil, but they have never tasted it. They know the stories from Old Earth before everything became newly restored. These stories are alive in the memories of the first Elders, a race of ancients, of a time long forgotten, a people of renown.

Under the wise guidance of the Elders of Zion and the benevolent government of the commonwealth of Zion, the Kristalians thrived…

Elder Shanielle had many wonderful stories to tell about the immortal Elders of Kristalis, exceptional people that the Sovereign has appointed as guardians of many worlds under the Galactic Commonwealth of Zion. The title of Elder was a misnomer because they hardly looked old. Who are the Elders, and why are they so esteemed by the people of the galaxy?

Shanielle put the book back on the shelf. She sat down at her desk and sighed. She had to get this done before the students arrived. She looked at her disorganized desk, cluttered with papers, which was the sign of a hard worker. Even after her Old Earth life, Shanielle had continued to work hard. She shuffled them in a pile and sorting them out. The trash pile, the filing pile, and the to-do-ASAP pile. Then she stopped and smiled as she read a typed essay from her sweet Descie, Daleah, as part of her admittance to the Academy. It was titled, "Who are the Elders?"

19314.6.4

Since I have visited Aliyah, I found the answers to the questions that weighed on my mind. The first question is, why are they called Elders? The name comes from an ancient scroll about the twenty-four Elders who reign with the Everliving One in Nova Zion. Many millions of the eldest Elders from Old Earth are 20,314 years old. A simple way to figure out their age is to add one thousand years to today's date, written at the top of the letter. Everyone knows how to write the date in that order: the years After New Earth or ANE for short, the month, then the day of the month. The resurrection of the first Elders happened one thousand years before Old Earth became transformed into New Earth. I am only fourteen years old, an infant compared to them!

The second thing that has always perplexed me was, why do they have white hair, and why do they always wear white? The color white represents purity and holiness. The Elders have no blemishes or stains because they are without sin.

The third question is, why are they different from my family, even though they are family? Why are they taller?

The Elders' inner bodies are made of pure Light, which makes their hair white. Elders are more like the angels, although I have never seen one. They are about eight feet tall. Sometimes they change shapes. I have seen my Ancie Shanielle glow on joyous occasions. One time, I saw her become shorter when something made her sad.

Can they change into an animal, like my wolf Lupel? My Ancie thought this question was hilarious, but I got my answer. She can only change her size and her facial features a bit.

Also, Elders can't marry or have children. But they have adopted many children at the resurrection long ago, children who died young and never had a full life. Some Elders have many descendants. If they married during their Old Earth life, they can visit these children and their descendants. Some of these children have become Elders. My Ancie has stopped counting her descendants a long time ago. To the Elders, all children are their children and anyone much younger than a hundred is a child of hers. We are all like one big happy family.

What are the things that the Elders can do? Ancie Shanielle was uncomfortable answering that question. Elders don't talk about their special powers. She does not think of them as powers, but as gifts from the Everliving Creator. In her own words, Elders are "endowed with different supernatural gifts, all from the same Spirit, much like the first Apostles. The Elders wielded these gifts, depending on what they needed to do, and they never used them for selfish purposes."

My Ancie can travel instantly anywhere in the galaxy. She calls it being "carried away in the Spirit." These words came from the Ancient Holy Writings. They happened to the ancient prophets Ezekiel and Elijah, to the Apostles Paul, Philip, and John.

I have also seen Ancie grow a whole fruit from one seed and I have seen her multiply food to feed my family. My one favorite thing she did was to bond telepathically with the animals. These are wonderful gifts!

I asked Mama when I can become an Elder like Ancie. She was so surprised! We can't become one until we've had a full life as a human. We all must grow up first. We learn about everything first. Then we get married, have children, a few careers, then several hundred years later, we will be ready for Eldership. There is plenty of time and no rush to become an Elder!

Someday, when I am ready, I will read the Book of Eldership. According to my Papa, the book is only for those who are ready to become an Elder. When I go to the Academy next year, I will learn more about them. My story has only begun. For now, I will enjoy just being myself.

Shanielle smiled as she finished reading the essay. It was the work of students like these that brought her joy.

At the edge of the village, Elizon stood with his favored winged steed, Blazer. With a light hop, Elizon got on the Lipican. Blazer excitedly galloped and jumped over the edge of Aliyah, flapping his fluffy white wings rapidly. After three days of intense prayer, Elizon felt invigorated. Blazer delighted in soaring over the lush growth beneath them. Elizon spotted their shadows moving over the forest of blue pines sprinkled with red maples. They soared around a large water geyser. Elizon felt the mist on his face as Blazer flew around it. Ahead of them, smaller geysers sprouted from the ground, continuously watering the vegetation of the cloudless planet. Together, rider and Lipican soared over the rainbows reflected in the mist's light from the geysers.

Elizon looked at the perfect landscape, recalling a time when he viewed another land from an airplane. Nothing here like Old Earth to mar the perfect symmetry of the land. *No poor villages, no polluting industries, no destructive mining, and no overcrowding. It was as Eden was.* Elizon and Blazer flew over the family estates that dotted the landscape, each of them surrounded by edible gardens, nestled between meandering rivers that shone like ribbons of silver.

Blazer neighed as he saw a herd of fluffy white Lipicans running on the wide-open space of the prairie, strengthening their muscled legs. Elizon sensed Blazer's excitement and allowed him to dive lower, flying over the Lipicans swiftly. The herd unfolded their wings and lifted off the ground, catching up with Blazer and Elizon.

They flew together over herds of antelopes and hairy elephants with large curly tusks. Winged white lions were crouching in the prairies, watching the antelopes, but not chasing them. Elizon smiled, remembering. *These gentle lions are nothing like Old Earth's predatory lions.*

Elizon and Blazer were nearing the floating village, visible under the arch of the sparkling halo. The Lipicans separated themselves from Blazer as he approached the village. Blazer landed on the grassy edge of the village, retracting his fluffy white wings as he galloped toward the gardens. As Elizon dismounted Blazer, he saw the distant herd of Lipicans appearing like a solitary cloud amidst the cloudless sky.

Elizon stroked Blazer's flank as he spoke, "Your friends flew away! You'll see them again." He removed the straps from Blazer's head.

A brilliant flash of light burst before Elizon and Blazer.

A female Elder appeared with twin Elders, each in their white outfits, with luggage, and their travel staffs with its white stones.

Elizon registered no surprise and immediately greeted the three Elders. "Halo, I am Elder Elizon. The messengers sent you?"

The female Elder replied, "Halo Elizon. Indeed, we are sent here by order of our beloved Sovereign. We are the newly appointed Oracles of Zion. I am Moralee of Regalor." She said as she inclined her head respectfully.

"I am Benzi," then his twin responded, "and Zephan." The twins spoke their names separately, then simultaneously, "We are from Evanglar and honored to be here."

"Welcome to Aliyah," Elizon greeted them with extended arms, "We have been expecting you. The Headmistress will help you get settled. We have many newcomers at Aliyah this year." As an afterthought, he smiled toward the twins and added, "I am also glad that my sister Shanielle and I will not be the only sibling Elders at our Academy."

Then he turned toward his Lipican, stroking Blazer's fluffy head and a long goatee. He looked directly at Blazer's eyes. Thank you for the invigorating ride, Blazer. I am going back to the Academy now. Blazer understood, for he neighed and tilted his head toward the village as if telling Elizon to get going. Blazer snorted as he galloped back to the herd of Lipicans grazing on the field, his long white mane, tail, and feathered legs billowing in the breeze.

The other Elders noticed the silent communication between them.

"He is a beautiful Lipican." Moralee remarked, "How long has he been your companion?"

"I befriended Blazer as soon as I settled here several years ago." Elizon replied, extending his arm toward the path to the village, "Allow me to guide you." And they walked together. "Blazer was the first Lipican to connect with me immediately out of all the herd here. At our first meeting, he ran toward me the minute I emerged out of the village, as if he already knew me. The Lipicans here are special, able to link telepathically with Elders. They are the same breed that our Sovereign and his Elders rode at His second coming, but they were originally from this world. When the three of you settle here, you will have Lipican companions. I don't know if there are twin Lipicans, though." He grinned at the twins. The four of them glided more than they walked as if their bodies were weightless.

"We look forward to it. It is a precious and blessed thing to have such a telepathic companion," said Moralee.

"It's not much different from the communication bond between twins," commented Benzi, as they glided leisurely on opalescent streets.

Elizon expressed surprise, "You two share a telepathic bond?"

"Indeed," replied the other twin, Zephan, "we have been like this since we shared the womb. It grew stronger when we became Elders."

"It's more common for us Elders to share telepathic abilities with animals." Moralee remarked, "I have known the twins well. We have been on missions together."

"That's excellent news!" Elizon grinned at them, "Because I will need all the help that I can get! Here, let me carry your bag for you." He took Moralee's large bag as if it weighed nothing. Elders were super strong, but Elizon was not about to throw away years of good manners. Neither was it an act of chivalry, but the character trait of a courteous Elder.

The four Elders glided on a path laid with opalescent stones, through a colorful edible garden, with its abundant variety of trees and jewel-like fruits. They arrived at the village.

Moralee exclaimed, admiring the view, "What a picturesque village! Such beautiful opalescent stones!" Even the columned gazebos, the water fountains, and the benches were made from the same opals. They chatted as they went uphill toward the village center, waving and greeting the villagers.

They arrived in front of an imposing edifice, surrounded with tall colonnades, with cast-iron balconies jutting out of tall windows, and a flat roof surrounded by a balustrade. Above the entrance were the words, THE ACADEMY. Its pearly doors were open.

Elder Aaronia was a youthful Elder whose bearing reflected years of wisdom. She stood up from her office desk and walked down the hallway toward Elizon's office, her long, curly white hair swinging across her back. She found him busy talking to three new faculty Elders she had met earlier.

Moralee greeted her, "A bright Halo to you!" The twins spoke simultaneously, "Halo, Professor Aaronia!"

"Halo everyone! Elizon, I am ready to depart for the council meeting at the Lighthouse Space Station. How about you?" Aaronia asked, her amber eyes glowing.

"Indeed! I wouldn't miss it for the galaxy!" replied Elizon, as he straightened himself. "I am prepared to give my report. Elders Moralee and the twins will join us. Their messengers have instructed that we work on the mission together."

"You're in for a real treat!" Aaronia added excitedly. "I, for one, can't wait to hear news from the colonies about their exciting frontier adventures. And the ones from well-established worlds about the extraordinary things they have invented. It's all very exciting, but not always. There are also sad reports of fallen worlds struggling to regain their status under the Commonwealth."

The five Elders stood together—Elizon, Aaronia, Moralee, and the twins. Elizon held his hands out and asked, "My friends, are you ready?" They all nodded and held each other's hands in a circle. They glowed slowly and then disappeared in a bright flash of light. Elizon's office stood empty.

The Spirit of the Holy One carried the five Elders millions of light-years away in another part of the galaxy. Before Elizon appeared inside the Lighthouse station, he quickly glimpsed it from space. With its scintillating beacon, the lighthouse was a replica of the kind that beckoned the seasoned seafarers of Old Earth days. The lighthouse's domed shield protected the station and its natural habitat from the freezing void of space. Under the domed shield, a colorful paradise with edible vegetation surrounded the lighthouse.

THE LIGHTHOUSE

The five Elders reappeared under a large gazebo room filled with many Elders. They could see the stars through the domed shield and on one side, the tower with its scintillating beacon.

Other flashes appeared as more Elders arrived the same way. An Elder walked toward the five and beamed at them, "Welcome to our beacon of light for all spacefarers! I am chief councilor Elder Saludel. You must be Elders Aaronia and Elizon! Everyone here is excited about meeting our new members!" Elder Saludel was like all Elders—youthful, vibrant, physically fit, and energetic, with glossy white hair. The Elders were all dressed in their finest white garments and gold-striped mantles.

Aaronia greeted Saludel, "Pleased to meet you, Elder Saludel."

"As are we. I have brought three Elders, Moralee, Benzi, and Zephan." Elizon bowed respectfully as he introduced them.

Elder Saludel beamed, "You are welcome to get acquainted with our councilors. They are eager to meet you. We have no complicated rules for conducting our meetings. We share our reports in a relaxed manner. As immortals, time has no meaning." If one looked around carefully, the assembly hall where the meeting convened did not have a clock. Elder Saludel spread his arms and said, "Feel free to walk around."

Aaronia beamed and bowed graciously, "Thank you, Elder Saludel." And under the gazebo with its entwined vines, they met the councilors who had come from the far reaches of the Galactic Commonwealth of Zion.

Elizon walked around. It was the first time he had ever set foot at the Lighthouse Space Station. Surrounding the gazebos was an Edenic garden, a stream of living water gently running through it. As he walked on the soft ground of a well-established path, he spotted a man-sized rock with a fissure, water streaming out of it like a small waterfall, into a pond with multiple streams. One stream meandered toward the lighthouse. Elizon thought to himself, *That rock looked exactly like the one that Moshe hit in the wilderness!*

He continued walking the path toward a small bridge over the stream. The path led him toward a glowing tree that proudly carried fiery yellow and red foliage. The brilliant colors gave the tree the appearance of fire. He knew what it was. *The Tree of Life, its branch brought from Nova Zion and planted here.* He went toward it, looking at its fruits. They were small and ordinary, but he knew better. He plucked one and ate it. Suddenly, he felt himself tingling everywhere, transported into the presence of the Father of Light and the love that emanated from Him. Joy flooded his entire being. He looked at the garden and saw the glow from every plant and every living thing. He didn't know how long he was like this, but it felt like a long time. When he came out to rejoin the others, it was as if hardly any amount of time had passed.

☞ ☞ ☞

The emissary from Regalor was happy to see Elder Moralee, "I must tell you. We could not have asked for a better replacement. The children are in excellent care and curious about their new Elder."

"Glad to hear it, Elder Rolandel." Moralee said with wise eyes, "I will miss working with these sweet children!"

"You can always pop up and visit them anytime!" Rolandel said in jest, "No spaceship required!"

Moralee chuckled and remarked with a smile, "I'm not likely to forget where I came from."

"The next time you visit, you will bless us with your beautiful melodic voice and talented guitar worship again! They are what makes you unique."

"Of course! Elder Rolandel! Anytime!"

☞ ☞ ☞

A female Elder with short white hair and almost masculine features was speaking to Benzi and Zephan. "How are you two faring on Kristalis so far?"

"We've only arrived." Benzi replied and his twin Zephan added, "From what we've seen so far, it's an amazing place."

"No regrets about leaving Evanglar?" The Elder persisted with her questions, her demeanor showing concern for the twin Elders.

"Are you kidding? The weather's great!" Benzi replied and Zephan added, "For once, we can see the sun and stars! It's such a bright world!"

"You know me well, Benzi, Zephan. I am so thankful to Our Sovereign for giving us such precious Innocents like you two. After an Old Earth life with a barren womb, I have never been happier than when I was giving the responsibilities of raising so many precious children after the resurrection, children who never had a full Earth life. I have taken care of you for so long. I can't help feeling like a protective mother hen!" She finally smiled, her concern for the twins dissolving.

"Elder Sophira, we will continue to make you proud of us." Benzi said and Zephan added, "We thank you for everything you have done for us."

☞ ☞ ☞

The meeting was beginning. Inside the Lighthouse, Elders lined up to enter the round meeting hall. They were from all four corners of the galaxy. The room gleamed with gold walls, a domed silver ceiling, a copper floor, and sparkling lights everywhere. In the center of the meeting hall, twelve Elders sat at a round table representing the original twelve colonies. More tiers of occupied chairs surrounded the table, like a circular indoor amphitheater.

The chief councilor Elder Saludel stood up from the larger chair to preside over the council while everyone else sat down. He exuded a warm presence with his short white hair and beard. "Esteemed councilors of the Commonwealth Council of Emissaries, please note that this meeting is being held on the fourteenth day of the ninth month, year 19,314 After New Earth. Let us remember the wise words of the Royal Elder David of Bethlehem, as he stood along with the twenty-four Foundation Elders and addressed the first gathering of Kings and Elders twenty millennia ago..."

Long ago, our Sovereign Creator made some unconditional promises to me... that I will receive an everlasting dynasty and rest from all my enemies all around. Today, these words are being fulfilled before my very own eyes. Therefore, I, King David, of the former government of Israel, son of Jesse of Bethlehem, am honored to stand before such a multitude of people. I welcome all of you to the first council of Kings and Elders here on Nova Zion.

These are the words I prophesied: Let us praise Adonai Elohim with all our hearts in the council of the uprights and extol Him in the assembly of the righteous. How great are the works of Adonai, for they are pondered by all who delight in them. Today, I look at this great assembly of righteous remnant, and I see His exact words being fulfilled this minute. Our Elohim does great works! Let this Council begin so that His will may prosper. With the multitude of your counsels, His plan will succeed.

"And here we are, continuing this excellent Davidic tradition. This day, it is my pleasure to introduce two new members of this council, Elder Aaronia representing Kristalis, and Elder Elizon representing Indigor. We always begin with a report of the first-ever colonized world in the Galactic Commonwealth of Zion: Kristalis. Elder Aaronia, you may proceed. It is customary for new members to begin with a brief introduction of themselves."

Elder Aaronia stood up and addressed the council. "Thank you, Elder Saludel. It is an honor to be a part of this council. I am an Elder from the twentieth-century Earth and a Jewish survivor of the Holocaust. For a hundred and forty years, I was a consultant to Queen Valoria of Kristalis until eighty years ago when I transferred to the Youth Academy of Aliyah as a professor of ancient Israel history. It gives me great joy to be with young students, many of whom are my descendants at this excellent school." Aaronia's head of white hair glowed brighter as she spoke with warmth about her work.

"Now about Kristalis... We have been on Kristalis for over twelve millennia. The people are happy and prospering. Population growth, production, construction of new habitations, mining of opals and diamonds are about the same as they have been for the last millennia. Yesterday, I had a meeting with Queen Valoria, who has informed me of some exciting news." She continued as the Elders looked at each other, wondering what she meant.

"Although things remained the same since the colonization of Kristalis, there is something new on the horizon. Kristalis has arrived at an important crossroads. For the first time in our entire galactic history, humans and Elders are working side by side with the Seraphies." There was a buzz of excitement among the Elders at this news. Elder Aaronia waited until the buzz subsided to continue.

"As you well know, my predecessor has spoken to your

council of our relations with the Seraphies from the planet Serfaretz, the other habitable planet in the same star system. I have often consulted my dear friend Queen Victoria on how to approach a reserved species. For hundreds of years, we sent a representative to invite them to our Kristalis Council of Elders. Finally, a small group of Seraphies took part in our council three years ago. We have received them with warmth and they have given us excellent counsel. Then last year, they finally invited us to their council and have come up with a proposal." The buzz faded quickly.

Aaronia resumed. "For thousands of years, our adventurous people often visited Serfaretz for excursions, but the Seraphies have rarely ventured to meet the humans. This situation will soon be changing. What made them change their mind, you might ask? They have seen the excellent work the Elders have accomplished all over the galaxy. They realized they needed to grow as a people. They are descendants of the mighty Seraphim, who have humbly served the Sovereign Creator since time immemorial, but they are not an adventurous species. In contrast, humans have expanded to over two hundred worlds. Therefore, the Council of Seraphies has come up with a joint venture for a trial period. They have assigned four adults to work at our Academy and signed up twelve of their children to join our students as their new classmates. I have appointed one Seraphi as professor for the extra class, History of the Seraphies, and three others will assist him in developing the curriculum. If our venture becomes successful, they will send more Seraphies to other academies. This is only the beginning. The younger generation of humans who will grow with the young Seraphies and develop even better relations with them than we Elders ever had. They will step into an amazing future!" She ended the last part with a flourish. She saw the transfixed faces of her audience at this exciting news.

"I know how you feel. This historical milestone is a

surprise to our Academy Elders, too. For the first time in the history of the Galactic Commonwealth of Zion, our respective races will work side-by-side. The angelic race has always worked with us since time immemorial. For us, this undertaking with the Seraphies is untested. Therefore, I ask the council to pray for prosperity and bless our joint venture with the Seraphies." She ended on a more solemn note and stepped away from the podium to let the presiding councilor take over.

Elder Saludel stood up to speak. At first, there was silence. Aaronia's wonderful news was overwhelming.

"This is an auspicious time! You have our blessing. Let's go to the next report, but I think nothing will ever top this incredible news." His comment produced a few chuckles from the councilors.

The meeting went on. The representatives from each world brought their report. When it was Elder Elizon's turn to make his report, Elder Saludel stood up to introduce him.

"And here is our new council member, Elder Elizon, the Emissary for the inhabitants of Indigor."

"Thank you, Elder Saludel." Elizon stood up to greet the council, "I am honored that our Creator has chosen me for this council. Like my esteemed colleague Elder Aaronia, I am also an Elder from Old Earth, late twentieth century. Before my current position as Professor of Ministry and Missions at the Youth Academy of Aliyah, I was a consultant to the mayor of Kristalipolis and Crown City on Kristalis. I have been visiting Indigor for the past three hundred years under the guidance of the former predecessor of this council. Indigor was the sixth colonial world and the first to have fallen. Since year 13,337 ANE, our Creator has commanded the entire world of Indigor quarantined from the rest of the galaxy when its people rebelled and fell from grace. Corruption spread fast, especially after a comet crashed on Indigor. All these ecological disasters, wars, crimes, famines, and plagues, have reduced the lifespan of the Indigans to 105 years."

Elizon continued, "The Indigans rebuilt their world slowly. About five hundred years ago, their archeologists unearthed the old technologies of the first civilization and their scientists duplicated them. The age of reason and science emerged. The people questioned the stories of the Holy Writings. They viewed everything through the filter of science. A rift grew between those who practiced our faith and those who didn't. Certain rulers became involved, fearing a repeat of the first wars that wiped out much of their population."

"One of these powerful leaders, a charismatic man named Contrero Hadebar, enacted a law to ban the meeting places of the faithful believers, declaring such events illegal. He imprisoned those who resisted. When that didn't stop the faithful Indigans, Contrero established a special branch of the government to pursue these so-called radical believers. Contrero sent them to life imprisonment, but they remained faithful to the end. Then Contrero passed another law banning the ownership of the Holy Writings. His cronies have destroyed sixty-nine holy libraries. They relentlessly persecuted anyone who resisted giving away the Holy Writings. His police went door-to-door confiscating all the holy books. This action proved to be a more effective deterrent. Without the Holy Writings, teaching was harder. They enacted stricter laws. As of today, owning religious text, whether a book or a single piece of paper, is a crime that carries the death penalty. Gradually, the remnant who taught from memory died out. On an interesting note, Contrero Hadebar had fulfilled the true meaning of his given name, 'against the Word.' Before he died, he created another branch of government called BITE, which stands for the Bureau of Investigation for Technological Enforcement, but the people have nicknamed them 'Biters.' The succeeding leadership continued his ruthless legacy of forcing people into using technologies instead of paper and books."

Elizon continued addressing the council, his tone with a hint of sadness, "The last two hundred years have been difficult for Indigans. They have lost much of the knowledge about their Creator and the Holy Writings. Indigor has one remaining holy library intact, hidden underground, and kept safe by a remnant of the Brotherhood of Scribes and Keepers. People are still being imprisoned for less severe crimes, for a simple thing as owning a blank piece of paper and a pen.”

“A new generation of Indigans have come into a world that knows nothing of their origins. Their parents read them the old stories at bedtime, but in their hearts, they believe them to be the stuff of legends, myths, and fairy tales. They don’t know how to write. The schools teach them to use only electronic tablets.”

“Indigor has a vital resource called ethium, a rare element that is a source of long-lasting energy, which is used to make batteries for running a household. Although there are plenty of cheap ethium, technicians are a much more valuable commodity. A homeowner is lucky if he can find a technician to replace home appliances or a mechanic to fix his automobile. Knowledge of technology is more valuable than the energy that powers it. The technicians are in control and get what they want, often oppressing the people. They give away communicators for free, then they invade every facet of people’s private life, collecting personal information about their citizens, and storing it in a vast database by which they search using certain keywords.”

“On my last visit to Indigor, I spoke with the Brothers.” He paused briefly, then continued in a sad tone, “Two brothers have passed away recently. We will miss brother Sherman, as the Brotherhood considered him the wisest of them all. They are the last remnant of the Brotherhood in all Indigor. The Biters are relentless in their pursuit to rid the world of the remaining Holy Writings.”

Elizon paused, gathering his thoughts to convey his greatest concern, “I feel obligated to report that we need to train new Brothers. It has been seven generations since the destruction of the holy libraries. As my esteemed colleague Elder Aaronia mentioned, we are standing at a critical historical crossroads with our friends, the Seraphies. I have attained this position for such a time as this. Last night, the Holy One sent a messenger to reach me, and he confirmed everything that I have seen. The messenger also notified me of the three Elders who will assist me on the mission, also sent from the Holy One. They arrived here with me. That is my report. I ask humbly for your support and prayer." And Elizon sat down. There was a buzz of excitement in the assembly hall. Many of the councilors nodded their heads in agreement. Someone walked up to the Elder Saludel and whispered into his ears, and he nodded in approval.

As Elder Saludel got up, he remarked, "Elder Elizon's report has reminded me that this Council of Emissaries was founded to ensure that all the people in the Commonwealth are all spiritually connected with our Creator, that it exists solely to combat the forces of darkness effectively. We take extra care when the Holy One sends his messengers. Words spoken with the power of the Spirit through prayers and petitions to the Holy One have the power to change the destinies of fallen worlds."

An hour later, the Council adjourned. The Spirit of the Creator carried the council Elders back to their homes. Each of them felt blessed by the Spirit of the Holy One.

And the five were carried away by the Spirit again, back into Elizon's office in a flash of light. Their auras continued to glow. They didn't speak for a while as they savored the peaceful, lingering presence of the Spirit.

CHAPTER FOUR

NEW BEGINNINGS

In the beginning,
Elohim created
the heavens
and the earth.
~Adam the First

KRISTALIS, THE NEXT DAY

A new day dawned on a world that was but a minor part of the Galactic Commonwealth of Zion. The United Orion Interstellar Spacecraft was transporting the new Academy students across the vast distance of the galaxy. They saw the planet Kristalis through the portholes of the spacecraft, a glowing blue sphere with a sparkling white ring, in the orbit of a light-yellow dwarf sun. Some passengers were excited, and some were nervous.

For many of them, it was their maiden voyage across the vast cosmos.

The steward held his hand to his communicator and announced, "Please remain seated while we land at the Kristalis Galactic Spaceport on Kristalipolis. And here is a little historical background about this fair planet. The intergalactic pioneer colonized the first world, Kristalis, 7023 years After New Earth. Since that time, they have inhabited it for over twelve millennia. Kristalipolis is the largest city. Crown City is the capital. The ring of Kristalis has the largest diamonds in the universe which the Kristalians export to the colonies, along with its crystals and opalescent stones. The foundation diamonds of Nova Zion come from this world." The steward continued, pointing his hand toward the large windshield where the blue sphere was glowing.

"The Kristalians greet each other with 'Halo!'" The steward waved his hand and continued, "The word 'Halo' combines the old English word 'hello' with the name of the ring around Kristalis. Halo also is the crown of light surrounding an Elder's head. So, whenever you go, greet the Kristalians with 'Halo to you!' And you will make new friends." A few passengers chuckled at the steward's commentary.

The steward continued as the spacecraft descended toward the Kristalis Galactic Spaceport, "The name of the reigning monarch of Kristalis is Elder Queen Valoria. On Old Earth, we knew her as Jeanne D'Arc, a humble peasant girl, a woman of valor, who had the courage to obey the voice of the Creator. She led her nation, France, against the oppressive English armies and died at the young age of nineteen, burned at the stake for heresy. She died a martyr and resurrected at the end of the age to become a Royal Elder of the Commonwealth."

"Queen Valoria reigns from the magnificent Crown City. I encourage you to visit the capital city, which the Kristalians carved out of one enormous opalescent stone. The first Royal Elder planted the tree of life in the center of Crown City. It was first brought as a branch from Nova Zion. Welcome to Kristalis!"

The spacecraft made a smooth landing on a large platform. Viewed from the windows of the spacecraft, the city of crystals bore its name proudly. Its skyscrapers sparkled brightly against the backdrop of an azure sky.

A girl with striking violet eyes viewed the sparkling city through the porthole. Revelyn Trudy Pryor had not been listening to the steward, for she knew everything about the fair planet below. Mixed emotions fleeted across her pale face as she realized that the azure sky was without clouds. She felt exposed to the sun. She came from a cloudy planet where the sunshine was scarce and her skin was like alabaster. She thought, *I don't know what I am doing here. I will miss my homeland, my parents, and my friends.* The voyage entailed an emotional sacrifice on her part. Her home was her comfort zone, and she was now in unfamiliar surroundings. As everyone prepared to disembark, she stood up from her seat. She put on the silver-striped mantle over her violet blouse and swept back her long silky raven-black hair with her hands.

Revelyn sighed and picked up her carry-on bag. As she stood in line with the other young passengers to disembark, she determined to overcome her apprehension. She braced for the dawn of a new day in her life. A rush of courage rippled through her soul as she stepped outside. It was a bright and beautiful sunny day on Kristalis. The air smelled pleasant, of ozone with a hint of earth and pines. She saw a cloudless sky of such a brilliant azure blue that all clouds of doubt in her soul dissolved like vapor. She was ready to begin a life full of promises and adventures, eager to expand her boundaries.

Several rows behind Revelyn, a tall, dark-skinned teen stood up to disembark. Kato Elihu Obuni was a handsome teen with a long neck, generous lips, and warm brown eyes. He was smiling, ready for a new beginning, his sense of adventure heightened. He reached for his silver-striped mantle, putting it over the multicolored tunic that his proud mother had made from scratch from their little cotton field—spun, dyed, woven, and sewn together. He put on the matching multi-colored kufi cap on his head. The white mantle stood out starkly against his ebony skin, making his neck appear longer.

The new students in their white mantles disembarked from the spacecraft. They flocked through the debarkation room toward the hover shuttles like white doves, the silver stripes of their mantles shining softly under the bright sun of Kristalis. They were going to their destination—the Academy on the floating village of Aliyah.

Elder Shanielle was piloting a hovering shuttle full of wide-eyed students from the spaceport. She touched the display screen on the dashboard of the shuttle to turn on the communicator.

Daleah, at home, had just finished a bowl of fruit for her breakfast. The communicator on the wall of the kitchen rang twice before Daleah answered it with the click of a button. She had been expecting it. She smiled as she saw her Ancie Shanielle's face on the screen. She answered cheerfully, "Halo Ancie! I am so excited and ready to go!"

"Halo Daleah! We are all excited. I am on my way to your house now. Be ready at the front of the house in five minutes with your luggage." She signed off. Daleah's mother, who had been busy cleaning the kitchen, heard Daleah.

"Mama, Ancie will be here in five minutes. Time to get everyone to the front door!" Daleah announced as she rushed to get her luggage.

She walked to her bedroom. Unbeknown to her, while she had been eating breakfast, savoring the last hour with her family before leaving for the Academy, her three-year-old quadruplet brothers had sneaked out of their playroom into her bedroom. They were jumping excitedly on her bed. One boy accidentally kicked the latch on her suitcase. It sprung open, clothes flying all over the bed. Daleah's underwear landed one boy's head, another piece on his brother's hand, and another on his brother's thigh. It didn't stop them from jumping on the bed and flopping the suitcase on the floor, scattering more clothes.

Daleah gasped the minute she walked in, her expression horrified, hand on her mouth. She screamed, "NOOO!" Her older niece, Risenne, heard her yelling, and ran into the room quickly. She froze as she saw what happened.

"No, no, no!" Daleah yelled as she grabbed two of her little brothers off the bed, "Look at what you have done! How many times did I tell you, you are not allowed in my room! Get off the bed and get out!" Risenne was grabbing the other two boys. Her parents also heard her and walked in. Their mouths gaped at the scene.

"Mama, please do something!" Daleah was frantic. "Help me, Ancie is coming in five minutes!"

"Oh, Daleah!" Still dumbfounded, her mother exclaimed. "I don't know how the Quads sneaked in there! They were in their playroom."

Her father, who had the same reaction, quickly grabbed one boy and swung him under his strong-muscled arm and picked up the other boy with his other arm. "It's my fault!" Her father apologized, while holding them both under his arms, "I was watch them and went to the other room briefly to get my shoes."

"Risenne, please help Daleah pack her clothes," Daleah's mother led the two other boys away from their frantic sister, "and I will take care of this."

With the boys gone, Daleah gave voice to her feelings, "I am so glad I am going away!" She picked up and folded her clothes to repack her suitcase, her movements quick and determined, "I swear I will not miss my brothers, and I will enjoy the peace and quiet!"

"I don't blame you," Risenne quietly said while folding the clothes.

Daleah's older sister Mikalah came in and asked,

"Mama sent me to help you. What happened here?"

"A fiasco is what happened! The boys were at it again! Please help! Ancie will be here soon," Daleah lamented. "I spent all day yesterday packing and unpacking three times, and this is what I get for my effort!"

"Calm down! We are here to help you." Mikalah tried to comfort Daleah, quickly picking up the remaining clothes scattered on the floor.

The entire family gathered at the front door, barely in time. Even Lupel had shown up. Piloted by Elder Shanielle, the hovering shuttle landed in front of the house. Her mother, sister, brother, and niece were holding the hands of the squirming boys, who were excited to see the hover shuttle. Daleah quickly slipped on her handmade mantle.

Daleah's family hugged her, wishing her well, while her father carried the luggage to the trunk compartment of the shuttle. Daleah ran to Shanielle, hugging her tightly at the waist. Daleah was three feet shorter than Shanielle, for all Elders towered over fully grown humans by two to three feet.

"I am so happy to see you, Ancie!" Daleah exclaimed, still holding on to Shanielle's waist.

"I'm happy to see you too, sweetie. Let's go inside the shuttle. I would like to introduce you to your new roommate after I hug the family." The family was always happy to see their ancestress, giving her a group hug. It was always a great honor when she came to see them. Revelyn watched from the windows of the shuttle, amazed at Daleah's large family. As Shanielle and Daleah came into the shuttle, Elder Shanielle introduced them.

"This is Daleah Inara Joyce, and this is Revelyn Trudy Pryor. You two will be roommates." Then she announced to the rest of the students in the shuttle, "Everyone, this is Daleah, my Descie." The students smiled and waved at Daleah as Shanielle left for the pilot's seat.

"Halo! Nice to meet you." It was the first Halo that Revelyn had uttered since landing on Kristalis. It felt unusual saying it, like speaking an unfamiliar language.

"Halo to you too!" Daleah answered in kind.

Daleah put her backpack in the overhead compartment and sat next to Revelyn. They sat quietly together as they watched the family waving at them. Daleah couldn't say anything because she needed to catch her breath after the fiasco.

"You have such have a big family." Revelyn broke the awkward silence. "You are blessed!"

"You think so?" Daleah asked.

"Oh, definitely! Where I come from, I am the only child, and I have no cousins my age yet. It can be lonesome."

"Oh," said Daleah somberly, "I didn't realize." Revelyn's comment made her thoughtful. She might have been too harsh on her little brothers. It's not their fault. They are toddlers and don't yet understand. She sighed and looked at Revelyn, "Actually, my mother's pregnancy with the quadruplets was unexpected and came too soon. They are only eleven years younger than me."

"Ah, the age gap between siblings... You're right," said Revelyn, "that is unusually close. The average gap in years between siblings is 22 years. Still, your little brothers look adorable." She smiled.

"Adorable?" Daleah replied with a respectful tone, "I've heard that word so many times about the famous quadruplets! Just wait until you've experienced living with them for one month, then you wouldn't be so quick to call them adorable!" She frowned, unable to shake the frozen image of the disturbing moment of her undies atop her brother's head. *I am not going to share this private thought with my new roommate!*

Daleah's comment about her brothers made Revelyn laugh, an uncommon reaction that surprised Daleah. "What's so funny?"

"It's not really. You've made me forget my concern. I

miss my family already and you made me think differently. We will be best friends!"

"You think so?" Daleah asked, wondering how Revelyn would know.

"I know so." Then she leaned closer to Daleah and lowered her voice so that the others in the shuttle wouldn't hear her. "I will tell you a secret tidbit about the Elders. They have many amazing abilities that we humans won't have until we become one of them. We call one of these abilities shadchan. I know what you're thinking. The shadchan matchmaker is not only for matching a man and woman together for marriage. They do it for other situations, like matching roommates, friends, and coworkers. Sometimes they don't realize they are even doing it. That's how I know you and I will be best friends."

"Really, and I thought Ancie Shanielle was always wise." Daleah said as she eyed Revelyn closely, wondering how she got so smart, "You know this, how?"

"I can memorize a roomful of books about the Elders," Revelyn replied somberly. "It's not something I tell everyone."

"The Creator must have blessed you with much knowledge." Daleah said, impressed with Revelyn.

"There wasn't much else for me to do, being an only child. Your family is a blessing. See, I told you." Revelyn smiled, pointing her index finger at Daleah. "We complement each other."

And they chatted and laughed throughout the entire trip. Ancie Shanielle looked into the rearview mirror as she was piloting the hovering shuttle. She couldn't hear them, but she saw Daleah and Revelyn becoming friends. She smiled, knowing in her heart that she had selected an excellent roommate for her sweet Descie.

THE PLANET INDIGOR

Haro was riding his high-wheeler bicycle around the neighborhood. On his way back home, he stopped where a crowd of onlookers had gathered in front of a neighbor's house.

He dropped his wheeler on the lawn and walked over. His best friend and neighbor, Jamik Bond Tahaven, was standing with the onlookers. Haro and Jamik grew up as playmates, riding their wheelers and skateboards together. Haro hadn't hung out with Jamik outside of school since Jamik took part in sports. Haro preferred the quiet solitude of reading on various subjects he found interesting. Jamik knew nothing of Haro's genius.

"Hey, dude!" Haro said as he gently bumped into Jamik, "What's up?"

"Haro!" Jamik seemed pleasantly surprised. "The police are here."

"Strange... I know these neighbors." Haro inquired, "They are elders. Do you know why?"

"No idea," said Jamik, shrugging his shoulders, "but you see the officer in the grey uniform?" He said as he pointed to the man with the BITE emblem on the shoulder patch of his uniform. "That gent is one scary-looking BITE officer." Jamik and Haro watched as this gloomy officer barked orders to the blue-uniformed cops.

"Did they find anything?" Haro inquired further,

"Not yet. I arrived moments ago. Let's wait and see." They watched together with the onlookers.

"I'm sorry," said Jamik, "that I didn't attend your father's funeral."

"No big. It was two months ago."

"Family okay?" Jamik asked. "I know how close you were to your father. A tragic car accident!" Haro had been dwelling on his father's legacy for the past two months and keeping it a secret from everyone.

"Mom is still grieving. And you? Is the knee better?" Haro had heard about Jamik's recent knee injury at one of the school's games.

Jamik lifted his right thigh and stretched his leg, wincing. "Still not fully healed. Coach doesn't want his best player hurt until the knee's better. I'm going crazy at doing nothing!"

Haro's sister Ladya had shown up with her best friend Mei Herre, a tall teen with platinum blonde hair, both curious to see what was happening. Whenever they were together, Mei always interpreted in sign language for Ladya.

Mei spoke while signing, "What's happening?"

Jamik explained everything that happened. "Biters looking for evidence." They stood and watched, while Mei towered above the crowd.

The BITE officer came out of the house, carrying a transparent bag with the illegal items, a piece of paper with text on it and a pen. His heart skipped a beat, and his face almost drained of color. The items looked similar to the ones Haro found in his father's first wooden box. He kept his face expressionless, hoping no one would notice.

"There goes buh-bye to prison neighbors! All this fuss over a strange piece of paper!" Jamik remarked as the cops escorted the elderly couple, their hands handcuffed, to the police vehicle.

Haro answered him, "Haven't you heard? Owning a single piece of paper with religious text is a serious offense and carries a death penalty. If it's blank paper or pen, it's only one-year imprisonment." Haro was signing for Ladya.

"What?" The three of them looked at Haro in incredulous surprise, "No way!" Ladya's face showed a variety of emotions from surprise to disgust, then anger and sadness. She didn't need to sign what she felt, for it was all on her face. As the saying goes, if a person can wear his heart on his sleeve, Ladya's heart was on her face.

"Why would the Biters arrest people with religious text?" Jamik asked, "And how do you know this?" He was looking at Haro as if seeing him for the first time.

"It's a long story. I did some research. I'm surprised that it happened right here. It rarely happens now."

"Why research depressing topic?" Ladya asked, using her hand language.

Haro hesitated. "I can tell you more later. Why don't we get together at our house for some ice cream?" Haro didn't want the cops or onlookers to overhear them.

"You sure you want me there?" Jamik asked, "After ignoring you all year?"

Haro shrugged his shoulders, "No big! You were busy with sport activities. It wasn't my thing."

"It has been a year since we've hung together." Jamik remarked, surprised at the change in Haro. In the past, it has irked Haro that Jamik did not hang out with him. The four of them agreed and went to the Gallants' home.

In the kitchen, Ladya served cake and ice cream, and Haro brought their favorite drinks to their best friends. Haro was smiling happily, realizing how much he had missed his friend Jamik. Maybe with Jamik being out of commission, we might spend some time together.

They sat down to eat and drink in the family room, Haro told them of his research into the brief history behind the mass arrests that led to the prohibition of religious text, paper, and pens. He shared with them what he learned from the Indigonet, which wasn't much.

Then Mei excitedly shared some news with them, voicing and signing for Ladya's benefit. "Hey guys, guess what? I came back from Indipolis last weekend. The Queen invited me to the royal wedding! I got photos to share!" She took the camera out of her purse.

Haro looked surprised, "How come?"

"You remember not?" Ladya signed with her hands, facing Haro, "Me told you invite to cousin's marriage ceremony to King. She new Queen!"

"The new queen is my cousin twice removed!" Mei informed the group proudly, looking important, tossing her long platinum blond hair.

"I'm impressed," Haro said, raising his left eyebrow.

"Aren't they supposed to invite only close family members?" Jamik asked.

Mei looked at Jamik and said with hands on her hips, looking proud, "They didn't invite me at first. Then my other cousin got sick, so the bride invited me in her stead!"

Then Jamik snorted, voicing his disapproval of the

wedding, "My mom watched the whole wedding on the tele. It was long and tedious. I fell asleep halfway through it. I never understood the point of everyone wearing white outfits in public, white wigs, and sparkling stuff. Why bother wearing high heels if they are already tall? Why are the men wearing them too? Dumb traditions! I bet it makes them feel superior! They are a bunch of pompous misfits who waste our taxpayers' money!"

"Hey!" Mei looked upset at Jamik's comments, "That's not a fair description of the royals!"

Haro somehow found the conversation amusing and burst out laughing, which made Mei even more upset. Mei got up from the couch and ran off to the kitchen.

Ladya gave Haro and Jamik dirty looks and signed, "Now, see what you done!" She announced with a sarcastic facial expression, "You morons, wonderful people skill!" She followed Mei to the kitchen to comfort her.

"What now?" Jamik looked at Haro, shrugging his shoulders, "Should I apologize for speaking my mind?"

"They will get over it," Haro replied while shrugging his shoulder.

"At least," Jamik remarked, "you find this amusing."

"To tell you the truth, I missed those carefree days when we used to have fun." Growing up as playmates, they used to fight, but they always got along. Haro remembered, *I haven't laughed since my father's death. Maybe being together again will be good for me.*

Haro smiled at Jamik, lifted his drink, and proclaimed, "Well, here's to a new beginning!"

THE ACADEMY, KRISTALIS

The evening arrived. It was time for the welcoming ceremony. Daleah had her wild curly hair pulled into a ponytail. It emphasized her oval face. The freckles on her cheeks seemed less visible in the dimmer light of the evening. She smoothed her dress, feeling somewhat self-conscious. She slipped on a silky mantle over a long formal dress. Revelyn had dressed similarly, her raven hair done in a braided chignon, strands of straight hair framing her round face.

Revelyn remarked as she pointed to Daleah's prayer mantle, "Your tallit is lovely! Did you make it?"

Daleah replied as Revelyn handled her tallit, "Mama sewed it and I did the embroidery with silver thread."

Revelyn twirled to show off her own dress. "What do you think?

Daleah remarked, "You look amazing! I've never met anyone with fair skin like yours. You won't get sunburned tomorrow when we go on the tour?" It was Daleah's nature to be full of questions.

"The Academy sent me instructions on how care for my sensitive skin and eyes." Revelyn assured Daleah. "I hope to get a nice tan like yours!"

"What tan?" Daleah inquired, face perplexed. "It's the color of my skin! Everyone on Kristalis is like this."

"I know." Revelyn laughed. "Let's get going!" She took Daleah by the arm, and they walked together down the hallways with arms linked.

Daleah and Revelyn followed the throng of students walking toward the grand assembly hall. The crowd was abuzz with the excited chatter of students.

Walls of iridescent opals surrounded the grand assembly hall. Columns of gold, silver, and copper were a reminder of the Millennium temple that graced the Old Earth. Chandeliers with sparkling crystal icicles hung from the high ceiling, held together by a globe of light. They refracted tiny rainbows of light across the ceiling and walls. Silky white gossamer veils billowed from a gentle wind through the tall arched doorways that led to the colonnade outside, where some students gazed in awe at the breathtaking evening sky. The arch of the Halo was half-illuminated by a setting sun, changing the sky to a warm pink glow at the horizon.

The assembly hall was festive. A delightful assortment of vegetables and fruits decorated the tables, all beautifully laid out. On each round table was a festive centerpiece exquisitely carved from large melons and other fruits, in the shape of flowers and leaves. Everywhere, the tables displayed various well arranged food platters, each with an assortment of sweet dipping sauces, and many pies—fruit, nuts, and creamy pies. Each plate setting at the tables had tall glasses of smoothies topped with whipped cream, white plates shaped like large leaves, the finest flatware of gold, and sparkling crystal goblets for drinking the finest grape juice. The polished white tables looked like white marble, with intricately carved legs.

Many students gaped in awe by the lavish display. Their families served such elaborate dishes only on Passover and other appointed festivals with their families. The opening reception at the Academy was special. The waiters, with their copper-striped mantles over white outfits and copper sashes, carried the last of the food to the tables.

"This is amazing! Come on, let's find our table!" Daleah exclaimed as she took Revelyn by the hand to found their table. They sat down on the ornate chairs, next to a tall, dark-skinned boy, who courteously got up to greet them, extending his hand.

"Halo, my name is Kato Elihu Obuni from Ankatar. Delighted to make your acquaintance." He inclined his head and extended his hand to shake theirs.

Revelyn seemed shy toward Kato, so Daleah took his hand and replied, "Halo to you! I am Daleah Inara Joyce from Kristalis, and this is my roommate Revelyn Trudy Pryor from Evanglar."

Another boy from their table also got up and introduced himself. "Halo, I'm Enoch Beahm Walker from Leviatar. I'm Kato's roommate. Pleased to meet you!"

Revelyn offered a timid greeting, "Nice to meet you both." Daleah nodded, "Pleased!"

Then more introductions as students of all diverse backgrounds arrived at their table. They were all wearing silver-striped mantles over formal white outfits in the various styles customary of their home worlds.

When everyone sat down, Daleah looked expectantly toward the platform. The tall Elders sat behind a long table, on luxurious throne-like chairs. They had dressed in their finest white garments and gold-striped mantles. Daleah recognized Elders Shanielle and Elizon among them. Ancie Shanielle was smiling and looking at her. Daleah smiled back.

Revelyn leaned her head toward Daleah and remarked, "Notice there's an empty seat at this table? All the other tables have one empty seat each too."

Daleah looked at Revelyn with surprise. "You're right. I haven't noticed. You're quite observant."

An Elder stood up, and the chatter of students subsided. He signaled everyone with his hand to stand up. The Elder of Elders lifted a gold cup of wine. He recited the blessing in the ancient tongue, *"Baruch ata Adonai,"* his rich baritone voice carrying across the grand hall, *"Elohenu, Malech ha olam, borai pri hagafen."* He lifted the flatbread and continued, *"Hamotzi lechem min ha aretz."* He took a single large grape that was the size of his fist from the bowl. He squeezed the grape until its juice filled his goblet and recited, *"Uborai pri ha aitz. Amen."*

Everyone said, "Amen."

Then he recited the same blessing again in the universal language of the Commonwealth, "Blessed are You, Lord our God, King of the Universe who creates the fruit of the vine, and who brings forth the bread from the earth. Amen."

Again, everyone said, "Amen."

The Elder broke the flatbread into several pieces and put one piece each into several large gold bowls. Then, the ushers passed the bowls to the students' tables. Amazingly, the bowls had somehow become filled to the brim with more bread pieces. What started as one piece of bread blessed by the Elder had multiplied a thousand-fold. The ushers also brought the pitchers of water to the tables. Amazingly, the water also changed to wine that tasted like the sweetest grape juice.

Then the Elder of Elders announced, "Together, let us sit and eat and rejoice in His Presence. Headmistress Mariel has a matter of great importance to announce to everyone after the meal. She will also explain the reason for the empty seats at each table."

Everyone helped themselves to the food and chatted away. Kato asked the group at the table, as they finished pilling the food on their plates and began eating. "So, what do you think? Empty chairs for students from one of the faraway colonies?"

"No idea, but it's possible." Enoch replied as he ate the blessed bread.

"I thought this Academy accepts students only in the Orion Belt?" Daleah said as she ate a vegetable salad.

"That's correct." Revelyn, overcoming her shyness, interjected as she forked a piece of mixed nut pie, "That's what the Academy charter says."

"Whoever they were, the flights were most likely delayed." Daleah volunteered.

"Delayed? Maybe a few, but there's one empty chair on each table." Kato said as he sliced a large strawberry the size of an apple and dipped it in a creamy sauce.

"I have a theory." Revelyn volunteered, feeling less shy. "They transferred to another school at the last minute."

"How about desertion?" Enoch volunteered his theory.

Everyone looked at him strangely. "My Ancie told me this story of someone whose parents sent him to a college." Enoch explained, "Despite his protest, he wasn't interested in pursuing school, so he ran away."

"Let's wait and see who's right!" Kato grinned, showing white teeth that contrasted with his dark skin, "The one with the right answer will win a prize!"

Everyone smiled. "What's the prize?" Daleah asked.

"Ah, Freckles," Kato replied somberly, "Maybe either you or Black Beauty here might win an hour of suffering in my presence." Kato replied somberly. The group smiled, a few chuckled, and Daleah laughed. No one had called her

Freckles before.

"Hey," Daleah raised her glass of grape juice and declared, "let's toast to our new friendship with this sweet wine!"

They raised their glasses and declared, *"L'chaim!"* "To our new friendship!" And everyone shared stories of growing up on their homeworld. For the first time in a long time, Daleah felt carefree and not bound by her family responsibilities.

As the meal neared its end, the Headmistress Mariel got up to speak. The chatter subsided as the students looked at her expectantly.

"Welcome to the Aliyah Academy! I am Professor Mariel and the Headmistress of this excellent academy. I hope you are adjusting well to your new surroundings. This academy has a long history of inspiring students to find their true passion, and equally important, of nurturing a spirit of compassion. We have always striven to bring together young people of diverse cultures and worlds. Tonight is a historic day, beginning with this incredible news, the biggest news since Kristalis was first settled by the pilgrims from Nova Terra. This is something brand new for the entire galaxy too." Daleah glanced at Revelyn, her eyes saying, I have no clues.

"For the first time in our entire galactic history, humans will work side-by-side with a different species, the Seraphies." There was a buzz of excitement from the young audience. Elder Mariel waited until it subsided.

The headmistress announcement came as a shock to Daleah. She recalled her "accidental" encounter with a young Seraphi two years ago on a camping expedition with her family.

"Some of you might ask, who are the Seraphies and where are they from? Kristalis and Serfaretz are two habitable planets in this solar system. We, humans and Elders, have visited Serfaretz many times. The Seraphies are descendants of the mighty Seraphim who guard the throne of our Holy One. It is an honor to announce that the Seraphies, the Elders, and humans will work on a joint venture for the first time in the history of the Galactic Commonwealth, right here at this Academy." The buzz started again, and Mariel didn't wait long for it to subside, for everyone wanted to know the rest of the story.

"The Council of Seraphies has sent four new professors and twelve of their youngsters to our Academy. These new students will be mainstreamed into our Academy, taking classes with you. And here they are, our Seraphi friends. Let us welcome them." Elder Mariel ended with a flourish, her face radiantly glowing, her right hand pointed to the entry of the grand assembly hall. Everyone stood up.

All eyes turned toward the tall entry door. A row of Seraphies streamed through the hall toward the Elders, surrounded by the gawking students. The tall Seraphies, their wings folded, walked humbly toward the Elders. The first four Seraphies were taller, their bearing filled with years of wisdom, each with two pairs of wings. They were of four distinct races. One race had the face of a lion, the second an ox, the next an eagle, and the last the face of a rugged man. After them, twelve shorter, younger Seraphies of each race, each with one pair of wings, followed. They were all wearing the customary white mantles over neutral-colored knee-length tunics that accommodated their wings. One could see their furred or feathered legs. They were all without shoes or sandals.

As Daleah watched them, she suddenly remembered the dream she had the night before about meeting the Seraphi, a feline with the face of a lion. Her face showed surprise as she recognized the Seraphi. It was he whom she met two years ago.

The Seraphies had reached the platform. They stood side by side with the Elders, the older Seraphies of equal height as the Elders.

The headmistress continued, "I am pleased to introduce our friends. Professor Silvero DeTabor will teach a new class, the *History of the Seraphies*, with his three assistants, Axel DePastur, Sorael DeNestle, and Michael DeTerra. They have brought their children with them, who will be students here." Professor Silvero moved closer to Mariel to speak

"On behalf of all of us, we are honored to be here to work with all of you." His voice was deep. "Allow me to introduce our group." And he approached the first young Seraphi.

"This is my son, Rory DeTabor." He put his hand on his son's shoulder. Their resemblance was remarkable, their fur and mane of a glossy grey, like silver.

"Pleased to meet all of you." Rory greeted the audience, his voice not as deep as his father's. He smiled with his sharp teeth, inclined his head, and waved his paws.

The new professor moved on to introduce other young Seraphies, "Mona DePastur, Soraya DeNestle, Nataniel DeTerra..."

After the introductions, the headmistress invited the young Seraphies to join the students at their tables.

As Rory walked toward Daleah's table, she realized something more. Rory's coming here was part of a plan, like the dream she had last night. She watched him as he walked toward her table, looking directly at her. He hadn't forgotten our encounter two years ago on Serfaretz. He is here, the last place I ever expected him to be. Am I still dreaming?

"Guess no one won that prize." Kato spoke to the group at the table, louder than usual, "Looks like Rory is coming to meet us." Kato, excited to meet the young feline Seraphi, rose from his seat and was the first to extend his hand. Everyone at the table also rose to greet him. "Thrilled to meet you, Rory DeTabor! It is an amazing day for all of us." He began by introducing himself, still shaking Rory's hand enthusiastically. "I am Kato Elihu Obuni from Ankatar. This is Enoch Walker from Leviatar, Revelyn from Evanglar and..."

Kato stopped because Rory spoke up. "Daleah Inara

Joyce, it's good to see you again." He moved toward her, bowing his head respectfully. Although Daleah seemed somewhat dazed, she responded in kind.

Daleah's friends were dumbfounded. Kato spoke, "You know Daleah?"

Rory looked at everyone at the table. Upon seeing their surprised expressions, he explained, "I see, you don't know the story. Daleah and her family went camping on Serfaretz two years ago. She was gathering wood for the campfire and had somehow gotten lost. A powerful gust of wind led her away. These whirlwinds can happen suddenly on Serfaretz. She somehow ended up finding shelter in our small cave, surprising my friends and me. Being shy, I dared to come up to her and helped her find her way back to her family."

Although Daleah spoke while waving her hand, "It was nothing—more of an accidental meeting. We spoke briefly."

Rory's penetrating look made Daleah feel disconcerted. Rory spoke again, "Actually, Daleah, I have you to thank for this moment. Our brief encounter with your startling questions sparked me into making this thing happen."

"Me?" Daleah stared at Rory with wide eyes, and squeaked, "I did this? I don't see how this little humble me would do all this."

Rory laughed while everyone watched the two of them in wonder. "Nothing in life is accidental. That gust of wind was the Holy One's humorous way of showing the Seraphies we needed to get our heads out of the sand, as the famous human saying goes." Then he spoke to the group, "Daleah asked some questions that made me realize that our people needed to change. That's how I got my parents involved to bring us here."

"Thank you for the compliment, Rory," said a surprised Daleah, while trying to regain her composure, "I didn't realize what a big impact I made on you and your people." She understood. She felt out of her element, not used to being the center of attention.

Revelyn saw Daleah's discomfit and spoke up, "Why don't we sit down and chat? Rory, would you like to break bread with us?" Revelyn overcame her shyness in her desire to help Daleah. They all sat down, partook of the remaining food, and chatted well into the evening. So began the fellowship between the humans and the young Seraphi.

Elder Shanielle glanced at Daleah's table and leaned toward her brother Elizon, remarking with a radiant smile, "I believe this is the beginning of something extraordinary, over at that table."

Elizon followed her glance and commented, "I believe it. These generations are forging new paths."

ABSORPTION DAY

We are all absorbed in one Spirit.
Some of us are Jews, others are Gentiles,
But we all share the same Spirit,
Which made us part of the body of Messiah.
Some of us are slaves, others are free.
Each of us drinks from one Spirit.
Some of us are men, others are women.
The Spirit of the Holy One
Has immersed us as one unit.
~Elder Timothy of Lystra,
The Complete Epistles of the Apostles

KRISTALIS, THE NEXT DAY

It was morning at the Youth Academy of Aliyah. Daleah slowly woke up to the noise of Revelyn's movements in their shared dorm room. For the first time in her life, she was sharing a room with someone else. The night before, she could not fall asleep immediately, going over the events of yesterday's welcome ceremony. She wondered how she could possibly have been the catalyst for influencing the Seraphies to work together with humans. *Don't let it go to your head,* she told herself.

After a futile effort to go to sleep, she went to the sink to get some water. Revelyn, who wasn't asleep, heard Daleah and she turned on the light.

Daleah wanted to confide in Revelyn. "Listen," she began, "I have to tell you something. I had a strange dream the night before I arrived here, and I am sure there was an angelic presence in my room. Rory was in the dream." She described the details of the dream to Revelyn.

Revelyn had been looking at Daleah with newfound respect, impressed that she got a visit from an angel.

Daleah saw Revelyn's expression, "Don't look at me like that," she added, "I had nothing to do with this historical event. I realize that gust of wind that pushed me to meet Rory two years ago was all part of the Creator's plan. If I hadn't been on Serfaretz two years ago, Rory or his peers could easily have run into someone else."

"Still, I think you should tell him about your dream." Revelyn added thoughtfully, "There is more to it. Your dream shows we were all walking together in a wilderness. Don't underestimate yourself so much. I doubt I would have done the same had I been in your shoes two years ago. I don't have your inquisitive nature."

"I guess. It's been an evening full of surprises! First, the Seraphies being here. That was nice. Second, when I saw Rory, was unexpected. The third surprise was a shock... when he informed me I played a small but significant part in the Seraphies being here. That's enough for one night!"

"I doubt there will be any more surprises. All good things come in threes, did you know that?" Revelyn smiled as she laid down to go to sleep.

"No, I didn't. I am glad you are here to to tell me more stuff like this! It's getting late and tomorrow is our first day! Sleep well." Daleah laid on the bed and turned off the lamp. She felt better after talking to Revelyn.

"Good night!" Revelyn responded in the dark.

Daleah stared at the window, her eyes adjusting to the dark. She saw the light of the halo softly illuminating the room. She thought, *One thing that will never change is the halo.* It gave her some comfort. And she fell asleep soundly.

In the morning, she sat up in her bed, her curly hair all tangled and crushed on the sides of her face. Then she jumped when Revelyn cheerfully announced, "Good morning!" She was used to waking up by herself, needing no one to nudge her out of bed.

"Halo to you! Did I miss anything?" Daleah asked, fully alert. She saw Revelyn dressed in her white outfit.

"Not at all! Breakfast is in thirty minutes. Today is absorption day! I am so looking forward to the tour of the village and our Academy. The morning's perfect, the sun is shining!" Revelyn announced cheerfully as Daleah got out of bed, her bright pink pajamas making her look more childish as she walked toward their shared bathroom.

Daleah stopped and turned around to inform Revelyn, "I don't mean to point out the obvious, but the sun is always shining here on Kristalis. It's like this every day."

Revelyn answered cheerfully, "I know that... but seeing the sun makes me feel happy! Can't help it!" She was smiling widely with her palms up and her head tilted.

Daleah stood for a moment, then said, "I see. I'll be right back." She turned back to begin her morning routine.

In the grand hall, the group met at the same table again. The food wasn't as lavish as the evening of yesterday. Rory made his appearance, grinning with his long sharp feline teeth as he greeted everyone. Only his kind eyes made him look less ferocious. The students were not used to having different species around them. They tried not to stare at Rory or ask too many questions.

Daleah wanted to ask him about his wings. *I wonder why his parents have two pairs while he and his peers have only one pair. I will not ask today! The answers will come — in time!*

Headmistress Mariel got up to speak on the platform. "A bright halo to you this morning! I have two brief announcements today. Our new Professor, Lionel DeTabor will speak this evening right here in this hall. He will summarize the history of Serfaretz. There are things that even us professors need to know, so I expect the Elders to attend too! I, for one, am so excited to learn something new! Last, we would like to welcome a special guest this morning, our Queen Valoria! She has some words for everyone. Please welcome our Queen."

Everyone stood up. Queen Valoria walked with a regal demeanor toward the platform, dressed in a long medieval dress of white velvet and silk, embroidered in gold patterns, with an ornate gold belt, bell sleeves, and square neckline. Her head was adorned with a golden crown over long, intricately braided hair.

"Welcome everyone to the Academy!" With open arms, she addressed the students in the assembly hall, "I normally don't come here to welcome new students each time, but today is a momentous day. I am here to welcome our Seraphi friends and to speak words of blessing! I am so delighted to have the Seraphies on Kristalis. We are witnessing an amazing historical day. For the first time since we settled Kristalis twelve thousand years ago, our respective species are working together. I pray for prosperity, success, and multiplied blessings in this joint endeavor."

The Queen's speech was short and sweet. Then she lifted her hands toward the people and recited the Aaronic benediction in the ancient tongue first, "*Yivarechecha Yehovah viyishmirecha. Ya'er Yehovah panav elecha veechuneka. Yeesa Yehovah panav elecha viyasem l'echa shalom.*" Then she uttered the same prayer in the universal language, "May Adonai bless and keep you. May his grace and his face shine upon you. May Adonai lift his countenance upon you and give you peace."

And Queen Valoria hugged the Elders goodbye before she exited the platform, for she was a longtime friend of the Elders. No one needed to be formal and stiff with her, for she was warm and caring.

Daleah and Revelyn stepped outside of the Academy and walked side-by-side with arms linked, following Professor Shanielle's tour group. The villagers, who were all part of the academy's support staff, came out to greet the students. A small white lion with wings kept going back and forth between Daleah and Shanielle in excitement.

Revelyn inquired, "Why is the little lion acting like this?"

Daleah was laughing at the animal's behavior, "Snowflake is happy to see me again. Two years ago, Ancie allowed me to take him home with me. He can't forget the wonderful time we had with my wolf Lupel and our other furry friends. Here on Kristalis, we call the white-winged lion a clion. It's a cross between a cat and a lion, smaller than lions and bigger than cats, with wings."

"So cute and cuddly!" Revelyn exclaimed.

Daleah stopped to bend down as Snowflake came toward her. He lifted his paw in greeting. She shook it and hugged him, feeling his snowy puffy mane tickling her nose. "Snowflake! Look who is here! My new friend Revelyn!"

As Revelyn also knelt down, Snowflake lifted his paw toward her in greeting. She shook it and he moved closer, giving her permission to hug him. A surprised Revelyn looked at Daleah. "Funny, I was just thinking I wanted to hug him."

"It's all right to hug him. The winged creatures here on Kristalis are special and empathic."

Revelyn tentatively hugged Snowflake, and he licked

her face. She laughed in delight. "He looks like Rory! They must be distant cousins!"

"It's not surprising!" Daleah replied.

Meanwhile, Shanielle had stopped to chat with a villager, waiting for the girls to catch up with her tour group.

INDIGOR

The day after the arrest of their neighbors, the four teens got together again. Mei was feeling better, but still miffed over Jamik's disapproval of the royal wedding. She ignored the boys and stayed in Ladya's room to show off her photos of the royal wedding. Haro had invited Jamik over to play video games in his room. Haro and Jamik went back to being best friends. They had forgotten about the days when they didn't hang out for a year.

Ladya and Mei were laying on their fronts on the bed, looking at Ladya's laptop with Mei's camera connected to it. Mei was proudly showing off one photo after another, smiling and exclaiming at each one.

"And here's the floating palace!" Mei exclaimed. "They held the wedding there. The invited guests waited in line for it to land. It was important to be on time before it went up again. And this one of me, waiting in line with Mom."

"Your dress looks good on you!" Ladya commented in sign language, "I glad we shop together. Great choice!" Both girls had gone shopping days before the wedding, trying on various dresses. The photo showed Mei wearing a simple and beautiful long white dress, a sleeveless V-neck with a gossamer top underneath that covered her chest and stretched to her upper arms, but exposed her shoulders. Her dress was "mother approved" for a royal wedding.

Ladya reflected on the photo of the floating palace. It was strangely interesting. The palace nestled on a large circular platform suspended by four round purple blimps attached to metal cables. The balloons were the same color as the purple sky of Indigor, rendering them invisible, like a camouflage. The palace consisted mostly of one grand hall for the entire gathering. Anything bigger or heavier, it would not have been able to go higher than eight hundred feet above ground.

All the wedding guests were wearing white, although not as elaborate as the bride's dress. The wedding ceremony and the reception took place in the same grand hall.

Ladya turned to ask Mei. "Please send me digital copy photo?" She pointed to the ones she liked. "So interesting! Me order plastic printout. This too!" She pointed to the photo of Mei with her mother. "That photo old!" Ladya pointed toward an old framed photo of Ladya and Mei at her birthday party from two years ago.

"Of course! Anything for my best friend!" Mei remarked, while tapping the keys of her laptop to send the selected photos to Ladya's account.

☞ ☞ ☞

Meanwhile, the boys in the next room were playing video games until Haro said to Jamik, "Let's take a break."

"Unfair! You have been letting me win! I don't remember a time when you lost so many times! You used to be good. What happened?"

"I'm not that much into the games these days."

"Is that all it is?" Jamik eyed Haro carefully.

"Yeah, that's all it is, nothing more."

"You're still grieving for your father, aren't you? Maybe we should do something else."

Haro sighed, "I will always miss my father. There's not much I can do about it." He paused thoughtfully, "You can bring your games next time. That way, we play fair. I am going to the kitchen to get some juice. You want something?"

"I'll have whatever you have," Jamik waved his hand and answered back nonchalantly, "thank you!"

As Haro left to go to the kitchen, Jamik found the cat that was hiding under the bed. Haro's cat disliked strangers. Jamik bent down to talk to it, "Here Kitty! Remember me?" The cat responded by hissing. "Not very nice, are you?"

Jamik then flopped on Haro's bed. His head hit something hard. He looked under the pillow and saw a wooden box. He opened it. He frowned in puzzlement, *What's an empty box doing under the pillow?*

Talk about odd timing! Ladya was also walking by in the hallway toward the kitchen and saw Jamik holding the box. She stopped.

"Hey!" She voiced, then signed, "Where Haro? What that?"

Jamik answered her back with gestures. He wasn't an expert signer, "Brother, kitchen, drink." Then he shrugged as he held the box for her to see. He pointed at the pillow and gestured again, "Hit head, box under."

"Let me see." She motioned to give the box and took it from Jamik. The carving on the lid seemed familiar. She frowned. Then Haro walked in with the drinks and saw her holding the box. He froze. He had completely forgotten about the box.

Jamik looked apologetically at Haro and grabbed the box from Ladya. "Sorry, I laid down. My head hit the box under the pillow." He said as he rubbed his head.

Ladya turned to Haro and signed with her free hand while shaking the box with her other hand, "Where you get?"

Haro sighed. Unable to sign while his hands while holding two glasses, he set them down. Then he signed to Ladya without his voice, not wanting Jamik to get involved. "It was supposed to be a birthday gift for Dad." He lied.

"This gift?" Ladya said while waving the box. "Not new! Smells old. Why buy Dad old thing then hide under pillow?"

"Why do you care?" Haro asked as he scowled at his sister.

"Because me not think you buy, you stole it! How me

know? Because me know THIS." She pointed to the symbol on the box, "Me see before!"

"I DID NOT steal it!" He said, still scowling, and signed vigorously. Jamik could see that they were both getting upset, but he couldn't understand why. "That box belongs to me! Give it back!" He reached for the box. Ladya pulled her arm away.

"Me tell Mom about box!" She gave him back the box, hitting him firmly on the chest with it, and walked out the door in a huff.

Haro held the box as if it was a delicate thing and put it down on his dresser.

Jamik, who had been feeling left out, asked Haro, "What was that all about?"

Haro sighed and turned toward Jamik, "I have a nosy sister who's always asking too many questions. To be honest, I'm tired of people invading my privacy. Not only my sister, but the pesky authorities!"

Jamik, not wanting to upset Haro any further, said calmly, "I agree with you. It's nobody's business but yours."

"I've been thinking. We're having our school break soon. What do you say the two of us go camping and fishing at our family's cabin in the country? I used to go with Dad, and now with him gone and Mom grieving, I don't know what to do."

"Splendid idea! Coach won't let me play until my knee is better, so I need to do something else. So, let's go camping together! And fishing!" Jamik got up enthusiastically and patted Haro on the back, hoping to cheer him up.

Haro smiled, feeling relieved. "Yeah, I can't wait to get out of this town and absorb some sun! I always feel better after being outdoors and smelling the fresh air."

Jamik nodded in agreement. "Hey, I'm all for it. What are best friends for? Let's do things together!"

There was another reason for Haro to go to the cabin. Something his father mentioned often made him think there might be more clues at the cabin. In his bedroom was a framed photo depicting his father next to a sun sculpture hanging above the fireplace in their cabin. He didn't think much of that photo for years until he remembered his father's comment about the light. *When in doubt, look to the Light for understanding. The path of a righteous person is like the morning sun, shining ever brighter until midday.* Now, every time he looked at that photo, these words came to his mind.

Haro thought, *I need to get out of this town and start searching for more clues about the Brotherhood. I wish Dad had told me more in his letter, like, when was the last time that he visited them? How many are there? What if they're all gone by now? What did he learn when he was there?* Haro was uncomfortable with the uncertainty of not having enough information. It was enough to make him push forward to search for answers.

KRISTALIS

Later in the evening, the students had gathered in the grand hall again. They had absorbed the academy and its charming village. Daleah and her friends had warmed up to each other. Gone was the uncomfortable feeling from their first awkward meeting of the previous day.

After the meal, Headmistress Mariel introduced Professor Silvero DeTabor. He stood on the platform and began with a deep voice, "Greetings, everyone! Although Serfaretz is our homeworld, what most of you don't know is that Serfaretz is not our original home." The screen behind him lit up, showing a photo of the planet Serfaretz as seen from space. "Two years ago, after the discovery of some ancient caves here, we felt obligated to share with the Elders that Kristalis was our original home. We left this beautiful planet many millennia ago, long before the Elders and the sons and daughters of Adam settled here from New Earth. Our people made a mass exodus to Serfaretz. Why? According to the legend of the mighty Seraphim, our ancestors, we will tell you a story that explains why we left." He looked at the screen showing the old ruins with the backdrop of the halo in the sky.

"Shortly after Lucifer became the adversary of the Holy One, the exodus happened. When he was garnering allies for the war against the Heavenly Realm, Lucifer sent a message to the Council of Seraphies that he was planning to visit them. Lucifer came and went. Why? He wanted the Seraphies to join him in making war against the Holy One. Our people became outraged at his audacity and horrified at such behavior from angelic beings. We refused to join Lucifer. After Lucifer and his hosts lost the war and the Holy One threw him out of the Holy Realm, the Council of Seraphies warned him not to visit Kristalis. Still, we had no guarantee that he would listen. Lucifer and his host of fallen angels searched Kristalis and found us gone. Even after we had moved to our new homeworld, they continued searching for hundreds of years and never found us. We have become adept at hiding in the mountains of Serfaretz. Even the mighty archangels couldn't find us. We became a reclusive people. The planet's harsh weather and rough landscape suited us well. It wasn't until several millennia after the Holy One threw Lucifer in the Lake of Fire that we reopened our home to the hosts of angelic beings. After Kristalis became settled by the humans, it took us millennia to trust the Elders and the humans."

"In retrospect, hiding from everyone didn't help us grow as a people. While your people have colonized the galaxy, we have remained much the same. We must think about our children's future. We don't intend to hide forever in our mountains and become the stuff of myths and legends, giving you the idea that we are shy and solitary creatures. We want to be a genuine people to you. We have traveled to many places in the entire galaxy, but we have not considered settling other planets until now."

"Now about our planet... Humans have tried to settle Serfaretz in the past and failed. Some of the most adventurous and brave people have ventured to visit our planet. They dared to climb the massive cliffs of our mountains and surf the giant waves of our oceans. It is time that we welcome our new human friends into our homes inside the mountains. The traditions of our ancestors should not bind us. Being here is the first giant step forward for Seraphies."

"I know many of you are curious about our wings. Our young are born with one pair of small wings that grow larger as they mature. They don't learn to fly until they are about seven years old. The second pair of wings does not appear until about four hundred years later. Our oldest Seraphies have three pairs of wings, as do the mighty Seraphim. With four wings, we can fly through the strong currents of our world. Here's what our wings look like." He stepped away from the Elders on the platform and unfurled all his four wings. They were large, longer than his height. The grand hall buzzed, and some students gasped with wide eyes.

"Serving our Holy One has been a great blessing to the relations between our four races. We have been together since the dawn of time and always at peace with each other. Parents prayerfully select each child to grow up with three other companions for life, one of each race. We do so to ensure they don't get the ideas they are better than other races. Each group of children grow up together, play together, study together, and eventually work together in their chosen profession. This oldest tradition has always worked for our respective species." He looked behind him at the screen which was showing the inside of the caves, the part of their world that Daleah never got to visit.

"Over the millennia, our civilization has developed a giant network of sophisticated caves, which are the perfect shelters from rough atmosphere conditions of Serfaretz. You might wonder what our homes look like. They look like tall buildings carved out of the giant caverns, most of them about a hundred stories high. The inside of our homes is much like yours. They are cozy, but large enough to accommodate our physique. After Lucifer no longer posed a threat to us, we built new homes outside the caves. We carved skyscrapers on the outside surface of the mountains and built towers and sky spires over them. Most of these are workplaces, beacons of light, and landing platforms for our flying species. Some of these buildings have cylindrical revolving habitats protruding from their tops, high enough to see above the mist. We have a sophisticated network of subways, elevators, and skyways." The screen changed again.

"Besides being here with you today, we have also developed a division of tourism and cultural affairs for those who would like to visit our homeworld. I am inviting the people of this academy to come to visit us on Serfaretz after the semester. I have informed the Headmistress that we are giving our students permission to visit your family's homes."

Headmistress Mariel came up to him and announced, "The name of our program is the foreign student exchange."

"That's the one! It's much like what we do with our young Seraphies, by bringing the four races together. We extend that excellent tradition to all of you. Thank you for welcoming us." Professor DeTabor walked to his table.

Professor DeTabor's informative lecture and slide show enthralled Daleah and her friends. Daleah leaned toward Revelyn, "I have been wanting to ask Rory about his wings! Now I don't have to ask!" She smiled at Rory, who was grinning, happy about his father's rendition of life on Serfaretz.

Later that night, Daleah and Revelyn were in their room, chatting about the day's events while sitting on their beds. Daleah told Revelyn, "I never realized how big their world was. On our family camping trip to Serfaretz, we only saw a tiny part of that world. I had so many questions I wanted to ask since yesterday! What a relief, not to have to ask them anymore!" Daleah was happy and in the right place, learning more every day.

"You can still ask me questions." Revelyn nodded in understanding and asked, "Want to hear other interesting tidbits about the Elders? For example, why do they always wear white? Have you ever seen them wear any other colors?"

"Now that you mention it, I'm curious." Daleah would never have thought to ask about it.

"I read about this in an obscure chronicle of a little-known Elder," Revelyn began the story, "not long after the first group of resurrected became Elders, they discovered they stopped wearing colored outfits anymore. Several times after the Spirit carried them away to other places, they noticed the colors of their garments were fading. The good Lord knew that the Light they emitted was absorbing the colors, and He kept it a secret. He found it amusing to watch their perplexed reactions as they tried to understand why fading happened. It was His way of showing His sense of humor. They all laughed about it afterward and wore white garments whenever the Spirit carried them away." Revelyn ended her story with a satisfied smile.

"Interesting tidbits of information, for sure!" Daleah said as she walked to her wardrobe to get her bright pink pajamas. "We better get our rest for tomorrow will be another absorption day." She thought, *I can't wait for orientation day so I can begin my education.*

INDIGOR

Ladya was laying down in her bed, unable to sleep. She couldn't stop thinking about the wooden box, about the image on its lid. Although she threatened to tell their mother about the box, she didn't have enough proof that Haro had stolen it. *Still, why would he hide an old box under his pillow? No, it's probably best not to upset Mom further. She is still grieving over Dad's death. Oh, Dad, I wish you were here. You had a knack for always saying the right words.*

Ladya opened a drawer near her bed. She took out a child's purple tablet and turned it on. It had been a gift from her father. The diamond she saw on Haro's box reminded her of a bedtime story her father read to her long ago, about diamonds from the sky. The storybook had illustrations framed in diamond shapes, similar to the shape carved on the wooden box her brother tried to hide. She read it, cherishing the memory of her father telling her the story in sign language.

THE KING AND THE RING OF DIAMONDS

Once upon a time, there was a mighty king who lived on a planet that was encircled by a white ring. The people of that world called it the diamond ring. He was a wonderful king who had everything, but he was lonely. So, he married the most beautiful woman of his world. Yet, she couldn't love him. She was vain, selfish, and chased after other men. He became heartbroken.

One day, he went for a walk alone in his sadness. He was ambushed by thieves and murderers, almost hung on a tree, but his servants rescued him in time. His heart stopped for a minute, but they revived him. Thankful that he survived, he divorced his wife and let her go. She went away, became lost in the wilderness, and never came back.

One day, he saw a beautiful, wealthy young princess not of his kingdom. She was from a far country. He wooed her and proposed to her, but she was not sure she wanted to marry a king. It was an enormous responsibility to be a queen. He promised to protect her.

Finally, one day she agreed. They were married and happy, but her family and the people of her nation wanted her back. She struggled to love the king, but it was hard. The king promised to give her everything. He gave her the most beautiful diamond ring and put it on her finger. It was like the ring of diamonds in the sky. He promised her he would build a beautiful mansion for her, made of precious diamonds fallen from the sky. She believed him and told her family she would not go back to them. They were angry and prepared to make war with the king, persuading the neighboring nations to join them.

The king amassed his army and went to war with the nations allied against him. He established a theocracy with all the nations as his subjects. Under his leadership, they built a beautiful mansion with the largest diamonds they could find. The king and queen lived happily ever after, in the mansion made of diamonds, filled with many children and servants.

Ladya thought of her dear father and his wonderful bedtime stories, unaware that those stories carried a hint of truth in them. Like many stories passed down through generations of Indigans, they became myths and legends, bits and more bits lost in the flow of time. Ladya's thoughts about Haro and the wooden box were drifting away. Being deaf and visual most of her life, her mind's eyes had always been imaginative. She rarely dreamed while she slept. She daydreamed of mighty kings, envisioned elegant queens, and imagined the wealth that came from diamonds in the sky. And finally, she fell into a deep sleep, both in body and mind.

CHAPTER SIX

JOURNAL OF A JOURNEY

I proclaimed,
"Praise Yehovah Elohenu,
God of Abraham,
because He has shown unfailing love
and faithfulness to my master."
~Elder Eliezer, the servant,
The Life and Times of Abraham

KRISTALIS, TWO WEEKS LATER

Daleah was at her desk, holding a book and running her hand over its colorful cover. She had bound the book herself and created the cover in her favorite colors of pinks and oranges. The title stood out in bring colors—Journal of a Spiritual Journey. She opened it to the first page, then flipped the pages to the last entry. Since taking the prerequisite class in penmanship, taught by Professor

Shanielle, Daleah's cursive handwriting had improved. Although it wasn't as elegant as the handwriting of the Elders, she was developing a distinctive style, as unique as a fingerprint. She enjoyed reading her journal, seeing the flow of words dance and sing on the paper, so different from the bland typesetting of an electronic tablet.

19314.9.29

We had an amazing day yesterday during Professor Bethuel's class, when he taught The Story of Our Origins in one of my favorite rooms, the Genesis Room. He finally let us experience the Memory Touch. I remembered my first time with Ancie Shanielle. Even then, I was still unprepared for another experience. Bethuel's world was so different from Shanielle's more modern world. Bethuel was a simple servant of Abraham who had learned much at the feet of his master. I never figured the Patriarch Abraham would teach his entire household about their Creator. Abraham imparted to them his gracious wisdom and everything about their origins, as he had learned at the feet of his Semitic ancestors, Noah and Shem.

When the Memory Touch began, Bethuel's glow grew and engulfed the classroom until we saw with our mind's eyes into his past. In the blink of an eye, we transported into Bethuel's world. We became fleeting shadows behind Bethuel as we watched him work with Eliezer, the other servant as they carried out their master Abraham's commands. Abraham excitedly welcomed the three strangers who had appeared near the grove of oak trees of Mamre.

The grove provided a shaded place for Abraham's household to settle in, away from the heat of the desert climate. The people in Hebron were rugged in appearance, their clothing rudimentary, with sand in their shoes, clothing, and everywhere. And how old the people looked! Their faces lined and spotted, so unlike the smooth velvety and clear skin of our people. Their hair of a strange grey color, brittle and thinned out. Their eyes were cloudy and squinting, their bodies bent slightly, and their hands calloused from years of hard work. I imagine water was scarce because we followed Bethuel carrying on his shoulders two large buckets of water on a pole. They lived in tents made of animal skins supported by poles dug into the sand. Their furnishing was simple, with carpets, mats, cushions, clay jars, utensils, and tools, and lots of bags for their nomadic travels. Beyond the grove of trees, I glimpsed the distant field where the animals were grazing: the camels, the sheep, and the oxen.

The three men who visited Abraham were different in appearance, wearing clean white vestments, much like our Elders. Abraham seemed particularly fascinated with one of the three men. He called him "My Lord," bowing to him. He invited them to eat and gave them water to wash their feet from the bucket that Bethuel had brought in. Bethuel saw Abraham run to get a fattened calf, telling his servant Eliezer to prepare the meat for the strangers, and Sarah to prepare the cakes to cook over the meat. His household had never seen him so excited.

That was when I got my first shock. I have never seen an animal butchered. The blood was pouring like a faucet from the cut in the neck of the innocent animal. I have never seen blood, not even my own. I never realized how bright red it was.

And when it was all over, that scene faded, and we were back in the Genesis room. We all sat quietly while Professor Bethuel seemed to know what we were going through. Bethuel told us that Adam and Eve experienced the same emotions when the Elohim made the first animal sacrifice as a covering for their sin. They too, went into shock at the sight of the bright red blood.

My friend Kato had a question about the innocent calf. Was it the custom of those days to eat meat daily, or was it a sacrificial offering to the One whom Abraham called Lord? According to the Professor, the answer was for both. It was common for people to eat meat in those days. For his guests, Abraham wanted to do something special from his heart. He loved his Lord so much he wanted to please Him. The offering was like the Mishkan's peace and fellowship offering. Next week, we will learn more about the Mishkan.

Daleah had reached the end of her last journal entry. Then Revelyn came into the room and called out to Daleah, "Are you ready to go?" As she held her journal close to her heart, she sighed. This is the best thing I have done in my young life. Thank you, Lord. Daleah got up from her desk and grabbed her backpack. She was ready for another spiritual adventure.

THE CABIN, INDIGOR

Haro's mother had dropped off Haro and Jamik at the cabin the previous day. Ladya, in the car, was still sulking about the hidden wooden box. Ladya knew better than to upset their grieving mother. Haro's thoughts about his pestering sister faded away as he slowly steered the bowrider, his father's motorboat into the boathouse. Jamik moored the bowrider, securing the rope tightly from the cleat to the post.

Jamik remarked as Haro stepped out from the starboard side into the boathouse, "That was cool! We should come here more often. This boat is a beauty! Your father did a wonderful job of restoring it! That motor runs smooth, better than the noisy ones out there!" It was a boat that caught many people's eyes, with the rich maple color of the boat's hull and gunwale standing out sharply against the green of the lake. Painted on the hull of the boat was the name Spirit.

Jamik asked, stepping off the boat, "Why is the boat named *Spirit?*"

Haro held the fishing poles while Jamik carried the pail of fresh fishes they had caught. A memory of his father came, unbidden, and with it, the heavy sadness that was part of his grief. *Father and I spent so much time together perfecting this beautiful boat.* Haro remembered how he helped his father modify the engines. He shook his head as if to shake off the memory. He replied to Jamik's question, "Father once told me a story about the Creator sending his Spirit to hover over the water when He created the world."

Jamik looked puzzled at the answer but said nothing. Haro continued. "These fishes will be tasty with some root vegetables from Mom's garden. I will dig some from the ground and meet you at the cabin." They walked on the gravel path from the boathouse toward the large rustic log cabin. Haro stopped briefly to dig some carrots, onions, and potatoes from the edible garden.

Jamik walked toward the back of the cabin surrounded by the wrap-around porch and filled with outdoor chairs. The porch columns that supported the roof looked like small trees, with its branches still intact, its bark removed and stained in the same reddish color as the borders of the cabin.

Haro came in and showed Jamik how to gut and skin the fishes to prepare them for cooking on the barbecue pit, telling him the history of his family's cabin.

☞ ☞ ☞

It was night. Jamik slept in the guest room. Haro crept silently out of his room toward in the family room. He looked carefully at the carved wood sculpture of the sun hanging above the fireplace. Then, he took it down to look at the back and saw an etching of a tree, but no message. There was a little diamond shape at the bottom. Haro sighed, That diamond is a clue. I'm on the right track. *What now?* He looked at the etching of the tree carefully. *It looks familiar. I have seen this tree somewhere. It must be from around here.* He remembered his father saying the wood sculpture was from a tree on the property. Other than fishing and camping, wood carving was one of his father's other hobbies. Haro took a photo of the etching with his camera. *Tomorrow, I will search for that tree.*

The following day, Haro dragged Jamik around for a hike. Jamik had almost recovered from his knee injury. "We won't be going far." He told Jamik while pocketing his camera.

There was the tree with the tire swing. Haro looked at the photo on the camera. *Nope! Not that one!* There was the tree near the river, with a rope hanging on it for swinging and jumping in the river. *Nope! Not that one either!*

Jamik inquired, "Are you shooting photos of trees for a project?"

Haro didn't want to lie and replied, "Yes, for research purpose. I'm looking for a particular tree."

"Anything I can help you with? Not to say I'm an expert, but Mom used to work at the arboretum. The way Mom talks about trees, it's like they are family. We have a new tree planted whenever a newborn joins our family. Mom chose a juniper when I was born because she believed I would grow to be tall. She was right."

Haro hesitated, thinking how much to share with Jamik. "I will tell you as long as you keep my nosy sister out of it." He showed him the photo of the etching on his camera.

Jamik replied with a grin and a wink, "Agreed." Jamik took the camera and looked at the photo closely. "Judging by its shape, it looks like an oak tree. Didn't we pass those on the way here? Several of them, on the sides of the driveway, past the gate?" He gave the camera back.

"Let's go!" Haro said, walking ahead briskly, not waiting for Jamik. "You think you can keep up?"

"It's not too bad!" Jamik replied, "I think the exercise is helping my knee injury."

When they arrived near the gate, Haro instantly identified the tree by the number and shapes of its branches. He held the camera before it.

Jamik looked at the camera, then at the tree. "They're exactly the same!" His voice registered surprise. They walked closer to it and saw the carved initials, M.G. inside a carved elongated diamond. Jamik exclaimed, "Why, that's your father's initials! Looks like you and I have the same family tradition!" Haro walked to the other trees, and found his grandfather's initials, also carved inside another diamond shape. There was also another tree carved with a diamond, but no initials. Jamik grinned, patted the tree and said, "Look like this one is yours! Your father wanted you to carve your initials inside this diamond shape!" Still grinning, he took his folding survival knife out of his pocket, flipped it on his palm, and gave it to Haro.

There seems to be a pattern here of hiding the boxes under trees. How can I dig under the tree while Jamik is here? I wish Mom would allow me to come alone. Haro furiously carved his initials on the tree. *How can I find the Brotherhood when everyone is watching me like a hawk? Should I take a chance by telling Jamik, maybe the two of us would be safer together?*

Haro had finished carving his initials, H.G. He turned to Jamik, who was resting under the shade of the tree, chewing on a blade of grass. Haro had finally decided to tell him, but Jamik spoke first. "Wouldn't it be great if we were to go on an adventure, looking for treasure?"

Jamik's question caught him off guard. *Maybe this is the confirmation I needed to tell Jamik about the secret?* Haro sat down next to Jamik, asking with furrowed brows, "Are you serious?"

"Maybe," Jamik answered nonchalantly, "but it will be more fun than video games. Things have become boring lately."

"Why do you say that?" Haro went through the same phase after his father's death. The usual things had lost their appeal. He was curious what made Jamik change.

"Ever since our neighbors got arrested, I wanted to find out more about the mass persecution of religious people." Jamik looked somber, which was unusual for him. "I asked my grandparents, but they were suspiciously close-mouthed. They told me to forget it. It didn't make me forget. It led to more questions."

Haro smiled, and Jamik looked at him at that moment. "Why are you smiling?"

"Looks like I have found a kindred spirit in you." Haro replied, "There's something I have been meaning to tell you for a while, but first, let's go back to the cabin for our midday meal." And they walked back to the cabin.

KRISTALIS

Daleah and Revelyn arrived at the Genesis room a little late. The other students were at their desk, their notebooks and quills in hand. Daleah and Revelyn sat down breathlessly, scrambled into their backpacks for their notebooks. The classroom was unusual. The walls of the classroom was designed with a panoramic mural of the genesis of creation, depicted with the massive hands of the Creator creating and shaping the creation. Daleah was in awe of the room. It made her feel as if she was there, at the beginning of spacetime and matter.

Elder Professor Bethuel looked like a typical Elder. Both his hair and beard were curly and shone like silver.

"Today," he began, smiling at the students, "we have a special guest from the Lighthouse Space Station, a close friend of mine who used to be a professor here. Please welcome Elder Todiah. He will share about his life experience on Old Earth."

A tall, thin, impressive-looking Elder came into the classroom and stood next to Professor Bethuel. Unlike Elder Bethuel, he was sporting short-trimmed hair and beard. They both carried the same countenance, youthful and regal.

"My name back on Old Earth was William Tyndale." Like Professor Bethuel, his face was glowing softly, filled with the Spirit of the Holy One and years of wisdom. "I was from a country called England. In my days, many poor people were illiterate. Only the wealthy aristocrat class and the clergy could read. The priests had a responsibility to teach them the Holy Writings, but they failed. They read the Holy Writings to the masses in Latin, which was the dominant language of the Roman Empire, but not the language of the people of England. The Holy Writings were laboriously copied by hand in Latin, years before Gutenberg invented the printing press in 1450. About a hundred years prior to my time, a man named John Wycliffe translated the Holy Writings from the Latin into English. The Church of Rome rejected the English translation and declared Wycliffe a heretic. They banned his writings and excommunicated him. He died in 1384."

"I was born 1494 years after Messiah, shortly after the invention of the printing press. I grew up in England in the early days of the Reformation movement. In those days, any unlicensed possession of the Holy Writings in the English language incurred the death penalty. After I graduated from seminary, I worked at various jobs. I became a gifted linguist, fluent in eight languages. Like my predecessor, John Wycliffe, I also saw how the Church of Rome kept the people ignorant of the Holy Writings. I became a Protestant reformer and a translator, with one difference. Wycliffe translated the Holy Writings from the Latin language. I translated them from Hebrew and Greek into English. The Church of Rome and the Anglican Church considered my work to be heresy and banned it. I and many others like me escaped the persecution and traveled throughout Europe to avoid getting caught."

"I continued to print my work in secret for many years until someone whom I thought was a friend betrayed me. Unknown to me, the church authorities sent him to search for and befriend me into revealing my work. The Church wasn't interested in justice. They sentenced me to death to rid of me and continue to keep their position of power. Exactly like the Pharisees at the time of Messiah. Despite all these obstacles, I did the right thing."

He paused briefly and looked out the window toward the graceful white halo of Kristalis. "It's time for a Memory Touch. What you will experience is not pretty. This memory happened the day before my execution." While he had been talking, a white dove flew in from the window and landed on the Professor's desk. Elder Todiah held out his hand, and the dove jumped onto his hand. He continued, "Be ready." And he glowed until infused the entire room with his glow. The dove flew away.

Daleah, Revelyn, Kato, Enoch, and the other students stood up and braced themselves to become observers in an unfamiliar world. The classroom with the creation mural dissolved. Daleah saw a stone-walled room bare of furnishing except for a straw mat. A grey pigeon stood on the barred window of Tyndale's gloomy prison and flew away into the dreary, cloudy sky. Tyndale had awakened by the prison guard loudly knocking at his door. He was shivering, cold, and miserable, his tattered clothes and threadbare blanket hardly enough to keep him warm.

The guard peeked his face through the small barred window of the door. "You have one remaining day until your execution! Finish your porridge!" His breakfast of porridge was on the floor near the door, crawling with roaches. He didn't care, for he was hungry. He reached and clattered the bowl to scatter the roaches. He determined to enjoy his moment of comfort with food, no matter what happened. Daleah and her classmates stood like shadows, watching Tyndale in his unrecognizable and wretched state. As soon as he finished his meal, the prison warden unlocked the door. A priest came in, richly dressed in a red silk robe with an elaborately embroidered border at the hem and sleeves, with matching cap and gloves. His face expressed the proud arrogance that Tyndale had seen so often with priests. The bright colors of his clothes amidst the dreary prison had jarred Tyndale fully awake, but he still did not bother to get up. His body was stiff from the cold. The prison warden, a simple man dressed in shades of grey, disliked Tyndale's attitude. His face showed his disapproval.

"You will get up and address His Eminence!" The warden kicked Tyndale with his foot and pulled Tyndale up by his ears. Tyndale got up slowly, wincing in pain. Daleah watched, shocked at such abusive treatment.

The priest spoke up. "Warden, that's enough! I will speak to the prisoner in private." He motioned with his finely gloved hand to the warden to go away.

"Yes, your eminence, please forgive me." The warden bowed and left quickly, leaving both men to stare at each other in silence, one proud and the other humbled.

Finally, the priest spoke first, "Do you wish to confess?"

Tyndale looked at the priest with amusement. "Yes! I confess that I was stupid enough to get caught!"

The priest sighed and pronounced formally, "William Tyndale, you have been found guilty of spreading heresy against the Church, of collaborating with the heretic Martin Luther, of printing and distributing unlicensed work in English, of participating with the enemies of the Church, and of escaping from the Church authorities. If you don't confess and repent, the Church will refuse your body a proper burial on holy ground."

Tyndale replied assuredly, "Haven't you heard? The Good Book tells us not to be afraid of those who kill the body. You should be afraid of Him who can destroy both body and soul. It doesn't matter if my body ends up in a pile of refuse, because I know Jehovah is with me. Is Yehovah with you?"

The priest's stance remained unchanged, his heart hard and proud, "I do not have to answer your questions. I am an appointed member of the Church, that's all that matters. You lost your position in the Church long ago.

Once again, I ask you, do you wish to confess?"

"I have nothing to confess to you. I am at peace. You and your kind do not differ from the Pharisees of old. You are a brood of vipers, children of the adversary! You priests preach to convert others to a dead religion. You teach them to follow the laws of the Church, yet you neglect the weightier matters of the laws of Yehovah, such as justice, compassion, and mercy toward the destitute and the unlearned. You look clean, but inside you are filthy. You exhibit righteousness, yet you are wicked. You profess to love Yehovah, but you have hatred and murder in your heart. I do not need your service! I would rather obey the laws of Yehovah than the laws of the Pope. Just go! And may Yehovah forgive you!"

The priest's face became white as Tyndale spoke, then red with anger and shame. He slapped Tyndale's face hard with his gloved hand. Tyndale flinched but remained resolute.

"Very well. I have nothing more to say to you." The priest replied huffily, trying to constrain his anger, turning to leave.

Then Tyndale shouted, "I have one more thing to say! I pray fervently that someday, a young boy farmer will know more about the Scriptures than a priest like you does!" Not wanting to hear more, the priest knocked on the door urgently, wanting to leave.

Then Daleah saw the grey walls of the prison dissolve. She was back in the Genesis classroom again. The students came out of the world of darkness and into a world of light. Their innocent faces expressed relief.

Daleah saw William Tyndale as Elder Todiah, with the same features, but more youthful and radiant. Todiah's story fascinated her.

Todiah spoke, "I stopped the memory here because the next part would not be easy to watch. After the priest left, I felt more exhilarated than I had been in a long time. The pain went away from my body. I remembered how I felt like the first time I held in my hands a Greek manuscript of the Holy Writings and realized that our Almighty Father was showing me my destiny to translate it into English. I have accomplished what I set out to do. I had no fear of death, even though I died a horrible death. Before I died, I cried, 'Lord, please open the eyes of the King of England!' My captors didn't want to hear my prayer, so someone came from behind and strangled me. Thankfully, I did not have to feel the burn of the fire at the stake. It had been a quicker death." He paused, surveying the faces of the students before him. Daleah blinked and felt something on her cheek. It was a tear. She held the wetness on her fingers, bewildered. It was the first time she had ever cried with sadness.

"About a year later, King Henry authorized the publication and distribution of the Gospel of Matthew, most of which I translated. Four years later, the Holy Writings were translated into English, again at the request of the King. My prayer came true. I brought something to show you." He held a tattered book. "What you see here is the famous *King James Bible*, published only 75 years after my death. I acquired this from a friend of mine after the resurrection. The word Bible here means books. It became a bestseller for many hundreds of years in the English-speaking world. About three-fourths of this book is drawn from my translation. My work continued to play a key role in spreading the Reformation ideas across the world. I was also the first person to use the true name of God, *Yehovah*, in my translation. Unfortunately, Bible scholars chose to ignore this name in the later English translations. Most of the people didn't know His true name until Messiah came back."

"Eventually, the boy farmer and many young people from all walks of life learned to read the Holy Writings. Many became more versed in the Holy Writings than clergymen. And you, young people, are all living proof of that."

After finishing their midday meal, Haro told Jamik everything that happened since his father's funeral—about finding the letters and following the clues. He repeated to Jamik, all from memory, word-for-word, what his father and grandfather had written in the letters—about the origins of the people of Indigor, the Brotherhood, and the Creator. Haro suspected there was another wooden box under his father's tree. He watched Jamik's expression change from surprise to shock to awe and then to respect.

After a long thoughtful pause, Jamik finally said something, "Why, this is big! Better than treasure hunting! I finally understand why everyone is so quiet about this religious thing. Who is the Creator?

"I believe He is the One that created the universe and humanity. Our species didn't evolve here on this planet as our school indoctrinated in us. We know that before the comet crashed into Indigor, the previous civilization was quite sophisticated. That is enough proof, no matter what propaganda they feed us at school. I've had much time to think about this since I found the letters. Many of the stories my father told me are finally making sense."

Jamik paused, thinking over what Haro had shared with him. Then he got up and announced excitedly, "What are we waiting for? Let's get a shovel and dig this thing up! Then maybe we will find the Brotherhood and meet these aliens!"

Haro laughed at Jamik's description. Then he said, "Let's do it! But do me a favor and don't call them aliens."

Thirty minutes later, they were digging under the oak tree, the one carved with the initials M. G. They were about one-foot deep when Haro said, "We should hit something soon. I found the first box under a rock." No sooner had he spoken, they heard a loud clunk as Jamik hit something hard. They both looked at each other and bent down to dig with their gloved hands.

"You're right," Jamik remarked, "it's a rock. Probably to protect the wooden box from breaking." As they pulled out a flat rock, underneath it was a rectangular-shaped box thickly wrapped in thick plastic with tape.

Excited, Haro cut the wrapping with his survival knife. "It's the same as the other wooden boxes. See the carving on the lid?" It was the pointed hand inside a diamond shape.

He removed his dirty gardening gloves. Both Haro and Jamik sat down as Haro slowly opened the box. He frowned, not sure what the object was, and picked it up. It was a bound book, its cover made of distressed brown leather. "Wow! A real, honest-to-goodness book!" Jamik remarked.

Haro opened it gingerly. In all his fourteen years, he had never held a book. He looked at Jamik and opened the book in the middle. "It's my father's handwriting." He said as he flipped to the first page at the beginning, the title. "Here it is. It's called, *The Journal of my Spiritual Journey*. It's thick. Dad must have trained a long time ago. I can finally get some answers."

Jamik looked at the handwriting and frowned, "Can you read it? This handwriting is strange, very curly."

"It's called cursive handwriting. I got used to reading it. Let's put the dirt back in and go to the cabin where people won't find us with this book." Haro told Jamik as he put the book back inside the box, then in his backpack.

After filling the hole in the ground, they walked hurriedly back to the cabin in silence, shovels in hands, pondering what Haro's father could have written in his journal. As soon as they locked the doors and sat down comfortably in the family room, Haro read the first page aloud.

19297.7.21

> *I have finally completed my training in calligraphy and penmanship. Everyone in the Brotherhood, including Brother Sherman, had been very encouraging. I have learned so much during my time with them. I don't know where to start in my*

journal. My father isn't here to teach me. He felt it would be safer if we don't talk about it when we are outside of the Brotherhood, as we never know who might be spying. Should something happen to one of us, the other will continue to carry the legacy.

The first thing I learned was the name of our original home—Earth. It became Nova Terra later. It was the first world that the Everliving One formed 27,000 years ago. In the beginning, He created the universe and everything in it. He finished in six days, and on the seventh day, He rested. He created the first man and woman. Soon after, the first man and woman rebelled. They became separated from their Creator. They lost their immortality. Death resulted from that sin, but the good news—He promised them a redeemer, a mediator who would reconcile the people back to Him and restore everything. First, they had to fulfill his promise to be fruitful and multiply. All generations received this sinful nature. It did not matter how good they were. For six millennia, there was never any peace on Earth. It was always war, violence, famine, diseases, and chaos. As the humans scattered over all Indigor, they had forgotten they were once His people. Only a remnant kept the knowledge of their origins, chronicling the essential events of their Creator's intervention for His people.

Finally, the redeemer, the Son of the Creator, descended on Earth to be born in the flesh. The good news was that He overcame death and rose on the third day. He who was without sin became the savior, the Messiah, taking the sin of the people on Himself. Anyone who trusted in Him would receive eternal life. Sadly, not everyone believed in Him or His wonderful promises. Those who trusted Him were raised to everlasting life. They became the blessed Elders, clothed with immortality. And when humanity established new worlds among the stars, seeding the galaxy, the Elders went with them, leading them in the way of the Creator. That was about 12,000 years ago. Indigor was the sixth colonial world and the second to have fallen, after Earth.

As of this writing, humanity has spread toward hundreds of worlds across the galaxy. We have been 'quarantined' because of our rebellious nature. When our sinful nature corrupted this world, many of the Elders departed. Overtime, we have slowly forgotten about our origins. The Elders are unique in that they are capable of instant travel across the vast distance of the galaxy.

The Elders visit our Brotherhood regularly. They keep us strong. Without them, we would not be here. We must keep the faith and continue to preserve His Holy Writings in our last remaining library, hidden from our world. We are working to disseminate the Holy Writings so that all Indigor will know the truth. The redeemer died not only for the people of Old Earth but also for all people on Indigor. We must put our trust in Him. And together, we will be raised to a life of immortality. It has been too long since Indigor has fallen, more than 7000 years ago. The Indigans can change things with help from our friends the Elders. The Creator has not forgotten or forsaken us, but we have forgotten Him. He is more powerful than the authorities who have taken control of our world. The time will come when the corrupt age of Indigor will end, and we will rejoin our family among the stars.

Haro finished reading his father's first entry. Haro looked at his captivated friend Jamik. There was complete silence as Haro and Jamik absorbed the account of humanity's genesis. For them, it was the beginning of their spiritual journeys.

CHAPTER SEVEN

FORMED IN SECRET

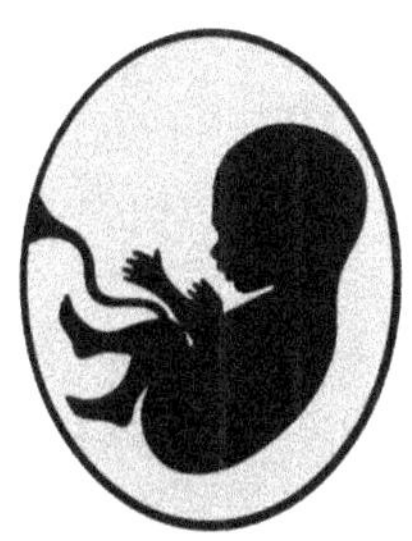

You have formed my inward parts and
You knitted me together in my mother's womb.
I exalt you because I am fearfully and wonderfully made.
Your workmanship is amazing and my soul knows it intimately.
You did not hide my frame when you formed me in secret.
You wove me intricately in the dark of the womb.
You saw my unformed body.
You recorded every day of my life in Your book.
You saw every moment of my life before they happened.
~The Complete Psalms

KRISTALIS, THREE DAYS LATER

It was morning. Daleah sat at her desk, finishing her journal entry of the previous day.

19314.10.2

Yesterday, Professor Bethuel shared his memory
with our class, of a time when he was with the

patriarch Abraham. We watched as the matriarch Sarah gave birth to Isaac, with the help of Bethuel's wife, the midwife. The professor called it a "twice-shared" memory. His wife had shared it with him long ago. Then he shared her memory with our class. Sarah's labor was so different from the time that Mama gave birth to my little brothers. Sarah was screaming in agony, giving birth to Isaac in her old age. Poor Revelyn was in shock, for she had never witnessed a birth of any kind, with labor pain or without. I tried to comfort her last night. I promised her she would never have to endure any pain, as my dear Mama never did. Professor Bethuel explained it —that labor pain was the curse pronounced on Eve for her rebellious act in eating the forbidden fruit. Our people have not experienced this curse since the time of New Earth. I witnessed Mama's labor while she gave birth to the quads three years ago. The room glowed and our loving family surrounded Mama was. It was a beautiful, joyous time, and free of labor pain. A few of the older family members saw the angels in the room with us, even though I and my siblings did not see them.

For once, it was my turn to teach Revelyn something. My wonderful roommate has shared so much knowledge with me. However, I learned that book knowledge is not the same as wisdom gained from experience.

It was surprising to discover that Rory, like Revelyn, had never witnessed a birth either. He was so quiet after Bethuel's memory share.

Even though I am blessed to have a large family, it's still hard for me to believe on Old Earth used to have families of ten or more children, within one or two years of each other. It's important to have balance in life, never too little, and never too much. Thank you, Adonai Elohenu, for my family!

Daleah and her friends had gathered at the table for the morning meal, excitedly chatting about yesterday's class. Revelyn had been quiet all morning, still unsettled after seeing the birth from the Memory Touch. The image of the birth stayed with her all night and into the morning.

"Remember what I told you, Revelyn. My Mama never experienced an ounce of pain!" Daleah said with emphasis, to correct Revelyn, "You will be fine when you give birth! Not IF you give birth, but WHEN." Revelyn looked relieved.

Then Kato grinned and said, "For sure, you will have a bunch of babies, like Daleah's mother! A quadrupled blessing! If you stay around Daleah's family long enough, that blessing might be contagious!"

Revelyn's expression changed back to uneasiness, "Is that possible?"

Daleah looked annoyed at Kato and declared with her pointed finger, "Kato, you are not helping! Don't say another word!" She turned to Revelyn with a reassuring smile, "You know Kato, he's always jesting." Daleah flipped her hand at Kato. "Ignore him! Our wonderful Creator knows your heart's desire. He won't give you too much or too little."

"When did our little Daleah become so wise?" Rory, who had been listening in silence all morning until now, remarked with a smile.

"How about you, Rory? Are you all right after seeing this painful birth?" Daleah asked Rory out of concern.

Rory's lifted his paw to his chin, its claws combing the long fur under his chin. He replied thoughtfully. "It was a bit of a shock because I witnessed none Seraphi births, not even in my own feline family."

"How come?" Daleah asked in puzzlement.

"Since the Seraphies were created, we have always produced one child per family, never more," said Rory, his eyes sad. "The fathers are the only witnesses to the births and the new-to-be-mothers instinctively know what to do."

Kato intervened, "Imagine this! Rory with a litter of little silver lions jumping all over your house, and your wife pulling out her fur, chasing after them." Even Enoch grinned at the picture that Kato presented.

Daleah frowned, "Really, Kato? You're exaggerating!"

Kato replied, grinning, "You should have learned by now not to take me seriously!"

"Actually, Kato isn't far from the truth." Rory interrupted, "I've dreamed of having a large family like Daleah's. Especially after I saw her family two years ago."

"Have your parents have arranged your marriage to a beautiful feline?" Kato asked, still the jester.

Rory smiled, enjoying the thought of a feline companion for life and answered, "My parents will arrange my marriage someday. It's still too early."

Daleah spoke, "See there! There's plenty of time to think about having a family later on!"

Rory went back to being serious, "We should do some serious prayer, such as asking the Holy One to change the destiny of the Seraphies and allow them to have larger families."

Kato and Enoch have stopped smiling. Kato spoke, "Rory, that's a weighty matter. We're just a bunch of fourteen-year-old kids. It's up to the adults to decide that."

"Our families have talked about colonizing the galaxy. It's only a matter of time before such changes are possible. Let's pray about it in private. I will discuss the matter with my father." Rory answered, his deep penetrating eyes surveying the group. And they ate their breakfast in thoughtful silence.

THE CABIN, INDIGOR

Haro had hidden his father's journal inside an old computer after removing most of the inside parts. Since the discovery of the journal, Haro and Jamik read Mardochi's journal entries together.

We face challenges each time we get the Gospel out. Continuing the Great Commission has always taken precedence. Long ago, the Adversary persecuted and hunted the believers on Old Earth. They persisted and met in secret, away from enemies who tried to stop the spread of His Holy Writings. The Brotherhood must continue to do the same—to share with the people about the Creator and his commandments, about loving Him and loving one another. His Word is Life. Without Him, there is no life. Slowly and overtime, the Brotherhood became a hidden secret to guard His Word, hoping that someday it will go out to all corners of our earth. I have shared many things with my wife about the Creator, but there is one thing she does not know: the existence and location of the Brotherhood. She does not know that I am a member. To protect the lives of our families, the brothers must keep their secrets.

Haro flipped the pages of the journal and a piece of paper fell out. Jamik saw it and asked, "What it says?"

Haro picked it up and answered, frowning, "Janov Diversi. *Hacker and Trafficker of Information.* It's my father's handwriting."

Haro and Jamik looked at each other, both thinking the same thing. Janov might have a link to the Brotherhood.

Moments later, Haro and Jamik were riding their high wheelers into town to look through the phone directory at the cafe. Haro didn't want to risk using the Indigonet from the cabin. Haro knew the cafe had a phone directory not connected to the network. He copied the address into his navigation device.

After they left, Haro showed Jamik how to use the device. "See this... I've removed the antenna. See this little icon? That's the antenna icon. It looks active, but it's not. It's only an animated image. The device has all the maps data. Search the location by dragging and zooming the map. It's a slower method. With this modified device, no one will track us."

Jamik remarked in awe, "That's ingenious. I'm impressed." Jamik had finally learned about Haro's genius with electronics and has sworn to keep it a secret.

Haro added, pointing his finger, "This is Janov's location. It's about twenty minutes away from us. If we take our bike, we might have to leave early in the morning."

And they rode their bikes back to the cabin.

KRISTALIS

Daleah opened her backpack to take out her notebook and calligraphy pen. The room looked like an old barn with distressed wood, paintings of farm animals, and a floor that looked like golden straw. Professor Mariel had named it the Manger Room.

"A bright halo to you this morning!" Professor Mariel began immediately, "I hope each one of you is ready to experience one of my spiritual adventures. Today I will share with you a precious memory—the first time I met my Messiah! Emmaus was my home long ago. The Messiah often went to preach in Emmaus. When I was a young woman, I would often go to Jerusalem to visit my older sister's family and watch over my little nieces and nephews. My friend Ruth told me about this man from Nazareth. I heard rumors that he was the Messiah, coming to take his rightful place as King of Israel. I was determined to meet him. We learned in our previous class that his first coming was for a different purpose. Let's be ready."

Daleah put her pen away and braced herself for another unfamiliar world. Her classmates did the same. Mariel's glow grew across the room, her radiance engulfing them. Daleah saw that she was on a road lined with palm trees, shadowing a different-looking Mariel, with dark brown hair. She was walking, holding her little niece and nephew's hands. An older child and another woman were also holding the little children's hands. They walked on the footpaths that flanked the dusty stone-paved road, away from the carriages, horses, and donkeys. They arrived at the outer court of the Temple. Amidst the throng of people was the glare of the metal breastplates and galeas of the proud Roman soldiers. Their shiny outfits made them stand out from the crowd of simple folks.

"He is not here at the Temple." Mariel's friend Ruth declared, "He is preaching somewhere else. Let's try the other place." The child she was holding had become cranky. Ruth picked him up and continued walking.

Mariel followed her and said, "Coming here with the children was a bad idea."

Ruth stopped and faced Mariel with determination, "It's never a bad idea to meet the Messiah, no matter who you are!" She resumed walking with the child in her arm toward a grove of oak trees. A crowd of people was dispersing. In the center stood an ordinary Jewish man in his thirties, with long wavy brown hair and beard, brown eyes, in the garb of a Jewish teacher, the tzitzit or fringes of his garment hanging out.

"That's him!" Ruth exclaimed enthusiastically. He was neither remarkable nor glorious. Mary stifled her disappointment. Surely, it cannot be this simple, humble man? He hardly had the appearance of a formidable, powerful man. The men were leaving. The women with babies and little children gathered around the man. His disciples were rebuking them and attempting to shoo them away.

"Let the little children come to me," said the man to his disciples, "and do not hinder them, for the Kingdom of Elohim belongs to such as these. Truly I tell you, anyone who does not receive the Kingdom of Elohim as a little child will never enter it."

It was not his physical appearance that made an impression on her. He was a contradiction. He looked humble, yet he spoke with power. He smiled radiantly and gently gathered the children to himself, holding them with such love and affection, as a woman would. His disciples frowned at him in disapproval, as if he had better things to do. Miriam knew these men did not understand, for they were men of labor. By tradition, Jewish men left the care and raising of children to their wives. Not so with this man —he understood. His actions surprised and delighted her. She became excited and beamed at Ruth, who smiled back in understanding. They guided the children to meet him. He touched the head of each child and blessed them.

Then everything dissolved, and Daleah was back in the Manger Room. Mariel's memory touch had ended.

"Welcome back to the present!" Mariel resumed her teaching, "Now you know what He was like in the flesh when He walked among us! I have treasured that memory forever. It had sustained me through the later years when I lost everything. I had no children of my own during my time on Old Earth, but the good Lord gave me many children during the eons of New Earth, children from the second resurrection. Many of these children died during childbirth, or during pregnancy, multitudes of them, so many that we couldn't count them. Our Creator gave these unborn children to the Elders, and we became their guardians, protégées, disciples, and apprentices. We gave these children a peculiar name: the Innocents. Why? Because they have never experienced life on Old Earth, and the Creators gave them fully mature bodies when they resurrected. These Innocents have been with us for many millennia." She paused and smiled radiantly, her eyes toward the door. "And it is my pleasure to invite Benzi and Zephan here today!"

The twin Elders walked into the classroom. Daleah recognized them from Elizon's class as the professor's assistants.

Mariel added, "Please feel free to ask them

any questions."

Daleah lifted her hand immediately, "What was it like for you to move so swiftly, from birth to death, then to resurrect in new bodies?"

The twin Elders with the cherubic faces were both uncannily alike. Benzi spoke first, "Actually, we were never born. Our lives were abruptly terminated when we were in the womb." Then Zephan added, "Our mother chose to terminate our lives. Although it was wrong, in those days, people mistakenly believed it was a common birth control procedure for unwanted babies."

Daleah and the other students were shocked. A pause ensued as they absorbed what they had just heard. For the first time since the semester started, Revelyn raised her hand timidly. "I'm sorry. I can't imagine such things. Can I ask why your mother didn't want you?"

The twins took turns speaking, "You may ask, but you might not like the answer. The question didn't bother us anymore after we met our biological mother years later. We have forgiven her because we wanted her to receive the love of the Creator."

"At the time it happened, she was still young, unmarried, poor, scared, and confused. After she went to the abortion specialist, she realized how wrong it was and lived with regret for years. She is fine now."

Benzi spoke at length, "People didn't understand that life started at conception. In the beginning, childbirth was difficult, and many women and babies died. Miscarriages were common. Later, medical advances made childbirth easier and saved lives. Then came the generations who were only interested in pleasing themselves. During the latter age of Old Earth, abortion was encouraged as a method of birth control. In the Creator's eyes, ending those unborn lives for selfish reasons was wrong."

Zephan added, "The psalmist David once wrote about the soul of unborn babies being formed in secret. My brother and I remember feeling secure inside our mother's womb. One minute, we were drifting in the water sac, and the next minute we felt this intense pain. Then death came. We slept peacefully for a long time, floating in a warm light until the resurrection.”

Daleah remembered the first time she held her little brothers in her arms. They were so innocent and sweet. As they grew, she liked them best when they slept and weren’t getting into everything. Still, she couldn’t imagine how anyone would want to hurt them.

This time Kato lifted his hand, “How were you able to make the jump to full-grown bodies? Was it strange?”

Daleah raised her hand quickly, intervening to add, “Yes! I’ve watched my baby brothers grow. It took one year for them to learn to walk. Were you able to stand like that, in one day?”

Both twins looked at each other, rubbed their hands together and grinned, “Now is the time for another memory session!” Benzi said, then his twin added, “We don’t have to explain in words what we experienced!”

As the glow from the twins spread throughout the room, Daleah saw herself floating in soft, warm light. The twin’s memory was more powerful than the Elders. She couldn’t see the shadows of her classmates as they shared in the memory. She felt like she was inside the twins. Then she heard the loud blowing sound of a shofar, one long blast, then the sound of a multitude of voices together like the roar of the ocean. She felt herself being pulled through a tunnel, toward a brilliant light. Then, in the blink of an eye, she stood before a throne. It was the Holy One, but she could not see His face because it was shining. Beside her was the other twin in the same physical form as hers, clothed in white. She looked at her hands and they were real. She touched her face. It was real. She wasn’t standing on any surface, but floating. She didn’t feel the gravity or any physical barrier even though she knew she was in a new body. She looked at the twin and saw his mirror expression of wonder. She saw her arm moving to touch his arm. It was real.

The luminous figure of the One sitting on the throne

spoke, "Come to me, little ones. Don't be afraid anymore. No one will ever harm you again. Your lives were stolen before you were fully formed. You never had a chance to experience the world. I am giving you wonderful parents who will teach you everything. You will always be by my side. My Kingdom is for pure souls like you. Welcome." The One on the throne introduced them to two Elders dressed in white who led them by the hands through the throne room. Then everything faded. Daleah was back in the present reality. She was back as herself.

After the silence, Kato was naturally the first to speak, "Wow! That was the Holy One! So different from seeing him through Mariel as a human!"

"Indeed." The twins spoke, then Benzi. "Many of us Innocents didn't know what happened to us. The Elders were wonderful to us. We grew up and lived with them for many millennia and we learned all about agape love from them. Now, we are free to explore many worlds throughout the galaxy."

Zephan spoke, "We didn't feel physically limited. As Innocents, everything was instinctive. Even language wasn't a barrier for us. My brother and I share a telepathic bond. We need not speak to each other."

Professor Mariel got up and announced. "Thank you so much, Benzi and Zephan for sharing." For Daleah and many other students, the lesson was a revelation.

THE CABIN, INDIGOR

Haro and Jamik were sitting on the couch reading the journal. They froze when they heard an unexpected knock at the back door of the kitchen. They heard the noise of the key being inserted. Haro scrambled to hide the journal under the couch, while Jamik quickly picked up the tele's remote to watch a martial art class. There was no time to hide the forbidden journal.

Haro said to Jamik with a worried look, "I think it's my sister. Mom probably told her to come here to check on me. She never announces herself, using her voice."

Sure enough, it was Ladya unexpectedly showing up with a flustered and nervous Mei. Ladya peeked from the doorway, elbowed Mei, and signed, "Please announce, we here."

"Hello, boys? We are here!" Mei yelled.

Haro responded, "Come in! We are watching the tele!" As Ladya and Mei walked into the family room, Haro voiced and signed to Ladya, "Did Mom send you to check on me?"

Ladya signed back, "Of course! Me big sister, me responsible adult now! Mom wants garden tools in shed. Me go there now."

"I will help you." Haro said, getting up from the couch. He turned toward Jamik, his back to the girls, his eyes pointing at the journal, his lips moving silently, "Watch it!"

"Go ahead," Mei told Ladya, "I am staying." When Haro and Ladya left for the barn, Mei started searching in the kitchen.

Jamik put his hands behind his head, stretched his long legs, and nonchalantly lounged on the couch, his feet on the ottoman. The clattering noises from the kitchen alerted him. He shouted across the room, "Mei, what's going on?"

There was no answer, but Mei came into the family room and nervously told Jamik, "I lost an expensive ring in here for the girls' slumber party. Have you boys seen it?" The one thing Mei was afraid to admit—that she had never been a tidy person. Hence, she often misplaced her items. Even Ladya repeatedly pointed out that Mei's room was a mess.

Jamik replied, "No, we didn't see a ring."

"Back to the kitchen to finish looking." Mei went back to the kitchen and made more noise.

Jamik tried to ignore the clattering noise while watching the cartoons on the tele. Then Mei came back, walking through the family room to go to the bedrooms. Jamik sat up and yelled, "Where are you going? You can't go in there!" He worried she would find the old desktop computer in Haro's room. Haro had unscrewed it to take the hidden journal out, and it wasn't screwed back.

"Why not?" Mei asked as she faced him, hands on hips.

"Ask the owner's permission first."

"Ladya knows I am here to search for my ring."

"Hold on. How about you let me help you find it?" Jamik sat up.

"YOU want to help ME?" She asked suspiciously, pointing at him, then at herself. "Why?" She hadn't forgotten the things he said about her royal family. "No, I don't think so."

"Hey! I can be a nice guy if I want to!" He got up.

"Fine! Prove it, and I will forget that you ever called my family a bunch of pompous misfits." She said as she turned away from him, her long blond hair swinging.

"I didn't call your family that! I said, them, not you!"

"Same thing! They are MY family!"

"Alright!" Jamik threw his hands up and said, "I am sorry! I won't repeat it again! What does it look like? The ring?" He asked as he went with her toward the bedrooms.

"It looks like a ring with a diamond the size of a knob." She said with a mischievous smile.

"What? Really?" Jamik asked, his eyes wide.

"No!" Mei sighed as she opened the door to Ladya's room. "Look for an ordinary ring that looks out of place. I might have dropped it somewhere. A bunch of us girls used all the rooms for the slumber party. It could be anywhere."

"I will start with Haro's room," Jamik said as he walked down the hall to Haro's room and quickly screwed the computer together. Then he searched the bedroom. Moments later, Mei peeked in to ask Jamik when he was searching the guest room, "Found it yet?"

"Nothing. Why are you so obsessed with that ring, anyway? Aren't you the one who wears cheap jewelry?" Jamik replied, looking under the bed for a second time.

Mei said to Jamik, averting her eyes nervously. "It's a

family heirloom. Keep searching in the other rooms. I will search in the bathroom." While Jamik was searching the other rooms, Mei became frustrated at not finding the ring in the bathroom and went to the living room. Jamik didn't hear her leave the bathroom. The first place she searched was under the cushion. Curious, she picked up the leather-bound journal, not knowing what it was. Then her eyes widened when she realized it was a book.

When Jamik walked in, she was holding the book gingerly, jaw agape. Jamik yelled at her, "What are you doing?"

Mei jumped in alarm and dropped the journal. He retrieved it and hid it under the cushion. Mei looked nervous, "What was that thing? It looks like a religious text. Isn't that illegal?"

"Of course, it's illegal!" An angry Jamik replied. "You weren't supposed to find it! It belongs to Haro's father and if you tell anyone, his family can end up in jail or worse. Promise me you will say NOTHING!"

Mei still looked upset and confused, "But how..."

Jamik looked angry and almost growled, "Say nothing! Tell me you understand."

Mei jumped at his angry words, "I get it." She was about to cry. "You don't want me to say anything! Does Ladya know about it?"

"No, she doesn't! You will keep your trap shut about it!" Jamik insisted, still angry. "She is deaf and need not be involved!"

The remark stung because Mei was fiercely protective of her deaf best friend. "Ladya is deaf, not dumb... and why should Haro be the only one to know about this book? How did he find it? Why would Haro keep it after all that speech he gave us of the danger? And why are you involved in the first place?"

Mei's many questions maddened him. "Stop with the questions!"

Mei blurted out, crying, "I don't know how I will keep it a secret from Ladya. She is too good at reading body language! She might be deaf, but she has always been smarter than me! Don't blame me if she finds out!" Ladya's intelligence was something that Mei had always envied. She never admitted to anyone that she was sometimes jealous of Ladya, who often helped her with her homework. She was the beauty, while Ladya had always been the brains. Their complimentary personalities were the reason they became best friends.

There was no time to argue. Haro and Ladya had returned from the barn. Mei left the room quickly, avoiding Ladya's stare because her eyes were teary from the argument with Jamik. She quickly passed Ladya to wait in the car, saying nothing.

Ladya frowned. Then she spoke to Haro, "I am going back home now. Thanks for the help." She left to follow Mei to the car.

Jamik blurted out, "I am sorry, Haro, but Mei found the journal and knows!"

"What? How did that happen?" And Jamik explained it all to Haro.

Meanwhile, Ladya got in the driver's seat of the car. Mei looked uncomfortable and pretended to search her purse for something, but she forgot to fasten her seat belt.

She tapped Mei on the shoulder to inform her to put the seat belt on. While still searching her purse, Mei signed with her hand, "Wait! I am looking for something! Go ahead."

Ladya was undeterred and tapped Mei's shoulder again. Mei sighed, resigned to defeat, and turned to look at Ladya, her eyes teary.

Ladya's expressive face turned to one of concern. "You alright?"

"No!" Mei sniffed and blurted out, "I still can't find my ring! It's not in the cabin!" She took out her handkerchief and blew her nose.

Ladya replied, "Oh? That all? It only thing, not your life. No worry."

"No, that's not it!" Mei shook her head, her cheeks wet

from tears. "I know most things can be replaced. It was an engagement ring! Jonik proposed to me. And I am pregnant! I lied about the ring being a family heirloom."

Ladya's jaws dropped, expressing astonishment at this turn of event. "What? You can't pregnant! You only sixteen! You met Jonik two months ago. That, fast! Proposed, when?"

"You know how I dread not being able to find a boyfriend who wasn't shorter than me?" Mei signed fast because of her distress, "He was tall, handsome, and SO romantic! He told me I was the most beautiful girl in the world! I lied to my parents about his age. He was a little older and my parents didn't approve of him. They wouldn't let me go out with him, so we sneaked out to see each other. Then a few weeks later, he proposed!" She stopped and sighed in relief. She had been feeling stressed by the burden of carrying three secrets—the engagement, the pregnancy, and the journal.

"You sure you pregnant? Take test?"

"Not yet, but I am one week late! Please don't tell my parents!"

"Not my place to tell anyone, me not know if me should congratulate you or me sorry." Ladya wanted to offer a sympathetic shoulder, but she didn't know what to say. "We deal one day at time. We not talk about you pregnant until test positive, alright? We go cabin, search again? Me suspect ring will show up somewhere. You bad habit, misplace things, always!"

Mei hugged her best friend, "I am so relieved you understand. Yes, you're right. One thing at a time. I feel better!" Then she insisted, "But, I already looked everywhere in the cabin!"

"We search one more time, then you get pregnancy test." She paused and looked sad, "Me disappointed you not trust me tell me about boyfriend. Me your bestie!" Ladya and Mei got out of the car and walked toward the cabin. Ladya was walking ahead quickly, still miffed at Mei for keeping a secret. Mei tried to keep up with Ladya as she entered the cabin and walked through the kitchen. Mei grabbed Ladya's arm and turned her around so she could use sign language facing her, "Please, I am sorry I didn't tell you!"

Haro and Jamik saw that Ladya coming in, looking upset, and Mei's eyes were puffy and red from crying. Haro and Jamik assumed the worse.

Ladya blurted out to Haro, "Me glad Mei finally told me! Me sick of people keeping secrets! Bad enough, me deaf, ignored, not join conversations, but when people think me no handle truth, me ANGRY."

Haro and Jamik looked at her, crestfallen. They felt betrayed that Mei couldn't keep a secret. Haro spoke and signed simultaneously, "Calm down! I am sorry we had to hide the journal from you."

Ladya looked at him in puzzlement, "What?" She asked, signing with her hands.

Haro frowned and signed back, assuming she didn't understand him, which was a common issue with Ladya, "I am sorry we hide the journal from you."

Mei gaped and looked in horror at the boys. She realized the boys had blurted out their secret from a misunderstanding. She shook her head while waving her hand, and covering her mouth with her other hand. Ladya saw Mei's expression and realized what happened.

Ladya became even angrier. "You morons! Mei told me NOT about journal, told me about engagement ring!" Looking at each of them, "SOOO! Truth out!" She looked at them all, her hands on her hips. "You ALL hiding secrets from me! First, wood box, then Mei engaged, now journal?" Her demeanor changed to determination. She stomped her foot and said with a flurry of forcefully moving hands, "Me demand see journal NOW! You NOT stop me! Me WILL tell her!"

Haro groaned and slumped down on the couch with his hands on his head. Because Jamik couldn't understand Ladya's sign language, he asked, "What did she say?"

"She knows about the journal!" Haro replied, "Keeping

this secret has blown up in our faces! Mei had a secret about her engagement, and I assumed it was about the journal. Our secret is out!"

And Jamik groaned and slumped as Haro did. Oddly, Haro felt relieved. It wasn't enough for him and Jamik to carry this secret by themselves. He got up and lifted the cushion on which he had been sitting. He picked up the journal and handed it to Ladya.

"Here is the thing that Dad had formed in secret years ago." His face as somber as he spoke and signed simultaneously, "You can't tell anyone because Mom could go to prison for this." Ladya took the book and held it gingerly as if it was a fragile thing. She mirrored his somber expression.

And for the rest of the day, everything became revealed. Gone were the secrets between siblings and best friends.

☞ **CHAPTER EIGHT** ☞

HAPPY ACCIDENTS

You only live once.
~An Old Earth saying

KRISTALIS, THE NEXT DAY

Daleah was at her desk, scribbling in her daily journal entry while Revelyn was getting ready for their morning meal.

19314.10.3

Yesterday, Elder Moralee substituted for Elizon while he went on a mission to Indigor. She is such a sweet person. I have a hard time believing that she died from a car accident when she was only fifteen years old, a year older than me. Before her death, Moralee loved to sing at church and tell people the story of the Messiah and His wonderful promises. I don't know what church is, but I imagine it's like the little shul in my family's hometown where we gather on the Shabbat to experience His wonderful Presence. She was a popular girl at school, always friendly to everyone, and never had a mean bone in her body. She loved to talk for long hours to her friends on the phone, playing volleyball, and going to the mall. Although I am not sure what a mall is.

Professor Moralee wasn't sure at first if she wanted to share with us the memory of her car accident. She warned us it was bloody and shocking, that we might feel nauseous or sick. Most of us agreed, although Revelyn and Rory hesitated at first.

The mother was chauffeuring the girls from choir practice at church. Moira Lynn, as her name was back then, was sitting on the right side of the back seat, chatting with the girls. The car made a left turn when it shook violently with a loud crash. Everything went black. When Moira opened her eyes, she saw the blood, the bones jutting out of the flesh, and broken glass everywhere.

I have seen photos of human anatomy for homeschool and they weren't disturbing. The real thing was shocking, and I felt the strangest sensation in my body, of the morning meal churning inside me, going up my throat. Moralee's memories were horrific. I took a deep breath to feel calm.

The girls in the back seat were crying. The impact had crushed the right side of the vehicle that they crammed so tightly. One girl shouted toward the jammed left door, "Help us!" Moira passed into blackness again. She heard the high-pitched noise of the emergency vehicles arriving and opened her eyes again, blinking at the flashing lights. Moira could not move. She saw an emergency technician putting the neck brace on the unconscious driver and moving her to the stretcher. She heard the other man telling the girls, "Be patient, I will pry open the car door and get you out." She heard the grinding noise of the door being forced open, and the girls being carried out. Moira died at that moment.

Moira was floating in a warm light as in a dream until she suddenly jarred awake at the sound of a long and loud shofar blast. She saw the glowing figure of the Messiah surrounded by a cloud of glory. He had eyes the color of amber fire and white hair surrounded by the most intense aura. He didn't need to wear a crown, for the aura surrounded his head looked like a sunburst crown.

I look forward to hearing more of Moralee's former life story. To be continued...

Daleah and her friends were quietly eating their breakfast. Finally, Revelyn spoke. "I wonder how Professor Elizon is doing on his mission to Indigor. He didn't speak about it except to tell us it's a fallen and broken world like Old Earth was."

Daleah looked up, "I wonder too. I would be interested to hear his report. He instructed us to keep praying for the people of Indigor."

Then Rory showed up with his tray of food. "A good Halo to you!" He sat down and inquired, "What's your topic of conversation today?"

"Indigor." Kato replied, "You didn't miss much. Professor Elizon will share his mission report with us today."

"For sure," added Daleah, "I am looking forward to his report! The reason we are here it to pray for lost souls of Indigor."

"Well said!" Kato uttered in agreement, impressed with Daleah's wisdom, "You should become a professor!"

Daleah looked thoughtful and smiled, "Maybe I will!"

"I spoke with my father last night." Rory announced, "And he told me Grandfather once traveled many worlds. He visited Indigor during its golden age before it fell from grace. He had never seen such an amazing world. The people had advanced technologies. They invented the floating cities, a knowledge passed on to your people, the Kristalians.”

“How fascinating!” Kato replied.

THE CABIN, INDIGOR

Haro had no choice. Ladya and Mei insisted on reading his father’s journal to learn more about their family legacy. They postponed their personal plans for the school break. Even Mei made excuses to her boyfriend, Jonik.

Ladya and Haro were arguing. “You remember, Dad said, safety in numbers?” Ladya explained to Haro in sign language, “You much young search for Brotherhood. Jamik too! Us four go together, safer.”

Haro glared at his sister. “That was for wilderness survival training!” He replied in sign language, also voicing for Jamik and Mei’s benefit, “We are not going camping, we are going to the city!”

“Me know that!” Ladya signed with forceful hand movements, her face expressing determination, “Listen me, Haro. Same thing, no matter, wilderness or city! Everywhere danger! Me older, me responsible for you!”

“What will you do if we get separated, and you are alone?” Haro persisted. He did not want to admit that his sister might become a burden to him. It’s like recruiting a deaf man to become a soldier or a spy. It’s a recipe for disaster!

Jamik and Mei had been listening to Haro and Ladya argue, not wanting to make things worse by getting involved.

Ladya stomped her foot, hands on her hips, “Have phone!” She signed fast, “We text! Stop worry MUCH!”

Haro threw his hands up, “No, we CANNOT use our phones. They will track us. You wait here. I will show you!” Haro left and came back with a briefcase. He opened it on the footrest. It had compartments for a dozen different electronic devices. Jamik and Mei sat up, fascinated.

"This is what I have been doing for the last two months." Haro expounded on his plan, "I tweaked them so that nobody will track us." He pointed to six handheld radios with short antennas. He picked one and extended the antenna. "These are two-way radios that Dad used on his job site. We used them for camping in case we got separated or lost. They are mobile phones with one difference—all communication is private. They have a 30-mile range." Haro gave one handheld radio to Jamik. "I am going outside to call you." Haro left with the other radio through the kitchen.

"Hello, Jamik! Can you hear me?" Haro was calling Jamik through the radio.

A surprised Jamik answered. "Wow! Loud and clear!" He eyed a confused Ladya and pointed to his ear, as if saying, "I can hear this."

Then Jamik felt the radio vibrate. Jamik handed the radio for Ladya to read. Hello Sis! How cool is that?

Ladya took it and texted back, All right, genius! I believe you. Come back and tell us your plan. Unlike the language of hands, her written communication was perfect, word for word.

As Haro walked in, Mei signed with her hands, facing Ladya. "You are the one to talk about keeping secrets, Ladya! You never told me your brother was a tekkie genius!" Mei didn't look flustered anymore. She was back to being the beautiful, confident, and proud teen. She was wearing her lost engagement ring, which sparkled as she moved her hands. It had been at her house the whole time, fallen and lodged behind her dresser. Ladya had helped Mei find the ring and got her the pregnancy test, which turned out to be negative. Mei acted as if the pregnancy thing had never happened, which annoyed Ladya.

"Family decides, keep secret." Ladya looked directly at each of their faces with determination. "Not my secret! Family protects Haro so authorities not take him! You NOT tell anyone!" She finished, staring at them wide-eyed.

"What kind of person do you think I am?" Mei looked a little hurt that Ladya didn't trust her to keep a secret. "I won't tell! Let's move on and do something other than argue with each other!" Ever since Mei had blurted out her secret about sleeping with her boyfriend, there had been tension between Ladya and Mei. What Mei did was contrary to Ladya's family values. Mei ignored Ladya and spoke without signing, "So, are we going to call and visit this Janov guy?"

Haro sighed, "You haven't been paying attention!" He signed and spoke, "Before we go out there searching for this guy, we must all leave our phones here, so we won't be traced." He picked up another device. "Here, you recognize this? This was a navigational device. I've removed the antenna. Now, it's a device with maps. They won't track us with this device. Follow me so far?"

Jamik and Ladya nodded, but Mei looked doubtful. He showed them the display screen. "Here's where the guy lives. It's in a bad part of a town. You girls can't go there, especially you, Mei."

A puzzled Mei pointed at herself, "Me? I don't understand."

"Yes, you!" Jamik leaned forward and interjected, "You are tall, blond, and beautiful! What do you think these gangs will do when they see you? They will notice you! You girls can't go into that area. We can't protect both ourselves and you!" Not knowing sign language, Jamik gestured for Ladya's benefit—tall, hair eyelashes batting, an expression of lust, and pretending to grab something. Ladya understood. Mei's beauty, her tall height, and platinum blonde hair attracted much attention.

"That's correct," added Haro, "you girls will chauffeur us. You will stay in the car. However, Jamik promised to teach me some defensive moves so I can protect myself. We're not going until tomorrow."

"You, learn defense," Ladya looked unconvinced, "finish one day, impossible!"

"Fine!" Haro threw his hands up and sighed, "I should practice for one week! How about we go search next week?"

"No!" Mei and Jamik disagreed simultaneously. "Don't drag it out." "We need to finish this before school starts again!"

"Fine!" Haro held up his hand and gave up, "Tomorrow!"

After they had all agreed on the plan, everyone seemed calmer. While Jamik taught Haro some moves, the girls caught up on reading the journal.

"Me feel closer to Dad when read this." Ladya remarked to Mei with hand signs, "Like comfort. Mom sad since his death, CRY continues CRY. Wish tell her about journal."

Mei looked pensive. "Remember what Haro said, you don't want your mom to go to prison or worse." Mei signed back, "It's better if your mother does not know about your father. As minors, the authorities can't arrest us. If we get caught, we can blame it on your father because he is dead. I don't want to see you and Haro become orphans."

Ladya didn't reply because she knew Mei was right. She sighed. They read a journal entry together...

19297.7.30

I often think of my family, of what will happen to them if I am gone. I think about my loving wife grieving for me, about her raising Haro and Ladya alone. I am glad I shared my belief with her, the things my father and his father taught me. If I am gone, my wife and my children will have questions. Like, why would a loving Creator allow suffering to happen? Why do bad things happen to good people?

I would not want anger to overtake their soul. I would want them to understand that the Creator did not create evil and suffering. The first world He created was perfect. He created the first man and woman with the freedom to make choices. Sadly, they chose to rebel. That rejection led to evil gaining a foothold in that first perfect world. The early Indigans also rebelled, leading to the same consequences. Thankfully, the Creator foresaw this rebellion, because He exists outside of time-space. He made the ultimate sacrifice. The Messiah descended to Old Earth to be born as a unique sinless human and died a horrible death on the tree. ◇ He became a sin offering for everyone in the galaxy and conquered death by rising from the grave. Through Him, people can achieve redemption. Although he did not create suffering, he was intimately acquitted with pain, sickness, brokenness, hatred, rejection, sorrow, grief, betrayal, and rejection. He had gone to the greatest depth of hell for us, taking all our iniquities on Himself that we might have life. He is not a distant deity, but always within our reach. He cares deeply for us. All the tears we shed became his tears.

As Ladya finished reading. Her eyes glistened, and the tears came slowly. She held her palm on the page of the journal. Mei looked up and saw her best friend's tears. She put her arm around Ladya and held her close. Ladya said, "Dad, miss him much!"

"I never knew your father's beautiful words could pierce our hearts like that!" Mei replied somberly. She noticed a diamond symbol next to the word tree and pointed to it. "Do you know why your father added a diamond symbol?"

Ladya looked perplexed, "Don't know. Ask Haro later."

KRISTALIS, THE NEXT DAY

"A good halo to you all!" Professor Moralee's smile brightened the whole classroom. "Today, we continue our lesson on understanding the Holy One's purpose in our lives, and why bad things happen to good people. What did we learn yesterday after the memory share of my car accident?”

Kato raised his hand and Moralee nodded at him, “We learned that some people were angry at the Creator for allowing suffering.”

“Correct.” Moralee began her teaching. “They refused to believe in a deity who allowed suffering. For example, my mother grieved after I died. She turned away from her faith because she couldn’t carry the burden of a daughter being gone. I was her only child, so it was doubly hard for her. My mother blamed the accident on the drunk driver. She took him to court. The judge let the man go because he was a friend of the defense attorney and the judge. Everywhere she went, she was denied the justice she felt she deserved. The man didn’t stop drinking. In fact, his dangerous decision to drink and drive killed more people. All these things happened when driving under the influence was not yet outlawed. My mother lost everything, divorced, lost her job, her house, and became depressed. Many years later, she finally recovered from her bitterness, forgave everyone, and returned to her faith. Then one day, justice happened. The man who killed her precious daughter went to life imprisonment for killing a judge while driving under the influence.” Moralee sighed, pausing briefly.

“People had an imperfect understanding of who the Creator was. How would you respond to these suffering people? Why didn’t He create a world where suffering doesn’t exist?”

Daleah raised her hand immediately. Revelyn, who was sitting next to Daleah, was her usual reserved self. Daleah answered, “I would tell them He created a perfect world at the beginning! Adam and Eve lived in Paradise like ours! But they wanted to taste both good and evil.”

“Correct,” added Moralee, “the serpent deceived Eve first. He told her it would make her wiser. The world never became the same after they rebelled. For over six thousand years, humans constantly and consistently made poor decisions. They fought with each other over senseless things. There is no wisdom apart from the Creator. What else did we learn?"

Rory raised his paw and answered, "Suffering is only temporary. The Creator allows evil one to rule a fallen world for a time."

"Thank you, Rory." Moralee answered, "The Holy Writings tell us they only live once, then death and judgment follow. The famous Old Earth saying, 'You only live once,' used to mean doing anything they wanted, without worrying about the consequences. They forgot the law of reaping and sowing. If we sow to please ourselves, we will reap destruction. If we sow to please Him, we will reap life everlasting." So ended the lesson as the school bell rang from the speakers like the sound of a trumpet.

ON THE ROAD, INDIGOR

They were ready to go. Haro, Jamik, Ladya, and Mei were in the car as Ladya was backing it out onto the gravel road when it made a squealing noise.

"Stop!" Haro yelled and signed with his hands in front of Ladya. "Mei, you came here with Ladya, did you hear that noise yesterday?"

Mei looked confused. "Maybe, but it wasn't as bad as now."

"And you didn't bother to tell me?" Haro got out of the car and opened the hood of the car to look. He announced loudly, "It's the drive belt. It's loose. You wait here, I am going to the shed for the toolbox."

Ladya looked at Mei's contrite face and said with a smile, "Don't worry. Haro is an expert at fixing car problems."

As Haro came back with the repair tools, Jamik remarked. "That's another thing I know about Haro—fixing cars. I'm impressed!"

They were finally on their way, but the highway was congested because of multiple collisions. Because Haro felt uneasy about staying on the highway, he insisted on driving on the country roads to their destination.

He looked at Jamik, "I can't shake the feeling that if we had left earlier, we would have gotten stuck in that accident, or worse."

"Looks like," Jamik replied somberly, "someone is protecting us."

"It was bad enough that Dad died in one." Haro tried to shake off the grief that was weighing him down.

Haro and Jamik were in the inner city of Rivertown. The streets were filthy and littered, graffiti sprayed everywhere. It smelled of urine, smoke, and other strange odors. A rundown city, windows barred everywhere, shop boarded up and out of business. People hung out in groups. Children and women were nowhere in sight. What used to be a thriving neighborhood had become a dump.

Jamik and Haro had come prepared. They wore dark clothes to avoid attention. They had packed their skateboards, slung over their shoulders, in case they needed to take off quickly. Ladya and Mei anxiously waited for them three blocks away. Jamik and Haro hunched into their jackets with heads down. Their wary eyes kept watch as they walked the busy street in a decrepit area. They turned left onto a quiet street.

Haro was looking at his navigational device and exclaimed, "We're on the wrong street. The number isn't here. There's another street of the same name. This must be Goron Street, not Goron Trail. The street sign is missing, so I can't be sure."

Jamik looked at Haro, "What should we do?"

Two older men with threadbare clothes came shuffling down the street toward them. One of them was limping with a cane.

Jamik said to Haro, "Should we ask them?"

Haro looked doubtful, "I don't know."

Jamik reassured Haro, "There's no street sign, so it won't hurt to ask. Let me do the talking." As they approached the two men, Jamik stepped toward them and inquired, hands in his pockets as if trying to look tough, "Hey, dudes! Do you know where Goron Trail is?"

Unknown to Haro and Jamik, these two men were not the ordinary people of the inner-city neighborhood. They came to pray and to survey the town. One of them was a Brother, and the other an Elder who had transformed into a tall, middle-aged man.

The shorter man answered, "It's two blocks back there to the right, but you don't want to go that way. We passed a gang that's looking for trouble. Take a detour on Malia Street. It's a parallel street on your right. From there, turn left on Goron Trail."

Jamik grinned and thanked the man, "Thank you for your advice, sir!" And they went their ways.

The tall man remarked, "What are these nice polite boys doing here? They are not from here."

The other man frowned, "Elder Elizon, I can't shake the feeling that the shorter boy we encountered looked familiar. They must be new to this neighborhood. I hope they'll be okay."

As they shuffled along, Elizon replied confidently, "Brother Mateo. If there is something I learned during my lengthy life, it's that there is no such thing as a coincidence or a chance encounter. On Old Earth, we used to call them 'happy accidents.' You might save this boy from being beaten up by that gang, or worse. I doubt you have ever met him before today, as he looks too young for the Brotherhood. He might be someone's son. Maybe you've met his father?"

Then the older man stopped dead in his tracks and looked at Elizon, who also stopped walking. He said with wide-eyed wonder and burst out, "It's Mardochi's son!"

Elizon raised his left eyebrow, "I remember Mardochi. This boy looked like his father!"

Mateo exclaimed, "We should go back and make sure they are okay!"

Elizon said calmly, "Indeed. We will. Obviously, he is

looking for someone or something. Let's pray for the boys. Does the boy know about his father being a Brother?"

Mateo's voice had a hint of anxiety, "I am not sure. Mardochi died two months ago in a car accident. The boy isn't old enough to know about our Brotherhood yet, but sometimes we recruit and train them at a much younger age. We have searched for a new Brother since the death of Brother Sherman. Our resources are stretched thin. The boy might have some valuable skills we could use."

Elizon remained calm and said, "Brother Mateo, we are doing everything to help you. Stay focused on our prayer walk for now. We don't know which building the boys went into and we won't find them until they come out, then we will keep our eyes on them." And they continued their walk.

Haro and Jamik stood before the heavy metal door. There was no doorbell. They looked at each other, not knowing what to do. Haro knocked on the door and waited. He knocked again moments later. Then Haro looked around and saw the security camera hidden under the outdoor light. He smiled, waved his hand, and announced, "Hello, we are here to see Mister Diversi."

Finally, the heavy metal door opened and a gaunt, disheveled man in his twenties peered out, looking at them suspiciously. "What do you want?"

Haro tried to use a pleasing voice, "Pardon us, we are looking for Mister Diversi. Is he available?"

The thin man looked suspiciously at the boys, "What is it about?"

Haro, "It's about my father. He was supposed to meet Mister Diversi. Are you Mister Diversi?"

"No, I'm not. Wait here." He closed the door.

Jamik looked at Haro and said with a worried frown, "I hope we don't have to wait long. I don't feel comfortable on this small street."

The door opened and a burly, tired older man with

spectacles and bushy eyebrows stood before them. He asked the boys in a gruff voice, "Your father sent you? Aren't you too young for my service?"

Haro anxiously asked the man, "Actually, he didn't send me. He passed away two months ago, then we found your name and number. Can we talk in private?"

Janov stood there trying to decide and then said gruffly, "Alright, come in!" He led them into a room full of dormant computers lying everywhere, even under the tables. He told the gaunt man, "Please go out and order the usual for lunch."

After the man left, Janov spoke, "Now, we have privacy. Please sit." He offered the empty chairs in front of his desk.

Haro introduced himself. "My name is Haro, this is my friend Jamik." Jamik waved a hello.

Janov asked, "So, who was your father?"

Haro answered, "Mardochi Gallant."

The man's face registered surprise. He slumped into his chair and ran this hand through his hair, expressing his dismay. "I am so sorry to hear about your father passing. He was a good man, but still, you didn't have to come. I see the resemblance now. What brings you here?"

Haro smiled, but serious eyes told a different story, "We found your name and contact in a private place. It said you were a hacker. You seem to know the reason my father came to you."

"Shh!" Janov looked alarmed, "Be careful, we don't use that word here! What I do is illegal. Here, I run a computer repair shop. The powers that be have spies everywhere!"

"So, my father was working on something big with you?" Haro didn't want to stop, "Was he planning to break through the authorities' wall of defense and bring the truth to the people?"

Again, Janov looked surprised, "How did you know? Aren't you too young to be involved?"

"I came across my father's secret by accident. I didn't

know he was involved until after he died. I know it's a something important that will bring the truth about our origins to the people. He didn't share more with you?"

Janov looked pensive. "He and his brothers were working to transfer some old writings into digital files. My plan is to upload these digital files to a server that's hidden from the authorities."

Jamik queried, "Brothers? Haro, your father had brothers?"

Haro looked at a puzzled Jamik, "Yes, you know, those Brothers."

Jamik caught on, "Ah, yes. Those Brothers!"

Haro turned to Janov to continue his inquiry, "So these files, did he give them to you already? Do you have them?"

"Unfortunately, I don't." Janov replied sadly, "That's what he would have done next, to bring this information to me in a mobile storage device. He died before that could happen." He sighed, looking more tired than ever. "We have been under this oppressive regime for a long time and I was looking forward to this break."

Janov opened a drawer and showed them a storage device the size of his thumb. "This is what it looks like. If you find one like this with your father's things, please contact me. Your father came to me because we used to have a family connection." He gave it to Haro.

"What's the best way to contact you?" Haro asked as he took the device.

"Glad you asked. Don't use the home phone. Don't trust anyone, not even my assistant."

He paused, and his face brightened as if he had an idea. He opened a drawer on his desk and gave Haro a phone. "Before you go, take this. You can reach me through this encrypted phone, it can't be traced. Use the code word 'freedom4all' to unlock this phone. Next time, we won't meet here. And be careful out there."

Then the radios in Haro and Jamik's pockets vibrated. Haro picked his radiophone and answered. "Hello?"

Janov was alarmed. He put his finger over his mouth

as if to say, "Don't answer."

"It's okay." Haro said calmly, "It's my sister and her friend. We're using a private channel. Yes, Mei, what's up?" Janov looked relieved.

"Your sister is getting worried." Mei asked with a hint of anxiety in her voice, "Have you found Janov?"

Haro answered, "Yes, Janov is here and we will be on our way to you soon." He put away his radio.

"That's clever." Janov remarked.

"One more question." Haro asked, "Did my father tell you where this information came from?"

Janov shook his head, "No. He never mentioned who he was working for."

They all stood up and shook hands. The man who had looked tired when he had welcomed them didn't seem tired anymore. Hope shone in his eyes.

As the door closed behind Haro and Jamik, they saw that the end of the alley blocked by three unruly men. They wore black clothing, tattoos, and pierced skin, and didn't look friendly. One of them quickly approached the boys with a shout, "Hey, you! Give us your money."

Jamik stepped in front of Haro to protect him. He stated confidently, "Sorry, we don't carry money."

The gangsters looked menacing. One of them said in a rough voice, "No matter, we will take your backpacks. Hand them over." They approached while Haro and Jamik backed away toward the other end of the street.

Jamik looked at Haro, whose face expressed fear, and said, "Run!" They turned to run, but the closest gangster grabbed for Jamik, who deflected his movements and yanked the gangster's arm. Jamik used the gangster's weight to turn and slam him into the second gangster.

Surprised, the two gangsters momentarily staggered as Jamik ran after Haro. The third gangster chased Haro and yanked his backpack. Haro felt the jerk and panicked, not knowing how to defend himself with his back turned. He held on to his backpack.

Using his running speed, Jamik slammed into the third

gangster sideways into the wall. As Haro tried to gain his balance, Jamik grabbed Haro and yelled, "Keep running!"

They both ran toward the end of the alley, the three angry gangsters chasing them. What they didn't see were the two tattered older men they had encountered earlier, who were pretending to talk to each other. Elizon and Mateo had seen the gang confronting the two boys. They moved between the boys and the gang.

Mateo swung his cane at the feet of one gangster who promptly fell flat on his face. Elizon pretended to falter and grabbed the second gangster and bumped him into the third gangster. All three gangsters went down on the ground. The two old men had expertly made it look like an accident without fighting.

"Oh, please excuse my clumsiness!" Mateo said apologetically to the gangster he had knocked over with his cane.

Elizon helped another to his feet, "Are you alright? You should watch where you are going!"

The gangsters uttered profanities as they got up, angrily sweeping the dirt off their black jackets, "Stupid old men! Don't you have better things to do than to wander like filthy bums!"

Elizon had his hand out, his head bowed, "Care to spare us old men some cash? We're hungry!"

"No! Get away from us!" One gangster shouted angrily. They all left, forgetting about Haro and Jamik, who were long gone.

As the gang walked away, Elizon straightened and grinned, "Nicely done!"

Mateo chuckled, "I can't remember the last time I had such fun!" Elizon and Mateo then ran toward the direction where the boys had gone.

Haro and Jamik fled the scene quickly on their skateboards. Haro called Mei by radio. The boys reached the car safely with an anxious Ladya behind the wheel, Mei next to her. The two old men saw the four of them getting into the car. Before Haro got in the car, he looked out of the car window. He saw the two old men staring at them from across the street. Elizon felt something was familiar about the four young people.

Jamik and Haro looked at each other. Jamik remarked, relief written all over his face, "That was close, but we made it!"

Haro sighed as relief flooded him, "I don't think I am ready to fight as you did. Thank you for the rescue!" Haro said to Jamik. He remained pensive for the rest of the ride.

And without the four young people realizing it, they had a full day of "happy accidents." The Holy One had been watching and protecting them.

☞ CHAPTER NINE ☞

CHASING A LEGEND

As long as the sun, moon, and stars maintain their boundaries, the children of Israel will endure forever. Our forefathers obtained these promises from the God of Israel. As long as the luminaries remain in the heavens, He will not let His people perish. As long as the universe continues its course, He will never reject the descendants of Israel. Since time immemorial, the children of the promise have struggled against their enemies. Many nations have sought to annihilate the nation of Israel. They have endured because He has willed it. In the fullness of time, He has realized the hope of our people.

~Elder Jeremiah, The Book of Fulfilled Prophecies

KRISTALIS, TWO DAYS LATER

Daleah was at her desk, scribbling in her journal entry with a somber expression.

Professor Aaronia shared with the class a fascinating tale of her Old Earth life. At first, some of us didn't know what being Jewish meant, so she asked each person which original tribe they came from. I know I am a Josephite, of the tribe of Joseph, because Ancie Shanielle told me whenever she goes to Nova Zion, she always enters through the Joseph gate. Being her descendant, I will also be able to enter through this same gate someday. The Jews of Old Earth were of the three original tribes—Judah, Levi, Benjamin. Aaronia is a Judahite, a descendant of the tribe of Judah.

At first, I didn't understand why many people on Old Earth hated the Jews. Aaronia survived a horrible atrocity called the Holocaust. An incredible six million Jews perished in the Holocaust, during a devastating war that pitted many nations against each other. The remaining three-and-a-half million Jews survived. In my world, death is non-existent, and I find this enormous loss of precious life so difficult to comprehend.

Andrea was Aaronia's Old Earth name. Her father was a businessman who made women's purses and other accessories in Germany and in other parts of Europe. I imagine a purse is like my backpack, although I am not sure. Her family was well off, but not wealthy. Sadly, her entire family perished in concentration camps.

Professor Aaronia spoke with such sadness about a madman named Hitler. Andrea's family was much like the rest of European Jewry, who never believed Hitler's actions would lead to genocide. Everything happened gradually. When the world finally uncovered Hitler's real plan, "the problem of the Jews," it was too late. Her family was trapped without a way to get out. The first trouble began when the Nazi youth smashed her father's storefront window on Kristallnacht, the Night of the Broken Glass, five years after Hitler became the leader of Germany. Andrea was a scared seven-year-old.

This sweet woman shared with us a memory touch of her time in the concentration camp. It was brief, like a snapshot. She warned us we might not able to walk out of the classroom with sane minds. The memory was of the imprisoned Jews, looking emaciated, like living skeletons in dirty, ragged clothes. Soldiers in olive green uniforms and helmets were rationing them with water, food, and blankets. Seeing this horrific scene for a brief instant was enough. She was only 14 when the war ended, the same age I am now.

For many years after the Holocaust, Andrea struggled in understanding why the God of Abraham, Isaac, and Jacob would let such horror happen. That was the "God" as she understood Him back then. Toward the end of her life, Andrea finally found peace, love, and understanding through her Messiah. The Nazis failed in their plan to wipe out the Jews. The Creator promised that the descendants of Israel will remain throughout eternity as long as the luminaries remain in the cosmos. Aaronia's thousands of descendants have populated Kristalis and many other worlds. As promised to her forefather Abraham, the descendants of Jacob numbered like grains of sand on each world governed by the Commonwealth of Zion.

Professor Aaronia ended her lecture: "People like the Spanish Inquisitors and the Nazis hounded our people for centuries. The Adversary targeted the Jews because Our Sovereign chose them to protect the precious Holy Writings, which contains prophecies about the Adversary's ultimate demise... Since that horrific time, many new generations have emerged, people who have never experienced the atrocities of Old Earth. In some worlds, the

Holocaust story has become a legend. Although the Indigans have forgotten, their stories contain a bit of truth, mixed up with legends, myths, and fairy tales. We must chase such legends."

I understand the professor now. We must not repeat this tragic history, even after millennia have passed.

INDIGOR

Haro and Ladya's mother insisted on having them back home from the cabin. She didn't relish being alone. It was bad enough with their father gone. The absence of her children didn't sit well with her.

Haro was unhappy about being home for the remaining school break and locked himself in his bedroom. He was reading the journal, hoping to find some clues, when he heard knocking at the door. He knew it was Ladya from the way she knocked. He hid his journal under his blanket and peeked through the door.

"What do you want now?" Haro asked, glaring at her.

"Haro," Ladya signed to him, "me need show you something."

"What?" Haro asked impatiently.

She sighed with her eyes rolling, not appreciating his attitude, "I saw something in journal."

Haro's scowl disappeared. "A clue?" He perked up, let her in, and locked the door.

"I show you. Gimme journal." When he gave her the journal, she flipped the pages and showed him the diamond symbol written next to the word "tree."

Haro's gloomy demeanor suddenly faded. "It's definitely a clue!" He said as he got up excitedly. "We found this journal under the oak tree!" He hugged Ladya, taking her by surprise. "Now, all we have to do is look for other diamond symbols! That should be our next clues!"

Haro went back to his bed, flipping the pages to look for the symbols, ignoring his sister, who was standing with her head shaking, her hands on her hips. She stomped her foot to get his attention. He looked up at her while she signed, "Hello! You forgot important! Lock the door! Not want Mom see this!" She pointed to the journal.

Haro looked sheepish, "Oh, Sorry!"

As she left through the door, she turned to ask, "Come tell me if more clue?"

His face peeking through the door, he signed impatiently, "Yes! Yes! Go away now!" He locked his door. The rest of the day, he spent searching for more little diamond symbols in the pages of the journal. He read one of Mardochi's journal entries...

19297.8.3

One of our Creator's oldest commandments involves teaching our children about Him. He instructs to listen to Him, to love Him with all our heart, soul, and strength. We must commit ourselves earnestly to his instructions, to teach and repeat them to our children when we are at home, on the road, before bedtime, and when we wake up. I have done my best to teach my children in a world that does not allow us to teach about our Creator. Bedtime was my favorite time with my children. We have passed these stories through many generations of our family. ◇ My father used to read to me these same stories, as did his father and his father's father. We do not know how old these stories are. The best way to teach our children is in the form of parables. Our wise King told such parables when He walked in the flesh among them during His time on Old Earth. They were stories about His Kingdom. He taught like this to the mass of people because they were not yet ready for the truth. However, to his committed followers, he spoke face-to-face, without riddles. Someday, I hope these same stories will benefit my children when they are older and ready for the truth.

As soon as Haro saw the diamond symbol next to the word stories, he stood up quickly. *The bedtime stories! How could I forget?* And he immediately went to his father's office. He found his childhood's tablet in the same desk drawer where the first hidden wooden box was. Ladya saw him come down the stairs toward the office while she was in the kitchen loading the dishwasher. She followed him.

He got the blue tablet and scrolled through the list of stories. "There! Two stories about diamonds!" He pointed them out to Ladya, one story entitled *Diamonds from the Sky,* and the second entitled, *A Trail of Diamonds.*

Ladya gasped and pointed with emphasis at one story, "This, me remember! Two children follow trail, many dropped diamonds!"

As Haro skimmed the story, he commented, "I remember Father loved to read this story to us over and over, even though it wasn't my favorite!"

The story was about two children whose family owned a cabin. They found dropped diamond rocks on a narrow beaten path. Throughout their treks on the trail of diamonds, they stopped at various places. At the last place, they came upon a sign that said, "YOU ARE WELCOME TO BOARD IN THE HOOD."

"Yes!" Haro signed forcefully, looked at his sister, and beamed a broad smile.

"Shh! Loud?" Ladya gestured with her finger on her lips.

Haro shook his head, still smiling. He pointed to the words in large caps. "Look! A play on words! Board in the Hood is Brotherhood! This story is a map filled with landmarks! It will lead us to them! The two children met an old man with his brother! It all fits!"

He pointed at one line. "Look. Another clue about how far the place is! They arrived from the West and collected 70 diamonds. That means we go east for only 70 miles!" And he hugged his sister, taking her by surprise a second time. "Time to make a travel plan!" He couldn't believe the clues had been right here in his house, under his nose.

And Haro spent the rest of the day preparing for a trip and calling Jamik to come over to talk about his exciting find.

THE ACADEMY, KRISTALIS

Professor Elizon walked in, beaming like the sun. The students were under the colonnade. The sun's glare reflected softly on the glistening columns and warmed the iridescent stone floor. Gossamer curtains hung from the tall ceiling between the columns, rippling softly in the gentle wind. The students sat on the floor, on large colorful pillows. The students had laid their sandals in neat rows on the steps that led to the colorful Edenic garden beyond the colonnade. It was an ethereal place, perfect for a group of prayer warriors. Elizon had once joked to his sister Shanielle, making an Old Earth cultural reference to living inside of a Maxwell Parrish painting.

Daleah had finished the last entry in her journal. *The professor's approach to teaching is practical. Prayer isn't something to teach, but something that's done. According to him, "Practice makes perfect," is an Old Earth cliche that is still valid even today. Just do it. The Spirit of the Holy One does the rest.*

Daleah closed her journal and crossed her legs on the pillows, ready to listen to the professor. The students had been waiting eagerly for Professor Elizon's latest report of his mission to Indigor. They had learned to pray for the success of their mission since the first day of *Introduction to Prayer and Spiritual Warfare*. The students were ready for a bigger challenge. Moralee and the twins were also sitting with the students.

"A bright Halo to all of you!" Elizon began cheerfully. "Yesterday, we finished learning about the importance of angels. Whenever we pray during challenging situations, such as war, accidents, or serious illness, certain spiritual forces are present. Angels have appeared during those times, to fight against the opposing force of darkness. We learned that we do not encourage fighting with each other. No matter how wicked the others are, we fight only against the spiritual force of darkness." He paused, picked up a pillow, and sat down.

"We have approached the time when we must do strategic spiritual warfare." He continued, "We do not wait for the enemy to make his move. Therefore, we are bringing the fight to the enemy. Dreams and visions are a way for the Creator to communicate with us about his plan and strategies. Professors Moralee, Benzi, and Zephan will tell us about the visions they received the day before they arrived here. Then I will tell you what happened while I was on Indigor." He nodded toward the twins to begin.

Benzi began, "We saw a dragon transformed into a snake. It couldn't fly anymore." Zephan spoke, "It slithered everywhere on the earth, prowling and devouring whoever crossed its path on the land." Then the twins finished together, "One day, the dragon crossed paths with a group of children and chased them." Then the twin Elders looked at Moralee to continue.

"My vision was about a land so crowded with indigo flowers that the light won't shine through. The people trapped in the crushing darkness cried out." Moralee continued, "I saw the four faces of the Seraphies cutting a path through the land to let the Light shine."

"Thank you for sharing." Professor Elizon spoke again, "We will talk about how to interpret visions. I also received a vision the same day. It was a simpler vision about my role as a leader. Can anyone tell me the interpretation of the vision that the twins received?"

Kato, as usual, was the first to raise his hand eagerly. "The dragon is the prince of darkness who controls Indigor. Not sure who the group of children are."

"Would anyone else volunteer to answer?" He noticed that Revelyn didn't volunteer much. The professor liked to encourage his students to take part. "Revelyn? What do you think Moralee's vision mean?" He smiled as he asked.

Revelyn looked at Professor Elizon in surprise. "Oh?

Um... Indigor was named after the indigo flower, which is purple. People got stuck and lost in the darkness... and maybe the Seraphies will help that world?”

The professor beamed at her, “That's good, Revelyn!”

Daleah had been listening through it all. She raised her hand. The professor nodded his go-ahead. “You said the visions happened before you arrived here when the semester began? What if others received visions on the same day? Should we share them too?”

For the first time since he walked in, the professor froze for a nanosecond. It had been a long time since anyone other than an Elder received visions. “Yes. Please share. Any human can have visions, especially at a time like this.”

“I didn't receive a vision like you Elders. Not while awake.” Everyone looked at Daleah. “This one was more of a dream I received while napping.”

“Still worth sharing.” Elizon said, “Go on.”

“I dreamed I was being carried on wings and landed on a wilderness devoid of people.” Daleah continued, “Then I saw some people far away on the horizon and we were walking toward each other. One of them was a Seraphi with the face of a lion.” She looked at Rory, who looked back at her with a smile. “We walked together in an unknown country until we arrived at a place teaming with life. Then the dream ended. When I saw Rory the first day here, I knew I connected him to the dream.” Daleah exclaimed, “Oh, there's another thing! I had the strangest feeling someone was in the room.”

“Daleah,” Elizon replied, “your dream and what's happening now are intertwined. What you felt was the presence of an angel. Your vision was partly fulfilled. A horizon means an imminent event. That fulfilled part are the people here with you today. The wilderness turned to a garden teeming with life is the unfulfilled part. Indigor is still barren, with its people in a barren spiritual wilderness.”

Elizon nodded to Rory as he raised his paw. “I didn't

receive any vision," Rory spoke with reverence, "but I received a visit from a messenger of the Holy One who informed me that the time has come for me and my people to go to Kristalis. We arrived the next day. A messenger visiting a Seraphi is rare."

"Indeed." The professor spoke solemnly, "We Elders also received visions accompanied by visits from the angelic messengers. Not all humans can see them. The visions and dreams all had one thing in common." He paused, "Indigor."

"Now, here's my report. I went to Indigor to visit the Brotherhood of Scribes and Keepers. You all remember what I taught you about the history of Indigor?"

"They are the last remnant of a people who know about our origins while the rest of Indigor have forgotten," Rory answered. "Professor Aaronia reminded us this morning of the prophet's famous saying, that people often perish from lack of knowledge about His plan and His purpose. The Brotherhood, like the Jews, persevered despite all odds. Everyone else must chase after the truth, even if it is hidden in a legend or an old story."

"Indeedy!" Elizon continued with a wide smile, "And here's some excellent news! On my weekly prayer walk with Brother Mateo, we encountered a group of children. One of them is the teenage son of a former Brother who died in a car accident recently. The boy was with three other teenagers. The twins' vision confirmed that these children are an essential part of the Creator's strategic plan to defeat the prince of darkness on Indigor, as are all of you, Rory and his people here."

Daleah raised her hand. Elizon nodded at her, "How do you know these children are essential to His plan?"

"We go with what He has given us. Our way has worked for millennia. We don't sit back and wait for things to happen. The Holy One waits for us to make the first move, then He will direct us. Elders have done this countless times, and we have never failed." He paused and looked at the other Elders, who nodded, passing some kind of silent communication between them.

The Elders stood up and Moralee announced, "We are in time for the big announcement from the Headmistress. Remember, we shared with you at the beginning that our village that we will travel to the stars someday? Let's stand up." There were gasps, sounds of excitement, and some oh's and ah's as they stood up expectantly.

Professor Mariel's voice came out of the Academy's intercom. "Halo to all students, professors, and villagers! I am excited to announce that our village will travel out to the stars toward Indigor. We will orbit the planet and pray our blessing over it. The host of angels will join us. Please join us outside the Academy to witness a beautiful sight!"

Daleah leaned toward Revelyn to whisper, "Finally! My second trip to the stars on Aliyah!"

"Oh," A surprised Revelyn asked, "when was your first?"

"About two years ago," Daleah whispered, not wanting to brag, "Shanielle invited me here to visit the grand opening of the Lighthouse Space Station."

The whole Academy, students, and Elders came out of their classrooms, overflowing the colonnades and gardens. Even the villagers were out of their houses, standing on the streets of opal stones.

A gentle humming sound came from the ground, intensifying like music. Then a horizontal line of pink light appeared from the edge of the village, rising above, becoming a large circle, shrinking upward until it disappeared at the top. It enveloped the entire village under a transparent dome with a faint glow. Everyone could see the azure sky of Kristalis through a light pinkish haze.

The ground continued humming, then slight vibrations came from the ground, intensifying. A horizontal streak of bluish light appeared at one edge of the village, crossed over the village like an archway, and disappeared at the opposite edge. But it didn't seem to do anything.

Daleah announced, "It's circling below the village.

Wait.”

The bright bluish arch came back, then another appeared from the opposite direction and crisscrossed the first one. They picked up speed. A third arch came up, this time on the third side, then fourth appeared to crisscross it. Then all four arches crisscrossed each other, speeding until they became a blur and the upper atmosphere glowed a purplish color.

“They are like wheels within wheels.” Revelyn remarked.

Then suddenly there was a bright flash of light, and the azure sky of Kristalis disappeared. They reappeared in a night sky. Then Daleah noticed the stars drifted slowly, then realized it wasn’t the stars that were moving. Aliyah Village was rotating. They saw the purple sphere with pink clouds rising on the horizon. Then thousands of tiny sparks of light appeared.

Elizon announced to his students, “Our allies, the host of messengers have arrived. We are in orbit above Indigor.”

THE VOID, ABOVE INDIGOR

The last thing Locitan expected was a floating village full of Elders and an angelic host. In a panic, he called all his minions together. He knew he couldn’t fight the Elders and all his former friends, because they were too numerous. So, he commanded his minions to station themselves over all the cities and to watch for any unusual movements. Then he went over to the chief of the angelic host. To his surprise, it was his old friend Alaniel.

“You again?” Locitan asked Alaniel, in his usual domineering, overconfident way.

“Why have you approached us?” Alaniel was quick to the point, wasting no time in pleasantry.

“This is my domain,” Locitan answered him, “and I come and go as I please. You and your kind don’t belong here. Please command them to turn back.”

"I don't order these people. They are not under my command." Alaniel announced, "We are here as commanded by our Father. We are here to cross into your domain. See, your boundary ends over there." Alaniel pointed to an invisible boundary behind Locitan. "We will not fight you. We are here to protect the Elders and humans on Aliyah."

"What exactly are they doing here?" Locitan frowned suspiciously. Can't they do whatever they do somewhere else?"

"What they do isn't any of your business." Alaniel replied patiently. "The Elders have always led their people. Our Father commanded us to accompany them. And here we are."

Locitan conceded that he could not fight them unless the messengers or anyone else crossed the line. So he commanded Alaniel angrily, "Let me talk to an Elder!"

Alaniel replied, "You haven't talked to an Elder since you rebelled, and they won't talk to you unless you give back the planet to the humans. That was the agreement made long ago. Do you wish to change it?"

"Definitely not!" Locitan said, offended at such a suggestion, but still suspicious. "Why do they need to be here? Who are they trying to protect down here?"

"No idea." Alaniel replied calmly, "What they do is none of my business."

"Just beware!" Locitan retorted back angrily, "If any of you cross that line, we will fight you! I don't care if you are messengers, humans, or Elders." Locitan was unaware that the Elders had crossed the line numerous times on their missions, without his knowledge. He left in a huff, seething underneath. He did not like being powerless. He was convinced that some Indigans were about to wreak havoc on his perfect plan for world domination.

Locitan sought Woevil, Vexid, and Griop. "Report any unusual activities to me immediately," he ordered them, "any defeats where humans under our control are losing." And he ordered his other minions to line themselves at the edge of his domain between the floating village and Indigor. The good angels and the fallen ones stood face-to-face.

ON THE ROAD, INDIGOR

Ladya was driving with Mei and Haro in the car. They arrived in front of Jamik's house, but a group of Jamik's friends were blocking the street, holding on to their high wheelers. Jamik was talking to them, holding his backpack.

As Haro stepped out of the car, he signed to Ladya, "Let me find out what's happening." He walked over to Jamik.

A burly teen with a fuzzy crewcut spoke to Jamik with a sour voice, "... your knee seems healed. Why can't you join us in the practice games?"

Jamik replied, shaking his head, "Rogan, I don't think so. Mom is taking me to see the doctor next week. He will tell me if I am ready for physical activities again."

A tall, slim teen with short wavy hair pitched in, "Do you realize if you don't get back soon, we will lose the games to our competition? You are the best player on our team."

Jamik said, "Walto, it can't be helped, but I am getting better."

They saw Haro arrive. The ebony-skinned teen greeted Haro, "Hi, bro! What's up?"

Haro returned the greeting, "Hello, Raol!"

Rogan was still looking dour, "So you can't practice... How about you watch us play?"

Walto looked suspiciously at Haro, "What are you doing here, Haro?"

Haro didn't like the way Walto asked, "I am here for Jamik."

Jamik intervened, "Look, I appreciate you guys asking, but this isn't the right time. I must go now. I will call you guys later."

Jamik's three friends left grumpily on their high

wheelers. Haro looked at Jamik, "Everything's okay?"

Jamik looked concerned as they both walked to the car, "They're glum because I forgot them during school break. Don't worry, I didn't tell them what we are doing."

As Ladya drove by the guys on their high wheelers, Walto remarked, "It's not like Jamik to dismiss us like that! When did Jamik start hanging with Haro the nerd again? And these snotty girls?"

Raol shrugged and replied, "Haro and Jamik have been best friends since first grade. One of the girls is his sister, and she's hardly snotty. She's deaf and very nice."

"Who cares?" Rogan, still looking dour, announced loudly, "We can practice without him!" And the unhappy group of bikers rode off with their high wheelers.

Finally, they were on the highway. Ladya drove while Mei signed the directions to her. Jamik was reading the map device and giving Mei the directions by voice.

"So Haro," Jamik asked, "how did you persuade your mother to let you go?"

"It wasn't easy. I needed an excuse to find the Brotherhood. I told Mom I wanted to visit the old playground to write a homework essay about a childhood experience. She wanted me to pick another topic that didn't require driving. She's been overprotective since Dad's accident. Then Ladya interrupted Mom and told her she was going to a wedding dress store with Mei and could drop me off. Mom finally agreed."

Jamik uttered, "Good! What's the next clue? What happens in the story?"

"Once upon a time..." Haro read the story on his tablet.

Jamik interrupted, "Skip to the part after the cabin..."

Haro began the story, "One day, the children were playing outside in the woods and saw a diamond rock dropped on a narrow path. They were excited because they had heard about the legend of the diamonds..." Haro paused, then continued, "Skipping ahead... the sparkling rocks led them to a ladder up toward a treehouse made of twigs, near a berry bush. They had fun in the treehouse, eating berries, and looking at the view."

Jamik looked at the map on the device. "We have passed the cabin," he remarked, "and we're going east on the Indipolis thruway, so the next clue is a treehouse made of twigs? A berry bush? Where are those?" Jamik had a sparkle in his eyes. He was enjoying this as much as Haro, going on an adventure.

"Not exactly," Haro replied, "but our father used to take us to a playground park with various playhouses and treehouses, all made from flexible twigs. Afterward, he took us to a farm nearby where they grew various berries."

"I remember those places when I was a kid!" Mei had been listening. "The playground was so much fun!"

"And," Jamik asked, "what do we do once we get there?"

"We look for more clues, carved diamonds on the oak trees, or similar, for confirmation that we are on the right path."

"I see the playground on the map." Jamik remarked, "We've been driving for about sixty miles. We're almost there. Mei, we should take the next exit."

Mei's phone rang, and she answered. "Hello, honey, what's up?"

Haro wasn't pleased and signed to her, moving his lips, "No phone!"

Mei turned to face Haro, pointed at the phone, and moved her lips to say, "My fiancé!" She spoke on the phone, "Honey, I am on the road giving my best friend directions. Why don't I call you back later?" She clicked her phone off while looking back at Haro's glaring face.

"Didn't I tell you I don't want anyone else involved?" Haro forcefully ordered Mei.

"Relax!" Mei replied, "All he knows is that I am looking for a wedding dress!"

Haro continued to glare at her, "You didn't give him any specific information about our locations?"

"No, I didn't!" Mei glared back at Haro, "What does it matter, anyway? We might not have time to go to a wedding store!"

Haro looked frustrated, "That's because it wasn't the plan! Do I have to explain to you the concept of the government invading our privacy?"

Mei looked hurt, "I am insulted that you think I don't understand!"

"Fine!" Haro retorted back, "Then turn off your phone! I don't want anyone tracing us!"

Mei looked hurt. Ladya saw the look and reached out toward Mei's hand to comfort her, her other hand on the steering wheel. She signed, "Do what he says." Then Ladya looked at Haro in the rearview mirror and glared at him.

Mei snapped shut her phone and powered it off. Then she looked at Haro, "There you go! It's off!" She crossed her arms in a huff. Then she turned to Haro again. "Just so you know, if I get away from my fiancé too often, he will get suspicious!"

Haro sighed, "Then you shouldn't have come with us!"

"I wouldn't have missed this adventure for anything!" Mei retorted back, "A chance to know about my ancestors and all about the first royals who ruled many worlds!"

"Wait a minute," Jamik interrupted, "you didn't come on this trip so you would find out if your genes are better than ours?"

Mei was taken aback by the question, "What? No!"

"Good!" Jamik replied, "Because if you did, I will kick your royal personage out of the car!"

Haro guffawed as he did when the four of them first got together again. This time, Mei looked more annoyed than upset.

Mei glared at Haro, pointing her finger, "You keep laughing! You wait! One day, you will not be laughing anymore when the truth comes out!" Haro stopped laughing and thought, *I wonder about the Elders and their physical resemblance to the royals, with their towering height and white hair. Do the Elders have children after the resurrection? I can't be sure, but I am determined to chase this legend about the enigmatic Elders!*

Ladya looked into the rearview mirror, knowing they were talking and felt left out. Haro saw her looking and tried to smile. *It's best she can't hear us. It would have distracted her enough to drive off the road.*

They arrived at the playground park. There were playhouses and treehouses made of flexible twisting twigs, even the maze, the benches, the seesaw seats, and the swings. So were the roofs of the sliding forts and the merry-go-round with its twigged horses. The four sullen teenagers got out of the car, but they didn't seem as enthusiastic as the young children on the playground.

Meanwhile, high above the sky of Indigor, unseen and unknown to them, the students and Elders were praying for them. Could the tide be turned in favor of the four questers?

CHAPTER TEN

FRIEND OR FIEND

Our fight is not against any human enemy,
But against the rulers of the high places,
Against the spiritual hosts of wickedness.
~Elder Paul of Tarsus, The Complete Epistles

THE VOID, ABOVE INDIGOR, THE NEXT DAY

Woevil, Vexid, and Griop met in the sky above Indigor. Woevil chortled, "Our master will be pleased with our report!"

They flew into the void of space and approached Locitan with fear and trembling. Locitan had been in a foul mood since Aliyah village appeared near his domain. Locitan's countenance glowed a faint red, his light almost gone, ready to spark into flaming red anger. The three minions bowed before him.

"Honored ppp... prince!" Woevil stammered before the fearsome Locitan, "Forgive our intrusion! We are he... here... as you requested... to bring a good report."

"Hopefully, nothing too good!" Locitan remarked morosely, "As long as it doesn't benefit them!" He tilted his head toward the angels and floating village behind him. Then he barked impatiently, "Stop groveling and get on with it!"

Vexid replied with a whimper, "Mmm... magnificent lord, we are pleased to report of a sighting... ttt... two angels disguised as old men... days ago. They tripped up three gang members... who were under our influence."

Locitan asked impatiently, "And what could these two possibly want with a hapless gang?"

"Ghoulish master!" Griop answered, trembling. Then, realizing his embarrassing slip of the tongue, he quickly corrected himself, "I mean glorious master! Forgive me!" Locitan was scowling, his eyes flaming red while Griop continued, "We heard the gang talking. At first, they were angry and embarrassed at losing. Now they believe the old men were protecting the two boys."

Locitan's countenance changed. "Two boys?" He looked pensive.

Woevil, Vexid, and Griop nodded their heads vigorously. They sniggered, satisfied that their report finally got Locitan's attention.

Suddenly, Locitan barked his order again, startling them. "Search for the old men and the boys! Keep in mind, we have eliminated almost everyone who was part of the remnant. That was a generation ago. Do you want to see their teaching passed on to a new enthusiastic generation?" He shouted, "No! I want updated reports!" The three minions realized they had displeased the prince of darkness. They groveled low, trembling.

"Bbb... but... forgive me, please, my highly honored prince." Woevil stammered, "I regret to inform you, there are no records of these old men... bbb... but we will search for the boys! We aim to please you, master!"

"Stop groveling!" Locitan looked at them menacingly, his faint countenance glowing redder, "Get going or I will kick your derrières again! I don't want to see your ugly faces until you have something of value to report!" With that, Woevil, Vexid, and Griop moved backward to protect their derrières, only to bump into each other, which made Locitan madder.

When the trio were far enough away from Locitan's formidable kicking foot, Woevil said, "Let's go quickly and thwart the boys' plans!" And they turned toward Indigor.

THE ACADEMY, ABOVE INDIGOR

Daleah and her friends were sitting at their usual table for the morning meal. The tall, arched doorways in the grand hall revealed the starry night sky, half obscured by the planet Indigor.

Daleah finished eating the last wedge of her blood-red orange, starring pensively at the purple planet covered in swirls of pink clouds. Revelyn was peeling a green kiwi the size of a grapefruit. She looked at Daleah, "What's on your mind?" She asked.

"Something the Elders said about Locitan and his underlings. Wondering how far they are, what they look like, and what they are doing."

Kato, who had just arrived with his food, heard and exclaimed, "Even if we could see them, we wouldn't want to see their ugly faces!"

Daleah looked at Kato, frowning, "So they're ugly?"

"They are nowhere close by." Rory interjected, "Even if they were near, they're hard to see because they look translucent."

"I don't even know what ugly looks like!" Daleah looked more confused, "I can't even imagine it. Everything on our world is beautiful, as the Creator intended it to be."

Revelyn reached out for Daleah's hand to comfort her, "You don't want to see ugly. I went to an Old Earth museum once, where they had a display of masks. Long ago, people invented horror movies, and they made masks shaped like distorted faces. The images stuck in my mind forever."

"There you go!" Kato agreed, "Spoken like an Elder! You don't want these things cluttering your beautiful mind. Enjoy your innocence while it lasts!"

While they were talking, Moralee and the twin Elders walked toward their tables, surprising them. Daleah spoke, "A bright halo morning to you, professors! What brings you here?"

"A good halo to you all!" Moralee greeted them, "Professor Elizon has requested that you meet for an urgent prayer session before class begins."

"The enemy has gathered a stronger force to combat us." Benzi spoke, then his twin Zephan added, "He is trying to defeat our purpose here."

"The news is that Locitan's underlings might have discovered the young group of people." Moralee's countenance was sober.

Rory's whiskers twitched forward, and his brows furrowed, "How did you find out?"

Moralee answered, "An angelic messenger informed us. He saw the three demons bringing their reports to Locitan. Whatever the information was, it sparked Locitan's attention. We guessed immediately it was about the young questers. They will need the protection of our prayers."

Kato got up, "My friends, let's defeat the enemy's purpose!" And they left the grand hall, putting aside their morning meal.

THE CABIN, INDIGOR

The four questers were back in the cabin. The trip to the park with the large playground had not been the success they had expected. He searched for more clues in his father's journal. He sighed in exasperation because of the lack of clues. He read the bedtime story about the trail of diamonds again.

... The dog Dando missed the children and followed them, sniffing for their scent. The children continued to follow the trail of diamonds. It led them to a hidden pink boat on the river. The children found more diamonds in the boat and a map marked with directions.

But before they steered the boat out, they heard Dando bark. He caught up to them. They took him on the boat and sailed across the great lake, following the directions on the map. They passed a little island that was only twice the size as their boat. It had a swing under an oak tree. They stopped to have fun on the swing. Under the tree, they found another diamond. They continued to sail the boat on the great lake, with Dando happily sniffing the breeze.

Haro put the book down on his lap because Ladya was in the kitchen, unaware that she was making clattering noises, as usual. She was preparing the midday meal for everyone. Mei was sitting on the recliner, her feet up, sipping her drink, and reading a women's magazine on her tablet as if she didn't have a care in the world.

Jamik watched the newsman on the tele reporting the record number of suicides among teenagers. He watched another story about the Biters arresting an artist because she made an art project out of homemade paper. He expressed disgust and remarked, "More invasion of privacy!" He switched to the sports channel with the remote.

Mei perked up and exclaimed, "Will you look at that!"

Haro scowled at her, "I'm not in the mood for whatever's in your girl's magazine!"

"Not that, you dolt! It's the heiress of the berries farm we went to. She's in the magazine!" Mei exclaimed, "She also owns an ice cream factory. There's a pic of a pink yacht behind her!" Mei showed the boys the photo on her tablet. "She painted it pink, like the color of her favorite berry ice cream."

Haro and Jamik perked up and got up. Haro took Mei's tablet to get a closer look. "How did we miss this?"

From the kitchen, Ladya could see the three of them bending over Mei's tablet. She went to find out what was happening. When she saw the photo, she signed excitedly, "That next clue!"

"Mei, let me read it." Haro said as Mei handed him the tablet to read. Then he commented, "Apparently, we missed nothing. The farm removed the photo of her with the pink yacht from welcome sign. That's why we couldn't find the clue. That boat is four miles away from the farm."

"What a waste!" Jamik remarked, "All these hours searching for a silly pink boat at the harbor near the berries farm yesterday!"

"It made sense. We were on the right track," Mei replied, "We found the diamond carvings on the oak trees at the playground, then at the berries farm."

"What to do when find boat?" Ladya intervened in sign language, "Need permission, go inside!"

Haro said thoughtfully while reading the article, "Maybe we need not go aboard her boat. What do we know about this heiress?"

"The article said that she takes the boat to retreat to a little island." Mei said, "I wish we had a picture of the island, then maybe we will save ourselves a trip!"

Jamik was looking at the map device. "Wait. I'm looking at her boat's harbor and tracking the river toward the East." He zoomed in on the map device. "Look! There's a tiny island in the middle of the river and it's shaped like a diamond!"

"What?" Haro exclaimed. Everyone looked at the map. "So that's what the story meant about the map. The diamond-shaped isle is right there! We don't need the pink boat!"

Mei shouted, "Hurrah!" and Ladya threw her fists up, feeling victorious.

Haro also shouted, "Finally!" And everyone got excited at this discovery, grinning, jumping, and hugging each other.

A knock at the door interrupted their joy. They froze, looking at each other, wondering who would be at the door. Haro said, "Let me handle this." He went through the kitchen to answer the door.

To his surprise, it was Jamik's three friends, Rogan, Walto, and Raol. "Hello, guys!" He tried to stay calm, but he felt disturbed in his spirit, "What a surprise! How did you know about my cabin?"

"Oh," Walto was the first to reply, "we didn't know it was your cabin. We assumed Jamik's family owned it. We went to his house, and we overheard Jamik's mother in the backyard talking on the phone about Jamik being at the cabin to recuperate."

Raol added, "She was kind enough to serve us some drinks in her kitchen. We saw the phone number of the cabin pinned on the fridge and we searched for the address."

"Well, is Jamik here?" Rogan asked in his usual moody way, "Are you going to invite us in? Walto's brother drove us here. We can't keep him waiting!"

"Jamik is here." Haro replied tensely, "Let me get him. You should know, it's my family's cabin, not Jamik's. I will need my mother's permission to let you in. Wait here." And he shut the door and left quickly.

Haro went back to the family room. Jamik looked at him, his face somber, "We overheard."

"Not let them in!" Ladya stomped her foot and signed, "Mom said no permit other people. Cabin our private sanctuary!"

"I will get rid of them, but not quickly." Jamik said, "I like my friends, but they are putting a crimp in our plans. Ladya, Mei, why don't you bring some drinks and cakes for them? Then I can send them on their way without them being suspicious." He went to the door and played the naturally charming Jamik, "Hello guys, what a surprise to see you here! Why didn't you call to tell me you were coming?"

"Is that a way to greet your friends?" Walto looked suspiciously at Jamik, "You didn't answer our calls."

"Well, here I am, safe and sound! Why don't we go to the boat deck, it's nice out!" Jamik led Rogan, Raol, Walto and his brother outside sat them down on the outdoor chairs.

Meanwhile, inside the cabin, the girls served the drinks to the four uninvited guests. Then back inside, Haro, Ladya, and Mei ate their midday meal and got their backpacks, ready to leave at any moment's notice, while they waited for Jamik who was entertaining his friends outside.

"Here's what we will do..." Haro announced, "we will take Spirit, my father's bowrider and look for the next clue."

Mei asked, "And what's that?" Haro read the bedtime story again.

> *... They arrived at a little lighthouse on the coast where an old man dressed in white welcomed them. He would give them a diamond if they could answer one question. "How are diamonds made?"*
>
> *The older boy told him, "They form when big rocks collide together in space."*
>
> *The old man told him, "That is one good answer." He gave the diamond to the boy. The old man told them they could leave their boat anchored at his place if they wished to continue. They thanked the man and left.*
>
> *The children took the map with them and followed the marked path with Dando in tow. They found another trail with diamonds that led them around a field of corn, toward an old abandoned silo with a missing roof. When they entered the empty silo, they found a diamond inside.*
>
> *They followed the trail toward a farmhouse with a flock of sheep. They stopped when they remembered their parents' warning about the wolf*

*in sheep's clothing. So, they hid and watched the
sheep for a while. The boy held Dando under his
arm. They didn't see the wolf, so they walked toward
the farmhouse cautiously.*

Haro finished the story and said, "The next clues are a
lighthouse, a field of corn with an abandoned silo, and a
sheep farm."

Ladya answered the text on her phone, "It's Mom
again. She wants to know what we are doing."

Haro suddenly sat up, "That's it. We need to keep Mom
from getting worried. Let's take a photo of all of us
together with our guests. That way she will think we're
staying at the cabin for the rest of the day. I hate lying, but
this little quest of ours is important. One day, she will
realize that." So, the group took photos to send to their
parents. Even Mei sent one to her fiancé.

An hour later, the uninvited guests finally left, and
everyone breathed a sigh of relief. Jamik came back in and
announced, "How much time do we have left?"

"We have five hours," Haro replied. "Are you sure they
left?"

"Yes, yes!" Jamik said impatiently, "I saw them drive
away. Let's go!" He grabbed his backpack, and they all
went together to continue their quest.

The four questers took Spirit, the runabout motorboat
that belonged to Haro's father. The color of their
lifejackets stood out brightly. The girls, their hair pulled
back in ponytails to keep their hair away from their faces
in the wind, sat behind while Jamik stood next to Haro,
learning to steer the boat. They steered Spirit eastward
down the river, passing the town where with the twiggy
playground and the berries farm toward the diamond-
shaped islet had a tire swing hanging from an oak tree.
With his binoculars, Haro saw the carved diamond on the

trunk of the oak tree. They went past it.

The river ended and merged into the great lake. They sailed eastward, looking for the lighthouse. Vacation homes crowded the shoreline. Gradually, the homes became scarce and the greenery more bountiful. Haro watched through binoculars while Jamik steered the boat.

Then Haro saw something odd. It looked like a black horse until it spread its wings. Haro exhaled sharply and exclaimed to everyone in awe, "Look! It's a black-winged horse!"

"What? Where?" Jamik exclaimed while Ladya and Mei stood up instantly.

Haro gave Jamik the binoculars while pointing at the black shape along the shoreline.

Jamik remarked, "I see it! Such small wings. I don't think it can fly." They took turns looking at the horse through the binoculars.

Mei commented excitedly as she looked, "From the old stories, I thought these horses were white."

Haro got his binoculars back and looked at the horse again. "The horse's looking at us, but it seems sad."

"Maybe lonely? Not feel like belongs here. It rare!" Ladya replied. Most Indigans had never seen or heard of a winged horse.

"Maybe the Creator is showing us this special horse because we are on the right track?" Haro remarked pensively, still watching.

The black Lipican nodded its head as if agreeing with Haro and finally turned back toward the forest. Haro exhaled sharply again. Was it my imagination or did it just understand me?

They spotted the lighthouse, standing sharply on the seashore because of its black and white painted stripes. Haro steered the boat toward the lighthouse, toward the pier.

A man with grey hair and a short, well-trimmed beard came out to meet them, but he was wearing a striped sailor shirt and an ascot cap, not the white as in the story. He looked physically fit.

He greeted the four on the pier. "Hello! What does a group of children want with a stop at a lighthouse?"

Haro replied, "We are exploring the area for a school project. We'd like to know the history of this lighthouse."

"You are welcome! I am Nashon Korell, the lighthouse keeper." He beamed, happy that the children showed an interest in his place. Jamik secured the boat to the post, and they followed Nashon to the lighthouse. It was a cozy place with lots of empty shelves in what used to be a library. Knickknacks and useless stuff now cluttered the shelves.

Haro asked, "Do you live here?"

"Yes, my brother and I take turns caring for it." Nashon answered, still smiling, "Various individuals who believe in the history of this place have contributed to help us maintain it."

"I hope you don't mind my asking," Haro continued, "but what happened here? Was this a library at one time?"

"I don't mind you asking! I'm glad you did!" Nashon answered with sad eyes, "We used to have many wonderful books until those creepy people took them all. For generations, our family has maintained this place, one of the few historic monuments that survived the early disasters. People used to come here and refresh themselves in spirit."

"And by the creepy people, you mean the Biters?" Jamik asked.

"Yes, them!" He replied with a grimace. "They haven't bothered my family for a hundred and eleven years. Good riddance! So, what sparked your interest in this place?"

Haro, taking a chance with Nashon, revealed the reason for coming, "To be honest, it was my father who first mentioned it. He passed away recently. We have been exploring some places we used to go as kids."

Mei, who had been quietly interpreting for Ladya, intervened, "What can you tell us about this place, and what exactly is a lighthouse's purpose?"

"Oh, children!" Nashon smiled while rubbing his hands, "I'm happy to oblige! It's been a while since anyone took an interest in this place! You are in for a treat! There is an ancient legend that on another world far away, the first lighthouse was built in a land called Egypt, with strange buildings shaped like pyramids. Long ago, ships often became shipwrecked. The sea was treacherous at night and it was hard to navigate, to avoid crashing into rocks. It was a world with a large moon that caused tidal effects. So, someone got the bright idea to build large fires along the shoreline to guide the ships. Over time, oil lanterns replaced the fires, then electric lamps. They invented the lenses to intensify the light atop the tower. The beacons became stronger and more sophisticated. These ancients built lighthouses all over their world."

Then Nashon paused and asked the group, "Do you know why lighthouses also became libraries?"

The four questers shook their head at the question. Nashon continued, "The keepers didn't have much to do, other than maintaining the lighthouse. So they read many books. Over the years, their collection of books became libraries. The ancient world developed this tradition that lighthouses were beacons of light for understanding and gaining wisdom."

The four listened in fascination, "These ancients traveled to our world in spaceships. They brought their clever inventions and designed this lighthouse. With the books gone, we have no way of proving that these people were real. That's my story for today! And now, time to turn on the light!" He went to a dashboard and switched some buttons. Then he said, "Now, you can see the light from the top of the tower! You're welcome to look around and climb upstairs!" The four went to explore the lighthouse.

When they finished, they went back to Nashon. Ladya spotted a knickknack on the shelf, a carved wood sculpture of a pointed hand. Ladya became excited and waved at Haro to get his attention. He looked at where she was pointing. Surprised, he asked Nashon, "Where did you get that wood sculpture?"

It was Nashon's turn to be surprised. He inspected Haro and his friends closely before he said, "Ha, finally! I was wondering when someone will ask about this strange object! A man gave it to me five years ago and told me that one day someone will come and inquire about it. His name was Mardochi."Haro confirmed, "That's my father! Mardochi Gallant."

Nashon went to get the object and gave it to Haro. "Here, it's yours now. I'm sorry to hear of his passing. Your father was a good man. He told me the hand should point to the East, toward the sunrise. Our historic tradition is all about the Light of Understanding and Wisdom."

Haro was speechless as he held the sculpture. It reminded him of the sun sculpture and the wooden boxes he had discovered. Haro's eyes were tearing as he remembered his father. Jamik spoke for him, "Thank you, Mister. We'd like to ask you one more thing. Is there a corn farm nearby?"

Nashon answered, "There is a cornfield with an abandoned silo, about half a mile from here. I always drive past it, the sheep farm, and the apple pie factory on my way to the corner store. I will be happy to give you a ride on my way to the store."

The four questers looked at each other in silence, realizing that Nashon had volunteered the information they needed.

As Nashon drove them, they passed the cornfield with an old silo. It had a faded logo shaped like a diamond. They drove by a large billboard picturing an old woman in a white apron, smiling, holding a spatula, and an apple pie. The large words stood out, "Mama Wolf's Apple Pie." Exactly like the bedtime story. It welcomed visitors to the factory.

Haro remarked in wonder, "Why, that's the apple pie that Dad liked to eat! He used to bring them home after an out-of-town trip!"

They passed the sheep farm. They could smell the aroma of baked apple pies even before they arrived. They thanked Nashon for the ride as they got out in front of the factory.

From the driver's side, Nashon announced, "Hey, I will be happy to give you a ride back to your boat."

Haro bent down to the driver's side and said, "Thank you for your offer. If it's all right with you, can you come back in two hours?"

Nashon replied, "No problem, it's my pleasure! Your father has done so much for our family and I would like to do the same for his children!" And he drove off.

Jamik, Ladya, and Mei looked at Haro, waiting for him to tell them about the next clues. "Oh, right!" He took out his childhood tablet. He continued the story. "Alright, after the boy and girl saw the farmhouse..."

... The trail led them to an abandoned root cellar. They found one diamond inside. Then when they came out, an old woman wearing a white apron and holding a spatula was standing before them, asking them, "What are you doing here?"

"We were just exploring." The boy answered, "We like to explore new places."

"That's all right!" The woman said. "Would you like to eat my delicious apple pie?"

"Do you live at the farmhouse with the sheep?" The girl asked.

The woman replied, "Yes, I do."

The boy and the girl looked at each other. They were hungry, but unsure if they should accept the old woman's offer of a sweet apple pie. "Maybe later we will have your apple pie." The boy said to the woman.

"Play here as long as you like. Watch out for the wolf!" The old woman told them.

The children and Dando went back on the trail and found more diamonds. They went through an apple orchard. This must be where the old woman harvested the apples for her pies. They ate the apples instead of eating the woman's pies.

They entered a forest of tall pine trees and followed another trail of dropped diamonds. It led them to a commune of people living in tepees and old buses. The people were friendly. Their chief wore a white garment and a rock diamond necklace. He greeted the children, who asked him where they could find more diamonds like the one he had. He told them he found only one, on a trail near an oak tree. So, the children and Dando continued onward, but they knew they were on the right track.

They found more diamonds on a trail that led them to a cave, but it was dark. They walked back to the commune and asked for a flashlight, which the chief gave them. They walked back into the dark cave. They were a little scared, but they kept going. They found more diamonds, stuck in the cave walls, shining like stars, reflected by the flashlight. They didn't have the tools to pry the diamonds off the walls, so they kept walking. Railroad tracks appeared on the ground of the cave. They arrived at an abandoned subway. They found diamond rocks on the ground, along the railway tracks. There was an old empty train. Finally, they came to the dead-end of the subway. In front of them was a door, and an old fallen sign that read, YOU ARE WELCOME TO BOARD IN THE HOOD.

A man with long white hair and beard came out of the door, holding a long staff in his hand. He announced to the children, "My name is Tomas. You have arrived safely at your destination. You have both come a long way and you have passed the test. The old woman was the wolf in disguise. You were wise to avoid her. You have come a long way from

*the West collecting 70 diamond rocks.
Unfortunately, the diamonds aren't yours to keep.
You must return the diamonds to their original
locations on the trail. For the diamonds are for
others who must prove themselves worthy to pass
the test. Now, you are welcome to receive your
reward. My brother Yoshua will instruct you."*

Jamik asked, "So which clue do we look for first?"

Haro outlined the story, "An abandoned root cellar, then an apple orchard, the pine forest, and the commune."

Jamik looked at the map on the handheld device. "The forest here is many miles wide. I don't know. I think we need an entry point into the forest."

Ladya signed with her hands, while Mei interpreted, "Ladya suggests that we skip the abandoned root cellar if we can find the part of the forest near an apple orchard."

Jamik suggested, "Why don't we ask the tour guide if there is an orchard near the forest?"

Haro nodded in agreement, "Good idea!"

☞ ☞ ☞

Twenty minutes later, they arrived at the apple orchard. They searched for a carved diamond on the tree trunks, but couldn't find any.

Mei saw a bench and told Haro, "I'm tired of walking." Earlier, she had wanted to taste a piece of apple pie at the factory, then go to the souvenir shop, and the restroom. It was always one thing or another. And Ladya wasn't much help with Mei. She had looked at Haro and Jamik helplessly, shaking her head and shrugging her shoulders.

As soon as she sat down, Mei saw the diamond carved on the bench. "Hey, will you look at that!"

Jamik, who had become annoyed at her demands, asked irritably, "What now?"

Mei answered sharply, "It's a carved diamond, you dolt! Right here on the bench!"

They ran toward the bench to inspect it. Haro remarked, "It makes sense. It's made of oak, which is a hardy wood used for making outdoor furniture."

Jamik exclaimed with delight, "So we're on the right track!"

They continued east some more, toward the forest, following the gravel path that the tour guide mentioned. Haro was also holding a compass.

They walked through the forest, following the gravel path until they heard the siren of the police vehicles and saw the flashing lights. They stopped. Haro told them, "Wait here." He walked ahead to inspect and came back.

Mei asked, "What's going on?"

Haro said solemnly, "It's not good. I saw a Biter and the flashing light of a police car. The last thing we need is an encounter with them." They all looked disappointed.

Jamik suggested, "Can we go around them?"

Ladya held her hand to stop them, then signed as Mei spoke for her, "Ladya said she will check it out. The police won't arrest a deaf woman."

Haro looked doubtful. Mei said, "I will go with her. Wait here."

Haro said, "Be careful. We will wait for you at the apple orchard." He handed Ladya the souvenir cap he had purchased at the factory. "Here, put this on to look like a tourist."

Ladya and Mei went ahead. Ten minutes later, they came back and Haro sighed with relief.

Mei explained what happened, "Ladya was brave. She told a policeman and the BITE officer that we were visiting the factory and wanted to hike to get in shape for our school fundraising marathon. They did not allow us to go, because the area is under lockdown while they pursue members of the commune. We saw the buses and the teepees as described in the story. Ladya pretended to ask innocent questions—what is a commune, and the officer was happy to oblige. They said that living off the grid wasn't legal."

"Well, that's it for today." Haro sighed in disappointment, "We're stuck. Without the chief of the commune, we won't know where the next clue is."

"We can try tomorrow." Jamik suggested, "Hopefully, the place won't be crawling with cops by then. Let's hope the chief wasn't arrested."

They all went back to the pie factory, waited for Nashon's ride to the lighthouse, hopped into the motorboat, and sailed back to the cabin. And when they arrived home, Haro put the glass sculpture on the fireplace mantelpiece. He announced, "This quest seemed more like an outing. Let's eat and rest. Tomorrow morning, we will feel refreshed and search for the Brotherhood again."

THE ACADEMY, ABOVE INDIGOR

The prayer session concluded as Professor Elizon announced, "This has been an intense prayer session. How do you feel?" Daleah felt tired physically and mentally, which was unusual for her.

Kato was not his usual cheerful self, "A little tired. Is that normal?"

Rory spoke confidently, "I feel stronger."

"It is normal for humans to feel tired." The professor answered, "Elders and Seraphies usually feel more energized from praying. We are experiencing the effect of pushing against the spiritual forces of darkness."

The Elder twins stood up to speak, Benzi first, "We saw in our minds, the messengers and the fallen ones were standing in opposition at the boundaries, ready to battle." Then his twin spoke, "There was high tension in the air. They came so close to fighting, but they relented."

"And why would they do that?" Daleah frowned, "Why didn't they stay apart like before?"

Elizon looked at Moralee. There was silent communication between them. She answered, "It's a good question that deserves a satisfactory answer, Daleah. The fallen ones found out Haro's identity. While you were praying, the Spirit of the Holy One showed us what was happening with them. They came close to finding the Brotherhood, but had to turn around."

Revelyn was sad to hear it, "What will Haro do? Will he give up?"

Elizon smiled, "No, little one. Haro and his merry little band of questers will go back to search the place tomorrow. No one has given up. The path toward victory is to be vigilant and persistent."

A puzzled Daleah asked, "What did you mean when you said they were hindered?"

"Locitan's fiends sent Jamik's friends to the cabin to interfere with their plan to find the Brotherhood. They also sent other people to hinder their quest." Elizon turned toward the twins, "Please share what you saw during the prayer time."

The twins nodded and spoke. "The Bureau sent a spy to infiltrate a commune of people living off the grid. He pretended to befriend them, then betrayed them to the authorities. The police showed up with BITE officers."

"They arrested the commune people, right before Haro and his troop almost stumbled upon them. Fortunately, Haro's deaf sister got some details from a friendly cop without raising suspicion."

Daleah smiled, "And that's good news, Professor?" She looked at Elizon with hope.

"Indeed, little one." Elizon beamed, his face glowing. "It's excellent news! Remember what you learned from Professor Aaronia about betrayal?"

Enoch raised his hand to speak, "A German neighbor betrayed her family, a boy she thought was a friend. He told his parents she was Jewish, and they informed Hitler's henchmen who caught them and sent them to those horrible concentration camps. Aaronia met that boy many years later, and forgive him and his family."

Elizon nodded, "Thank you, Enoch, for the summary. This is how we are to respond when faced with people who betray us. Our Messiah told his followers to love their enemies, to do good to those who hurt you, to bless them who curse you, and to pray for those who abuse you. We pray for the spy, the cops, and the Biters to see the truth."

Then Moralee spoke, the Spirit of the Holy One glowing through her, "Our Messiah is forgiving to all, so must we be. The war between good and evil isn't waged against people. This war is against the spiritual forces of darkness, against the fiends who influence our friends."

"I see." Kato commented, "The Indigans don't know who is behind—a friend or a fiend."

The Elders smiled as the students understood.

Daleah, "Let's be watchful!"

And everyone agreed, "Amen!"

☞ CHAPTER ELEVEN ☞

SEEKERS AND KEEPERS

Ask and you will receive.
Seek and you will find.
Look and you will see.
Listen and you will hear.
Knock and the door will open for you.
~A Treasury of Messiah's Proverbs

THE VOID, ABOVE INDIGOR, THE NEXT DAY

Woevil, Vexid, and Griop met again, smiling smugly at their mischief. "For sure, our master will reward us handsomely after we give him this report!"

Locitan had been waiting impatiently ever since he received reports about the discovery of the two boys.

"You're late!" Locitan growled, "No report from you since I sent you to manipulate the boys' school friends to go to the cabin.

"Horrid prince," Woevil bowed low, then realizing his embarrassing slip, he quickly corrected himself, "I mean honored prince! We bring wicked news! After the cabin, we foiled Haro and Jamik's plan."

"Indeed, magnificent lord!" Vexid was no longer vexed. He grinned with glee, "They planned to visit a commune. We sent a BITE spy who is now interrogating them!"

"Glorious master!" Griop gripped his hands tightly, saying, "With the cops there, the boys couldn't get through. The cops have searched the commune."

Locitan eyed his three minions silently, one by one, making them nervous. Then he startled them by barking his order, "You know what you are? Nincompoops, all three of you! Do I have to tell you how to do everything?"

All three looked fearfully at Locitan, wondering what they wronged. They cowered low.

"These people are inconsequential!" Locitan began angrily again, "They are poor and without power! Let me ask you again, why I pushed to create the Bureau of Investigation for Technological Enforcement?" His three minions quivered.

"I... I... didn't forget, my prince." Woevil whimpered woefully, wringing his hands, "It was to search for that annoying remnant and... to destroy their pesky writings!"

"You got that right! I created the bureau to bite people!" Locitan smiled sarcastically, "They are my most successful endeavor. Why? Because I manipulated people in positions of power. Let me ask you, did the BITE officer find any of these pathetic holy books?"

"No, my lord." Vexid looked vexed, afraid to look at Locitan. He stammered, his left eyelid twitching nervously, "There were no books... not even a single device."

Again, Locitan asked angrily, "Do these people know about our Father?"

"Master," Griop gripped his hair while he groped for something to say, "I am sorry... bbb... but... there mmm...

must be something! We can.... get them tortured for... for crucial information!" He groveled to his master again.

Locitan smiled wickedly, satisfied at the fear he provoked in his minions. He commanded sharply, "Don't bother with torture. They know nothing! Now, go back before I do any more damage to your egos, then come back ONLY when you find EXACTLY what the boys are looking for. Search the area where they met these two suspected angels in disguise as old men. Don't waste time on insignificant people!"

And the incompetent minions left quickly to do their job as commanded. Gone were the rewards they had in mind to receive. For there were no rewards for the wicked.

THE ACADEMY, ABOVE INDIGOR

Rory was meeting with his Seraphi companions Mona, Soraya, and Nataniel for prayer, long before everyone had awakened.

They prayed with wings unfurled, covering and encircling each other. They alternated between prayer and praise, singing of the mighty Seraphim, "Holy, holy, holy is Yehovah Elohim, who was, who is, and who is to come."

The Elders, who were early birds, did not see the Seraphies, but they felt the power of their prayer. Something was happening. Toward the end, the intensity of the young Seraphies' prayer formed an orange glow at the center of their circle that went upward like a pillar of fire. It went out of the floating village toward the void, unseen by the students and the inhabitants of the little floating village. The angels saw the pillar of fire as it went toward Indigor. The pillar of fire appeared invisible to Locitan and his minions as it passed through their domain. Only the Seraphies, the Elders, and the angelic warriors of Yehovah could see it.

☞ ☞ ☞

Daleah sat at her desk, unable to write in her journal. She remembered something her Ancie Shanielle once told her about writer's block, then she scribbled in her journal —about her feelings.

19314.10.7

Yesterday's prayer session was so intense, it left me exhausted. The Elders and even the Seraphies seem energized by the prayers. I wanted to write yesterday, but I went straight to bed instead. I have never in my life ever felt like this.

One thing for sure—today another spiritual battle will wage over Indigor. It's not over until we win the battle and declare victory over the force of darkness. Will it be a brief battle or a long drawn-out battle? Who knows? Only He knows. One day, everyone on Indigor will revere the true Supreme Being, not the world leaders. May the Spirit of the Holy One help us all!

Daleah stopped scribbling and picked up the journal. It came as a surprise to her how a few words can have more impact. The words felt like a prayer.

Daleah became startled when Revelyn slammed her journal and lamented, "I am having a hard time writing anything down. Let's go to our prayer session!"

"I agree," Daleah said as she stood up, "let's go! Today, we will have a breakthrough!"

"How do you know?" Revelyn stared closely at Daleah who was smiling.

"I just know." Daleah beamed. And they left their room together, their elbows linked.

THE CABIN, INDIGOR

The four questers were in the cabin's kitchen, finishing their morning meal when Haro announced, "I would like to read one of my father's journal entries. I believe this one is significant." He looked at them solemnly and began reading, while Mei interpreted in sign language for Ladya.

19297.8.7

When I first arrived at the Brotherhood, I expected to learn more about our family's ancestors and the original world where we came from. Over time, I learned much more. I never fully understood why we needed a savior and why he had to die for our sins. I didn't even think I was a sinner. I believed I was a good person. I was wrong. Even though I grew up learning to do good, the Holy Writings are clear—ALL have sinned. The Creator is all-knowing. He sees into the hearts of men and looks for the humble truth seekers.

Discovering my Messiah was like discovering the greatest treasure in the world. The Ancient Holy Writings tell us He who was without sin became the perfect sacrifice for our sins. He became our redeemer.

In the beginning, Indigor was like the Garden of Eden, filled with perfect people without sin. They never experienced death until one of them rebelled. That rebellious nature spread like a contagion. The wage of sin is death. Since then, our people have experienced shorter lives as millennia went by.

If we Indigans continue our rebellion, our world will remain separated from the Creator and quarantined from the other worlds. Yet, we need not despair. There is a prophecy from the Oracles of Zion that the Messiah will come to Indigor at the end of the age and claim what rightfully belongs to him again. On that day, the Prince of Darkness, Locitan, will no longer be in control. I long for that day. We must continue to trust in Him and his promises, for the day when we will become like his chosen and special Elders, a royal priesthood. Ask and you will receive. Knock and the door will open.

☞ 201 ☞

Haro ended with a triumphant note in his voice. They had a moment of silence, their minds on the words they had just heard. Then Haro commanded. "Let's get ready for our quest!"

Everyone proclaimed cheerfully, "Let's go!"

☞ ☞ ☞

Unseen and unknown by everyone on Indigor, the orange glow had followed them like a protective cover. This time, they did not need to use the family's motorboat. While Ladya drove them, Jamik read the map and discovered another way to get across the river through a little-known bridge. The four questers stood in front of the apple pie factory. It was Haro's idea to wear hats and shirts from the factory—in case the cops stopped to question them.

Mei complained because she didn't like the souvenirs. She found them ugly and unfashionable. Instead, she purchased a souvenir pin. She said, "I don't see why we need them."

"I agree with Haro." Jamik said as he put on the souvenir hat, "It never hurts to be extra cautious. What if the cops are still looking for returning members of this commune? We don't want them to mistake us for them."

"I agree too." Ladya signed, "Haro, what next clue?" She purchased a souvenir bag, preferring not to mess her hair with a hat or hide her nice clothes underneath an ugly tee shirt. Even when going outdoors or camping, Ladya dressed nicely.

Haro reflected as he spoke, "We might not find the chief of the commune, so we will search for the oak tree ourselves. My best guess would be to keep going East." He put on the souvenir hat and got out his tablet to check the next clues. "We need to find the hidden entrance of a cave that leads to an abandoned metro station and a door with a welcome sign."

Ladya clapped her hands and signed, "Let's go! No time waste!"

☞ ☞ ☞

The four questers stood amid the remains of the festive little commune, with its cheerful teepees and colorful painted buses. It was as silent as a cemetery, except for the animals scavenging for food. The squirrels were sniffing the leftovers on the outdoor tables, and the raccoons were looking inside the toppled trash cans that littered the ground. They scurried away as the four questers approached.

"What shame!" Ladya remarked in sign language, with Mei voicing "Not bad. So colorful, orderly, well-maintained until yesterday."

"You know," Jamik grinned, "if we were ever to become fugitives, I wouldn't mind living like this!"

"Not me!" Mei added disdainfully, "Would rather live in a palace, thank you!"

Haro looked at his compass and pointed East. "Let's go that way."

They followed him when Ladya halted before them and signed, "You said, chief wore white garment, diamond necklace?"

Haro exclaimed impatiently, "So?"

"Well," Ladya hesitated, unsure, "what if garment is clue, not chief?"

Haro frowned, "How do you figure?"

"Look," Ladya pointed to the clotheslines where the commune members had left their clothes to dry, "Me think, we look for white outfit?"

"I don't see how a white outfit is a helpful clue!" Jamik remarked.

"We shouldn't overlook anything." Haro stood there, not sure what to decide, "Remember the orchard? We found the diamond carved on a bench, not a tree." He pointed at the largest teepee. "That's the chief tepee!"

Haro walked toward it. He opened the entrance flap.

The four questers went inside the leather tepee, huddling together. There was a bed with colorful pillows, a low table, and a chest for storing clothes. Amidst the colorful decor, one white color stood out. The inside of the tepee was covered in white fabric. Hanging from its center was a diamond-shaped lamp.

"Bingo!" Jamik grinned and turned to Ladya, "I am sorry I doubted you!"

Haro remarked, "It makes sense. The story said nothing about an oak tree. I assumed there would be more oak trees." And he looked into the chest. It had a diamond carved on top. "Look at this! Another diamond!" He bent down to open it while everyone looked. The inside of the chest contained colorful clothes. Only one item was white. It was a satin bathrobe with small diamond patterns on it. He unfolded it and checked inside its pockets. He said, "Well, that's it. They're empty. No new clues."

Ladya's eyes were sharp. She pointed at the label. "Look here!"

Haro looked closer. "It's the label with embroidered words!" *Made by Mardochi of Northfoundland.* "That's it!" Everyone grinned at each other. "The clue was here all along. My father must have given these items to the chief, in case something happened to him." Haro put everything back, and they walked out of the tepee.

Haro pointed the compass toward North. They were leaving until a loud commanding voice stopped them, "You there, halt!" They turned back in apprehension. A cop and a BITE officer rushed toward them.

THE VOID, ABOVE INDIGOR

There was tension in the void of space above the planet Indigor. Locitan looked angry and frustrated. He had commanded his minions to line up before the angelic messengers. He knew something was happening, even though he could not see the orange glow that had entered his domain. He confronted Alaniel and demanded, "Nothing is happening here. Time for you guys to leave!

And take your idiotic floating village back with you!"

"Locitan, I told you. It's not my decision. I am following orders."

Locitan became enraged, his red glow lighting up. "Then you gave me no choice but to fight you." He unsheathed and raised his sword to begin the fight. Alaniel unsheathed a flaming sword. And the fighting between Alaniel's angels of light and Locitan's menacing minions began. From Aliyah village, the Elders and the Seraphies witnessed the ongoing clashes and sparks of light made by the swords, and the lightning and thunder.

THE FOREST, INDIGOR

The BITE officer walked toward the four questers and asked harshly, "What are you doing here? Who are you?"

Haro spoke, "We are here to do some hiking. We were just passing. My name is Haro, this is my sister Ladya, and our friends, Jamik and Mei."

The BITE officer looked at the four of them suspiciously. He saw the souvenirs they were wearing from the factory. He stayed suspicious. "The four of you, come with me!"

Jamik, Ladya, and Mei looked at Haro for guidance, their eyes showing apprehension. Haro looked back at them with a confident smile and thought. *I better look confident. The last thing we need is to be afraid.* He beamed at the BITE officer and said, "Of course, Officer. Please lead the way!"

The officer led them back to the commune and made them sit at the outdoor table. He barked his order to the cop, "You keep on the lookout while I interrogate these youths." Then he directed his question to Haro and his friends while tapping on the table with his index finger and demanding, "Your identification, please!"

They took out their IDs and gave them to the officer, who scrutinized them. "You are all underage. Why your parents with you?"

Haro smiled confidently and answered, "We are here

on a school break to explore the area and do some hiking. Our parents are working. We have their permission to come here. We stopped to visit the factory and asked for directions to a hiking trail. We were told it was through here. Were we mislead?" He remembered something his father once told him. A neat trick to deflect a question was to answer a question with a question.

"No. We have arrested the people who lived here and we are in the business of looking out for anyone who might come back." Then he scowled. "I am the one asking questions here!"

"Of course, officer!" Haro continued smiling, realizing his tactic hadn't worked, "My apologies!"

"Do you know any of the people who live here?" The officer asked tersely.

"No, officer. This is our first time here." Haro replied politely. "What is this place?"

"Don't ask questions unless directed! Did you go inside any of the dwellings?" He asked unpleasantly. Ladya was looking nervous because Mei looked frozen stiff, not interpreting. She felt lost, so she looked at her brother instead. Haro's smile made her feel calm.

"Yes, we walked into the big tepee over there. It looked fun."

"Did you take anything out of it?" The officer continued to look dour and suspicious.

"No, officer. We were just curious."

"All of you!" He barked, "Empty your backpacks on the table!"

There was a flicker of fear in Haro's eyes, but he prayed silently. The group unstrapped their backpacks. The contents fell onto the table with clattering noises, including the radios.

The officer frowned. He ignored the radios, attracted by the colorful child's tablet. He said as he grabbed it, "Aren't you too old for this device?" He turned it on. Haro tried to stay calm, praying that the officer would not read the story with the clues.

Suddenly, the other cop yelled, "Officer! There's a fugitive getting away!" The cop was running, chasing someone. The four questers couldn't see who it was, but it looked like a shadow.

Then another shadow dashed by swiftly.

The interrogator realized he had to make a quick decision, either join his partner in chasing the fugitives or in continuing his interrogation. He looked determined. "Never mind. I am releasing you from my interrogation, but don't come back here! Is that clear?"

The four of them nodded. Haro replied, "Yes, officer. We apologize for trespassing." They took their IDs and devices while the officer chased after the second fugitive.

They walked away quickly from the commune, through the forest. Jamik bent down and exclaimed, "What a relief! I couldn't have handled that better than you did, Haro!"

The girls nodded in agreement. Mei remarked, impressed at Haro, "You saved us, Haro!"

"No, I didn't." Haro frowned, "I wonder what exactly they were chasing? The figures I saw looked like shadows. No matter! We are free!"

And the four seekers continued their quest, North bound.

☞ ☞ ☞

Unknown to the four questers, the orange glow that followed the four questers from their cabin like a protective cloud sensed they were in trouble. It transformed itself into two shadowy fugitives to keep the cop and BITE officer busy for hours, thus allowing the four questers to continue uninterrupted.

Locitan's unseen minions, Woevil, Vexid, and Griop witnessed the BITE officer interrogating Haro. They never saw the orange cloud. Their nasty smiles turned to gasps as they became confounded the minute the strange fugitives appeared, distracting the officer from the interrogation.

Above the void, the tension was mounting. Locitan's legion of minions stood face-to-face with Alaniel's angels, battle-ready if anyone moved past the invisible line. Locitan noticed the angels looking at something, but he couldn't see it.

Locitan faced Alaniel suspiciously, moving closer. "What were you looking at?"

"Have you forgotten our agreement? No crossing the line!" Alaniel reminded him.

"Seems to me that one of you crossed the line!" Locitan retorted.

"We are exactly where we should be!" Alaniel calmly answered.

Locitan struck his sword, pushing back Alaniel's sword and yelling, "Charge!" And the fighting began.

☞ ☞ ☞

The four questers had arrived at an impasse. Boulders interspersed with pine trees blocked their path toward the North. They circled the boulders until they faced the base of a high vertical cliff. Going up was impossible. There was nowhere to go except right or left of the cliff wall.

Haro stood there, unsure of the next step. Jamik suggested, "Why don't we split until we find something?"

"We should," Haro agreed, "because the entrance to the cave must be close by. I go right with Ladya. Jamik, you go left with Mei. When you find something call me by radio." He took out the radios from his backpack.

"If you don't mind," Mei blurted out, "I would rather go with Ladya!"

"Seriously!" Haro snapped. "This is no time to be picky!"

Ladya looked at Haro, her hands on her hips. Mei stood stubbornly, her arms crossed. He should have known better than to separate these two peas in a pod. Haro gave Mei the radio, his face scowling.

Haro walked with Jamik along the edge of the cliff until he found something—a carved diamond on the surface of the cliff. He called Mei by radio. "Hello Mei, walk back to us, we found the symbol."

Mei's voice came out on the radio, "We're on our way."

The four gathered again and followed the diamond markings along on the cliff. They found an entrance to a cave, hidden by a bush. Haro took out his flashlight, and they went inside. The cave had a fire pit the previous occupants had used. Graffiti covered the walls of the cave, not diamonds.

Haro's flashlight illuminated the graffiti, searching for a diamond shape. He remarked, "If there was a diamond shape on these walls, it's completely covered by graffiti!"

They walked through the natural corridor of the cave until they reached a tunnel with a timber door frame supporting its archway.

Haro remarked, "This is manmade. Let's follow it."

They followed it until it split in two. Jamik popped the question in everyone's mind. "Which way?" They all looked at Haro, who had been making all the leadership decisions ever since the quest began. "Naturally, we split up again, same as before." He took another flashlight out of his backpack and gave it to Ladya. He turned up the switches on the radio. "Call by radio when we see the symbol. They might not work underground, but I boosted the signals."

The girls found a diamond-shaped graffiti on the wall and called the boys. They got together and went through one more similar split in the tunnel.

They found curious drawings on the walls of the tunnels, but they weren't graffiti. They were older and faded, of winged horses, different mammals with wings, men with wings, men and women dressed in all white and holding long staffs, and what seemed to be a village floating on a disc.

Finally, they came out of the cave into what appeared to be an arched room.

Haro exclaimed, "This looks like our metro subway station in Indipolis!" Haro flashed the beam at the arched ceiling of the subway, its damage apparent from the missing colorful tiles that had fallen into the railway tracks. Haro recalled riding the city train, how bustling and noisy the station was, yet also brightly lit, clean, and cheerful. Here, he was in a forgotten station, eerily quiet, deserted, and damaged. They passed a broken booking window and rotting benches. They followed a path on the platform cleared of debris, evidence that others had passed through. Finally, they came to a dead-end, a plain metal door, with a placard that said, "YOU ARE WELCOME TO BOARD IN THE HOOD."

"YIPPEE!" Jamik hollered jubilantly, "WE HAVE ARRIVED!" He startled Haro and Mei, but not Ladya, who was deaf.

Ladya asked, "What to do now?"

Haro reached for the door handle, but it was locked. He knocked gingerly. "Tap, tap, tap." They waited. Nothing happened. Haro tried again, louder this time. "Bang, bang, bang." They waited.

"Well, Jamik," Haro said in dismay, "it seems your jubilation was premature."

"Maybe," Jamik frowned, "there's a doorbell, or a key hidden somewhere?"

Haro flashed his light around the door. There was no doorbell, but the knob had a keyhole.

Mei asked, "Didn't the story say something about passing a test?"

Haro looked at her, "No, the quest was the test. We passed." Haro looked pensive. "In the story, the man who opened the door said something about Yoshua. I wonder if it's another clue?"

Ladya tapped Haro's shoulder to intervene with signing hands, "Remember Dad's journal? Ask, will receive, knock, will open, Messiah, that who open door, name Yeshua!"

Jamik didn't know what Ladya said, so he tapped Mei's shoulder, "What did she say?"

"Sorry, I forgot." Mei interpreted what Ladya said.

"I see." Jamik asked, "So which is it, Yeshua or Yoshua? Is he the only way to go through that door?"

Suddenly, there was a noise, and the door opened! Two men in white mantles opened the door, surprising them. One of them greeted the questers cheerfully, "Hello, Haro! Everyone! My name is Brother Mateo. We have been expecting you. Welcome to the Brotherhood of Scribes and Keepers!" The four questers gaped at him. The door had opened because they had uttered the name of the Messiah. They had finally arrived. And the seekers and keepers finally came together face-to-face.

THE ACADEMY, ABOVE INDIGOR

Daleah heard the announcement from the Elders that Locitan and his minions had retreated to nurse their wounds. Everyone on Aliyah cheerfully thanked the Creator for the temporary victory.

Daleah was in the Outer Court classroom, a room with linen-like white walls on three sides and a woven curtain of blue, red, and white, decorated with cherubim, on the fourth side. The combination of woven colors made the curtain looked like lavender. There were also paintings depicting the Mishkan of Old Earth with its priesthood.

Professor Aaronia stood in front of the curtain wall, greeting the class, "A good halo to you all! We have a special guest, our own Professor Shanielle, who is also a survivor like me. Today, you will learn about one foundation of the faith—becoming an overcomer." Professor Shanielle came into the room with a long staff, a white stone attached to its top. Snowflake, the winged clion accompanied her. When he saw Daleah, he jumped to sit near her. Daleah smiled happily as she patted him.

"Halo, everyone! You all know me from your first class in penmanship. I am pleased to see your progress. Let's look at this white staff. What is the meaning of this special object belonging only to the Elders?"

The students had no clue, except Revelyn, whose shy

face revealed understanding. She didn't lift her hand, but Shanielle recognized the look. "Revelyn?"

"It's a traveling staff." Revelyn answered as she straightened, alert. "The writings of the Apostle Yochanan tells about the white stone. *In The Fulfilled Account of the Revelation of Yeshua the Messiah*, Yochanan wrote about the one who overcomes, who remains victorious until the end, will receive hidden manna and a white stone. I don't know why the stone rests on a long white staff."

Elder Shanielle said, "Revelyn, thank you for the excellent explanation. Indeed, there is a name written on that most precious gift, invisible to everyone but the Creator and I. The prophet Zechariah wrote about a special staff. He foretold that when the Messiah returned, old men and women will own long staffs. That's us, the Elders. The staff is the best place for Elders to carry the stone, as it is too cumbersome for a necklace!" Her grin was much like Elizon's.

Elder Shanielle asked another question, "What does it mean—to overcome?"

Daleah raised her hand, "Someone like Professor Aaronia?"

"Yes," Shanielle's smile brought a glow to her face, "an overcomer is more than a survivor. Many people who survived the Holocaust remained angry for many years at their oppressors and demanded justice. An overcomer is someone who has overcome these damaging emotions and has forgiven their enemies."

Rory raised his paw. Shanielle nodded at him. "What else can you tell us about your former life on Old Earth?" When Rory spoke, Snowflake heard, stood up, and languidly walked toward him. He was not used to seeing a Seraphi that looked like him. He stood there watching Rory for a long time, tilting his head.

"I faced many tough challenges in my life." Shanielle replied, "I grew up with an abusive and alcoholic father, I was forsaken by a husband, divorced, lost a child to suicide, survived cancer, I was widowed, and many other things... I also survived the end of that age when disasters and horrible diseases had overtaken the world, right until the Messiah returned. Through it all, I sustained my faith, trusting in His promises."

"I understand," Kato lifted his hand, "you are a survivor and overcomer. What is cancer?"

"Cancer is a disease with tumors in the body, caused by abnormal cell growth that spreads to other parts of the body. It's a common disease that happens only on fallen worlds."

Rory had been listening to the talk in fascination. Snowflake touched Rory's leg with his paw for attention, and Rory picked him up to pet his head. They seemed comfortable with each other. Daleah noticed Snowflake's movement and smiled. She thought, *Rory looks as if he is holding his own child!*

Enoch lifted his hand, "What is suicide?" It was another unfamiliar word for the students.

This time Shanielle sighed, "That's difficult to understand. It's the intentional killing of oneself."

The students' jaws dropped with shock. Daleah, without lifting her hand, conveyed her shock in one word, "What?" Her Ancie never told her about it.

"Indeed, I lost a child to suicide." Shanielle's glow disappeared. "At the time, I didn't understand how harmful depression could be, that it could lead to suicide. It's one of the many symptoms of a fallen world where people feel they do not have hope. Young people on Indigor also suffer from depression. A chemical imbalance or substance abuse can cause depression, leading to suicide."

"What?" Daleah asked her Ancie, "They have suicides on Indigor?"

Shanielle looked sad. "That's right. The people of Indigor suffers the same diseases as did the people of Old Earth. Without the Holy Writings, and the knowledge of a Supreme Intelligence, the suicide rate has increased. Parents are mourning their children. We must pray for the four young people on Indigor and their mission. It's not over yet." And another prayer session began.

THE BROTHERHOOD, INDIGOR

The fellowship of seekers and keepers had begun. The Brothers invited the four questers to the hidden underground dwelling. Brother Mateo welcomed and led them through a hidden room, a metro control room. They walked by the old electronic keyboards and screens covered in thick dust and rust. There was a hidden door behind a tall storage cabinet. It led to a stairway tunnel, going up. When they arrived, the other brothers had welcomed them all, delighted to meet the new seekers.

Haro, Jamik, Ladya, and Mei followed Mateo for the tour of their humble dwelling. There was a sizable room with comfortable sofas, armchairs, and ottomans. Numerous books filled the room everywhere, on all the wall shelves, stacked on the floor, tables, and even on the ladder. One brother was reading a book, waving at them.

"Wow," Haro remarked, "I have never seen so many books!"

"Believe it or not," said Mateo with a smile, "this is the only library in the entire world!"

Mateo led them toward another room, an eating area adjoining a kitchen, with an assortment of tables and chairs, all painted in the same color to give the room a sense of orderliness. One brother was cooking.

Jamik, who loved to eat, commented, "It smells good here!"

"You are welcome to have supper with us," Mateo informed the seekers with a smile, "but beware, don't expect any of us to be a gourmet chef! We take turns with the chores and the cooking." The kitchen looked spotlessly clean and organized with two large fridges.

Mateo remarked, "We use this area as a meeting room when we're not eating."

Mateo led them through the hallway toward two study

rooms, filled with many more books on the walls. Two brothers were working at their desks, scribbling, and shuffling papers. They waved at the group.

"This is our workshop area for book printing and bookbinding." Mateo continued, "There are our offices. Beyond this point, each of us received a private bedroom with adjoining bathrooms. There's two empty bedrooms. If you come and train with us for brief periods, you'll be living with us."

He led them toward a sparse, unoccupied bedroom. Mei remarked at the lack of decor, "It's not much, is it?"

He led them toward other rooms. "There's nothing luxurious about our humble adobe. We live minimally so we can focus on the most important aspect of our life—to study and write. No distractions."

Ladya signed her question, and Mei interpreted, "Do you mean to say women are a distraction? Is that why the brothers are all men?"

"That's not the reason," Mateo looked sad as he shook his head, "In the early days, before we went into hiding, our women worked with us. We have rotations so that none of us miss our wives or families. Some days, we hope men and women can work together." Mateo gave the girls a reassuring smile.

The small offices had desks with computers, laptops, and many devices, scanners, outdated phones, flat screens in different sizes, including a rare device—an old printer. Haro perked up. "What can you tell me about how you operate here?"

"This is one area of our work that we are struggling with for so many years now." Mateo sighed, "We scanned most of our books to digitize them, hoping to distribute them on the Indigonet someday. We need someone with more expertise in that area. We've done most of the legwork. There's no connection to the networks here, where the Biters can easily track us."

Haro remembered Janov Diversi, the hacker that his father was planning to meet before he died. "You need someone with experience in cyber and network security? Someone with access to a public network who can transmit your digitized data from a hidden, secure server, without interference from the authorities?"

"You know about that?" Mateo looked at Haro in surprise, "Did your father tell you?"

Haro shook his head, "No, he shared nothing about the Brothers. I found out on my own. Before he died, he was meeting with someone. I found a piece of paper with the professional hacker's name in his journal. His name is Janov Diversi. We met, and he informed me he has a hidden server ready. All we have to do is bring the data to him. My father planned it. Once the digitized books are out there, many Indigans will copy it and back it up. The good news will spread quickly."

Mateo looked doubtful, "You trust this man?"

"If my father trusted him, we can. He hates the Biters. Jamik has met him." Jamik nodded in agreement. "I have not found the digital data in my father's things, so I assume you haven't given it to him?"

Mateo replied, "That's correct. Your father was supposed to find a specialist first. Apparently, he already did."

Haro opened his backpack and handed Mateo the mobile storage device from Janov. "This is where you should save the Writings."

Mateo clapped his hands and burst out in joy, "That's splendid news about the hidden server! HalleluYah! I must inform the brothers!" He turned to leave and then stopped and turned with a grin, "Ladies! This is the answer we have been waiting for! If this works, our wives, daughters, and yourselves will join sooner than we think!"

He left his guests standing there. They stood silently, smiling at each other, amused at such behavior from adults. Haro knew he had completed his mission. He felt a sigh of relief and a weight lifting off his shoulders.

☞ CHAPTER TWELVE ☞

FOR SUCH A TIME

And Esther sent this reply to me, Mordecai…
Assemble all the Jews who dwell in Susa.
Hold a fast and pray for me…
Afterward, I will go to the King,
Even if it violates the royal decree.
And if I must die, I will die.
~Elder Mordecai,
Chronicles of the Babylonian Exile

THE VOID, ABOVE INDIGOR, THE SAME DAY

Locitan was nursing his wounded pride. His minions dared not approach him. The second-in-command of his armed forces, Sarotten, went to fetch Woevil, Vexid, and Griop because they had not reported in. Locitan's anger was getting the best of him. He had to control himself. It would not do to scare away his minions when he needed them to get the job done.

Locitan had many minions at his disposal to do his dirty work. He ruled over all creatures of wickedness, lurkers adept at deception, vexing spirits who worked up people's emotional wounds, and many more depraved spirits who caused damage to the human souls.

Sarotten was a big demonic henchman of Locitan, strong enough to force them to face Locitan. He squeezed the minions into his arms and threw them at Locitan's feet. They cowered before him in fear.

Locitan commanded them without anger, "Get up! I'm not mad and will not hurt you this time."

They looked up at him in surprise. He continued calmly, "Tell me what happened."

Woevil quivered, looking at Locitan. "Honored prince! We don't know how we lost. It was confusing!"

Vexid nodded, "Magnificent lord! We were doing well. After what happened with the deaf girl and the Mister Nice BITE officer, we sent a meaner officer in his stead. He caught the little group of children and was doing an excellent job of interrogating them."

Griop interceded, "Glorious master! It's true. He made the children empty their backpacks. He was so close to finding out what was on the devices. Then, out of the blue, these two fugitives appeared!"

Woevil remarked, "My prince! We tried to follow, but we couldn't see them. They were shadowy and disappeared as fast as they came. We realized too late that they had distracted the cop and the officer!"

Locitan had listened intently. "And you don't know where these two fugitives came from or what they looked like?"

All three shook their heads. The look of confusion was enough to convince Locitan that the matter wasn't their fault. He approached Sarotten closely, "What do you make of this?"

"Master, it is unusual." Sarotten replied, "I observed

everything during the battle from my position. I've not seen a single messenger cross the border, nor have I seen anything like what they described. Maybe it's a new strategy devised by our enemies?"

"My thought exactly!" Locitan nodded, "A new strategy to confuse my minions. I can't have them working down there with diminished mental capacity."

Sarotten grinned nastily, "You mean, working as retards? Why bother using fancy words?"

Locitan scowled, "Don't provoke me, Sarotten!" He returned to his minions, "I have another mission for you. I will give you some of my strength so you can do a better job." He blew his fiery breath on them and watched as the three insignificant minions became bigger. They no longer cowered and looked more confident. "Here is the assignment. Don't go back to the commune, but go back to where it all started, with the gang members. Get that gang emotionally worked up with revenge from their defeat by the old men who protected the boys. Also, watch the four children wherever they go. Report to me if they contact anyone important."

They all bowed. Woevil spoke for the three of them, "Thank you for choosing us, Master!" As they left, they didn't look wretched anymore. They looked smarter and determined. And that's what made them more dangerous.

THE BROTHERHOOD, INDIGOR

The brothers shared fellowship with the four seekers, showing them how to pray and breaking bread together.

As they ate together, Mateo announced, "If there is something you want to ask, go ahead. I'm sure you have many questions."

Then Mei spoke, unknowingly interrupting Haro, who had questions, "Actually, I have a question that has been weighing on my mind. When do we meet the Elders?"

Haro intervened, "I was going to ask the same question!"

Mateo smiled. "I believe you might have met one of

them. Haro, you don't remember me at all? I disguised myself as an elderly man with a cane when some gang chased you and Jamik. We protected you by blocking them."

"That was you?" Haro asked, surprised, "You were with that Elder? He didn't look like an Elder!"

"No, he transformed himself," Mateo replied, "because Elders are not human. They are more like angels. Their have bodies made of light, so they can transform into humans when necessary. You would have liked to have met Elder Elizon."

Mei still needed to know more. "About the Elders, is that why some of us, like the royals, looks like them? Because we are descended from them?"

"That's a whole different topic!" He replied, laughing, "I'm afraid you will not like the answer."

"It's better than not knowing." Mei looked at Mateo expectantly. "Just tell us." She continued to sign for Ladya, to keep her involved.

"All right," said Mateo, "here's the thing. Elders cannot have children. They're asexual, like the angels."

"Asexual?" Jamik asked, puzzled. "You mean like they don't have sexual organs?"

Mateo saw the look of surprise on the seekers. "Afraid so," replied Mateo, "but before they become Elders, before the resurrection, they were humans like us. They had children. Millions of their descendants are here. We are descended from them, not only Mei. The reason the royals are tall and light-haired is that our people randomly chose them to imitate the Elders. It's like role-playing. We were holding on to a glorious age when Indigor was part of the Commonwealth. We kept playing our roles long after we had forgotten why."

"Oh, I see." Mei looked blank. She didn't know whether to be glad or disappointed. "It's not the answer I was expecting, but I understand."

"There's an Old Earth adage," said Mateo, "I believe it goes like—imitation is the sincerest form of flattery."

"Me think," Ladya intervened, "makes sense. Kings, queens, imitate Elders."

"But," said Brother Jotham, speaking for the first time, "this doesn't make the royal family any less important. Mei, we will need your help. You are our link to the royal family."

"Oh," Mei smiled again, back to her old self, and feeling important, "sure, what can I do to help?"

"As soon the Holy Writings are ready to reach the people through the Indigonet, we need someone to deliver an important message to the king." Brother Mateo explained, "You see, the Biters are in control of the networks. They scrutinize all the messages written to the royals. We tried sending messages without success. We need someone to deliver the message to the king or queen in person."

"What exactly is the message," Haro asked, his eyes lighted up at fulfilling a mission, "and why would Mei need to deliver it?"

"You see," Mateo continued, "the king doesn't have the authority to abolish old laws. However, he has the authority to enact new laws. If we can get to the king first, the Biters can't hinder the new law, thus allowing the Holy Writings on the Indigonet."

A perplexed Haro asked, "Why do we need a new law that if the server is hidden and secure?"

"Because, Haro," Brother Jotham intervened, "we need the blessing of the king. We would not want to do anything illegal. The Creator's law says we must obey the law of the land. Even though His holy law takes precedence, still, we should do nothing illegal."

"We have prepared a letter for when we are ready to transmit our data on the Indigonet," Brother Mateo added, "along with a sample of the new edict to append to Indigor's constitution. It's all stored on a mini drive."

"Well, Haro," Jamik grinned, "we've got our work cut out for us!"

"You mean me, Jamik," Mei intervened, "Me, I, will

meet the king and queen with the message! Not you! You don't like the royals, remember?" Mei had a satisfied look on her face.

"Kids," Brother Mateo held his hands up, "no need to argue among yourselves! The plan is to split your team. Haro will go with one brother to meet Janov, and one of us will go with Mei."

"I volunteer to go with Haro!" Jamik was quick to answer. "I know the area, I've been there!"

"I will go with Mei," Ladya answered as she looked at Jamik with an amused smile. "Me hope, meet royal family!"

"It's settled then!" Brother Mateo announced. "We will split into two teams. Haro, Jamik, and I will go together. Brother Jotham will go with Mei and Ladya. Before we go anywhere, we must pray for the success of our mission. This is paramount. The enemies of the darkness are lurking around, ready to cause trouble."

ABOVE INDIGOR, A WEEK LATER

Daleah was sitting in the Upper Room for Professor's Elizon class. Elizon had arrived back from his mission on Indigor. He had shared his latest report and was now telling a story. "The king of Aram became enraged because Elisha, the prophet of Israel, predicted his army's movement and strategy against Israel. Before he could win any war against Israel, the king had to capture Elisha. He sent soldiers at night to surround the city of Dothan."

"Elisha's servant woke up that morning and saw the army of Aram surrounding his people. Elisha told the servant not to be afraid because the angelic army was in charge. After Elisha prayed, the servant's eyes opened to see the angelic army. Elisha also prayed for the enemy soldiers to become blind and led the blind soldiers to Samaria. They opened their eyes, they realized they were not where they should be."

Elizon paused, "Today, you will be like Elisha's servant. The Elders and I prayed for you. We felt it was unfair that you're unable to see the spiritual dimension of the battle, while Rory is the only student to do so. Therefore, your eyes will open, and you will see the warfare."

Rory raised his hand to remark, "I am glad. It's only fair."

Elizon nodded, "Not only that, all of you also will see the angel Alaniel right here, in this room."

"Alaniel," Elizon announced slightly loudly, "now!" Then the mighty angel Alaniel appeared suddenly. For the first time, the students saw an angel. They looked at him in awe. He was shining so brightly that he lit up the whole room.

"Greetings, Alaniel!" Elizon greeted the angel, "We asked Alaniel to come and give his report. This will help you pray better, to direct your prayer toward a specific purpose. He is a skilled warrior angel."

Alaniel inclined his head before the awestruck students. He smiled and turned to Elizon. "Truly!" His voice was powerful, reverberating through the room. "The story of the prophet Elisha, his servant, the soldiers, all that happened exactly as Elizon told you. I was there playing a minor part in that spiritual battle, leading with my horse and chariot of fire with other angels. We faced the Arameans with their horses and chariots to protect the Israelites. Elder Elizon, why don't you tell them what happened afterwards?"

"That's the best part!" Elizon continued, "The king of Israel asked the prophet if he should kill the Aramean soldiers. Elisha said no, but to feed them and let them go. The king did so. He prepared a feast for the Arameans and sent them to their home. They never bothered the Israelites again. The Israelites were merciful toward the Arameans. There is a lesson in this for all of us, especially the Indigans."

"Truly," Alaniel smiled, "you must continue to pray for them. Here's the latest report about the enemy's strategy. We couldn't to cross into their domain, but we saw where they went. The enemy is increasing surveillance activities among Haro and his friends. They are watching him at school and home, following him wherever he goes, keeping track of whoever is meeting him. Locitan is on the alert and ready for more action." He paused, looking at the still awestruck students.

Daleah saw an opportunity to ask a question. She raised her hand timidly. Alaniel saw her.

"Daleah, please ask your question." He asked, smiling at her.

Daleah, surprised he knew her name, asked. "What happens to angels like Locitan who rebels? Is there salvation for them? Will know mercy, like the Arameans?"

For a brief second, the light went out of Alaniel, like a flicker. He looked sad. "There is no salvation for angels who rebel. They have the same fate as Lucifer—the Lake of Fire. Resurrection is for humans, not angels because we don't have any physical bodies. The Messiah took on human form for the redemption of humanity, not angels. That is the harsh reality for us angelic beings. We are the closest to the Creator, and we should know better than to disobey Him. There's no excuse for rebelling. On the other hand, humans have a different fate, a better fate, because the serpent deceived them."

Again, Daleah expressed surprise, as did the other students. She regretted asking the question. Alaniel saw her expression and remarked, "Don't be sorry for asking, little one. We all need to know the truth." There was a moment of silence.

Then Elizon stood up and inclined his head, "Thank you for coming, Alaniel."

"It is always a pleasure to serve!" Alaniel inclined his head to the students, "I must be on my way. Farewell Elizon, my brother, farewell children!" He waved at them.

Everyone waved back, even Rory waved his paw, "Farewell!" And Alaniel vanished from the room, his light gone with him.

School break had long gone, and they were back at the cabin only for one day. The four seekers gathered around the kitchen table at the cabin where they had agreed to pray together once a week. They prayed the way the Brothers showed them. Jamik was uncomfortable because he was hungry. They had skipped breakfast after agreeing to fast and pray for the day. Jamik determined to ignore the desire of his gnawing stomach.

"We understand from this," Haro said as he tapped the journal, "that the answers to prayer can be hindered if we don't confess our sins and if there is any discord between us. We end our prayers in the Messiah Yeshua's name." He bowed his head to pray. "Let there be no discord between us. I will start by confessing my sin. Our Father in the Heavenly Realm, teach me to forgive my brothers and sisters."

Haro paused, praying silently, letting the Spirit of the Holy One reveal things to him. He remembered being bitter two years ago toward Jamik. He sighed because he was uneasy about unburdening himself, "I must confess that I was bitter and jealous toward Jamik last year when he didn't have time for me, after getting in sport activities. I confess to being impatient with my deaf sister. Forgive me."

Jamik looked surprised, "Sure, Haro, if the Lord is always forgiving, then I forgive you. I have sinned too I confessing to hanging out with friends who bullied while I stood by and did nothing. I will apologize to the people I offended." He looked at Mei and grinned, "I confess for insulting the royals."

It was Ladya's turn. "Me forgive Haro for impatience. Me repent too!" Ladya signed, "Repent for angry at people who mock me because me deaf. Me repent, angry at my best friend Mei for keep secrets. Me repent, angry at brother Haro."

It was Mei's turn. "I accept Jamik and Ladya's apologies." She paused, struggling with her confession. "I confess I have sinned. I confess to sneaking and stealing money from my mother's purse to buy clothes. Forgive me, Lord. Forgive my pride." She paused.

Ladya kicked Mei's leg gently under the table. Mei's face expressed annoyance at the kick. Ladya formed her lips, saying, "Tell them." Mei frowned, shaking her head. Ladya kicked her leg again, her lips pressed tightly together in stubbornness. Haro saw her expression and asked, "What's going on?"

"Mei MUST confess something." Ladya announced, with determined hand movements, "We MUST succeed mission. Confess everything."

Mei looked nervous, avoiding their eyes. They waited while Mei prayed, her head bowed and her hands clasped. Finally, she uttered, "I confess I am a sinner of the worst kind! I slept with my boyfriend before we made our vows of marriage!" She sighed, still looking down and not looking at her friends. She was embarrassed, but also relieved.

The boys were surprised, but silent, not wanting to blurt out anything that might hurt her feelings. After a while, they felt the loving and almost tangible presence of the Spirit of the Holy One on them. There was no judgment.

Woevil, Vexid, and Griop were watching from afar the four seekers outside the cabin. They were moving closer and closer until they suddenly became blocked and couldn't move any further. It was like an invisible wall. They looked at each other, knowing what it meant. Woevil uttered, "Woe to us! They've started praying!" The invisible wall grew thicker and thicker, pushing them further away from the cabin until they were so far away. They saw the cabin as a tiny dot.

A spiritual battle was waging. Daleah, Rory, and the other students watched the warfare, the purple planet visible at the edge of the horizon. They all stood in the Edenic garden of the Academy, watching in fascination. Rory was smiling, looking at the faces of the students more than he was watching the battle. He was happy that they could see the warfare. He wasn't the only one anymore. The Elders had prayed for them to see the spiritual realms, and now they could. The angels of the Light were fighting the dark ones, their swords clashing and creating sparks. Some dark ones were falling, clutching their wounds. Even though they were not flesh and blood, they could feel the piercing swords. They screamed in agony, falling away from the battle. They could see Alaniel and Locitan's brighter glows. Alaniel was a bright white light and Locitan a fiery red glow.

Professor Elizon watched with them, then he announced, "Children! It's time to pray! Do we want to win this battle for the Indigans?"

"Of course, professor!" Daleah replied excitedly while the students gathered on the cushions for prayer time, "Let's have victory in the name of the Messiah!"

"Good, but first things first!" Elizon commanded with a smile, "What's the strategy?"

Kato lifted his hand to answer, "The strategy is for Haro and Jamik to get together with Brother Mateo and give Janov the data."

"Indeed," the professor answered, "Don't forget, Janov must get the data safely to the hidden server. He will need our protection too. What else?"

Revelyn lifted her hand shyly, "You mentioned the story of Queen Esther? Something about her being in the same situation as the Queen of Indigor?"

"Revelyn is correct." Rory interjected, "we haven't yet heard the full story."

"It's true." Elizon replied, "I didn't finish. I will summarize it for you, then you can read all about it later.

We pray that the queen of Indigor will rise to the occasion for such a time as this, exactly as Queen Esther did."

He paused, "This happened to the exiled Jews who stayed behind in Babylon instead of returning to Jerusalem. Persia had conquered Babylon. One day, a Jewish orphan girl named Esther became the new queen to King Xerxes. Unlike the first queen who was vain and selfish, Esther was kind, beautiful, and intelligent. The king did not know that she was Jewish. She had an older cousin named Mordecai who was her guardian. To make a long story short, Haman, the King's chief official, was an evil man. He was so infuriated by Mordecai's refusal to bow to him that Haman plotted to kill all the Jews. Thankfully, Mordecai heard about the plot and told Esther." Elizon continued the story while engrossed students listened.

"Mordecai sent her a message, saying, if she remained silent, she and her house will perish. Who knows whether she had attained her royal position for such a time as this? As Esther faced this dilemma, she made a tough choice. In her time, people could not approach the king. Doing so would mean death unless he extended his golden scepter to let her approach. However, if she did nothing, she would perish, along with many Jews. So, she told Mordecai to tell all the Jews to fast and pray. They did so for three days, as did Queen Esther. When she was ready to approach the King, he was extremely pleased to see her. She invited him to a banquet she prepared for him and Haman. When the time came, she pleaded with him to save her and her Jewish people from Haman's wicked plot. And the King did. In the end, Haman was hung on the gallows he had ordered built to kill the Jews."

Daleah lifted both her hands, smiling, "Amen! Esther was very brave!"

"Grr... Amen!" Rory roared while clapping his paws, surprising everyone with his roar for the first time.

"Let's pray!" Elizon announced with a grin, loving the enthusiastic spirit of the students.

They were in the cafe, enjoying a casual conversation. Haro and Jamik watched as Brother Mateo handed to Janov Divers the data on a mini drive the size of a small pocketknife. Janov thanked Mateo profusely, "I have waited so long for this day, when we can speak freely without being watched and arrested!"

"Mr. Divers," Brother Mateo intervened, "it will begin soon enough, but it's not over yet. Please remember what Haro told you. Pleasure meeting you. We will keep in touch."

"Definitely!" Janov answered, smiling happily. And with that, he left the cafe.

High above the air, Woevil and Vexid watched the meeting with gleeful smirks. They saw the data exchange.

As Janov walked back to his workplace, a BITE officer was walking toward him around the corner of the intersection. Earlier that morning, Woevil and Vexid had made sure this officer began the morning in a foul mood. His wife had vexed him, and later, his boss had screamed at him. He was told to survey a specific section of the town, which was not in his usual surveillance route. As the officer walked, he saw Janov smiling happily and he didn't like it. No one should look this happy.

As the officer approached Janov, he barked, "You halt!"

Janov stopped, his smile gone. "Yes, officer?"

"Please empty your pockets!" The officer asked, scowling, but enjoying that Janov looked scared. He felt powerful.

"Officer, what's your reason for stopping me in the middle of the street?" Janov asked fearfully.

"Don't question me! I have my reasons!" The officer barked.

Janov reluctantly emptied his pockets of his key set, wallet, some coins, a mini drive, a pack of cigarettes, and a worn-out lighter. The officer took the mini drive without hesitation and opened his bag to reveal a tablet. He plugged the mini drive into the tablet and opened the files. It showed various photos of the town, with its endless art graffiti, the homeless, the gangs, and the closed shops. The officer asked suspiciously, "What's this? Why are you taking photos of this desolate and drab town?"

Janov shrugged, "Why not? I enjoy taking photos! It's a hobby. I am hoping to exhibit them in a show!"

The officer looked disgusted and handed it back. "They're ugly! An exercise in futility! Why can't you take photos of more cheerful things?"

Janov grinned and commented, "You'll be surprised at what people consider art! Look at this one, it's my favorite!" Janov pointed at one photo.

The officer expressed his disgust, returned the item to Janov, grunted, and left, still in a nasty mood.

Janov looked relieved. He walked back toward his shop. He walked past the alley when he saw a group of gangsters blocking his door. He had seen them often. It didn't faze him. He walked toward the other side of his building, whistling a tune, and walked into a tobacco shop. He waved hello to the owner who commented, "Trouble with the gang again?"

Janov nodded and replied nonchalantly. "As usual!" He walked toward the back and entered the owner's private office. He clutched a hidden latch and opened a bookcase, sliding it like a door. With his key, he opened the door behind the bookcase and walked into the restroom of his shop. The door was hidden behind a tall mirror. He was in his shop, safe, sound, and alone, without his nosy assistant around. Janov had ordered him to take the day off. His stubborn assistant insisted he could work while Janov rested at home. It had been a battle of the wills, but Janov won.

The vicious gang outside waited and watched, with no clue that Janov was inside his shop. He took out the cigarette pack and threw it in the trash. He wasn't a smoker. Then he took the lighter and opened a hidden slider at the bottom. The hidden mini drive that Mateo had given him was safe! He smiled happily. Then he moved a heavy desk to reveal a hidden panel behind it, which he removed. He crawled through the secret entrance and went down to the long-forgotten tunnels of the town. He was well on his way to the hidden server. And to freedom!

High above the air, Woevil and Vexid lost their evil sneers and looked confounded. They had lost track of Janov and the gangsters were useless. He wasn't in the tobacco shop anymore. They looked everywhere for him for hours without success. They weren't happy, but they hoped that Griop had better news.

☞ ☞ ☞

Mei and Ladya were having fun with the queen. Even though the queen was only three years older than them, at heart, she was still like a teenager. The queen was almost identical to Mei—the tall stature, the beauty, the platinum blonde hair. Unlike Mei, who preferred to let her hair down, the queen had her hair coiffed professionally, and she wore minimal makeup.

"I must say, Mei! I haven't had so much fun since the wedding. It gets lonely doing all these formal appearances. The royal family is a cautious bunch. They think I should keep my distance, but I feel more relaxed with you gals! Even my family had quickly adopted and adapted to the custom of the royals!" They were having tea in the queen's private sitting room, exchanging stories, family news. The Queen enjoyed learning some sign language to connect with Ladya.

"We enjoyed our time here too!" Mei said, signing for Ladya, who nodded. "I'm afraid we are taking too much of your time and keeping you away from your duties. We must be going."

"Nonsense!" Then she looked at the clock on the wall and gasped, "Oh, my! You're right. It's getting late!" She got up.

"Your royal highness," said Mei, raising her hand, "I'm

☞ 231 ☞

not leaving before I put on my lipstick.”

“Mei,” said the queen, “I wish you’d stop calling me that! You’ve always known me as cousin Enoka Malik. Our families promised we would always be warm to each other, even if one of us gets snatched up by royalty!”

“Don’t tell me you got snatched up!” Mei said as she put on her bright red lipstick. “You and your handsome king are definitely in love!”

“Oh, how I miss the color of that lipstick! It looks so nice on you!” Enoka lamented, “I can’t wear bright colors anymore. The royal family frowns on these things, saying I am a lady, not a prostitute! As if I didn’t know how to use colors properly and still look modest!”

Mei looked at the bottom of the lipstick. “Here’s the name of the lipstick.” She showed it to Enoka to read. “I have ten shades and I love them all! I even use the color names as passwords for my cyber accounts!”

Enoka looked shocked, her hand to her chest, “You shouldn’t tell anyone!”

“Why,” Mei shrugged, “I have nothing to hide, Enoka! I believe you need a long hug before we depart!” She hung her purse on her shoulder and got up to embrace the queen.

While Mei hugged the queen, she whispered some things for the queen’s ear only. Enoka looked surprised and was about to speak. Before Enoka could speak, Ladya put her finger to her mouth, forming the “shush” on her lips, and pointed to the phone that Mei purposefully left on the couch. Enoka got the message and smiled. Mei and Ladya said their farewells and departed.

Curious, the queen picked up the phone and entered the password that Mei showed her. She read the entire message from the Brotherhood and the sample of the new edict. Later that night, the queen had planned a special surprise for the king in their bedroom suite. Only, it was not the surprise the king expected.

☞ ☞ ☞

Brother Jotham was driving, praying that he hadn't missed Ladya and Mei as he arrived to pick them up. The girls came out of the palace just as he stopped the car in front. They were smiling widely. As they got in the car, they announced, "Mission accomplished!"

"What a relief!" He replied, "I almost left you stranded here. You wouldn't believe the trouble I went through while waiting for you in the parking lot! If it hadn't been for yesterday's bomb threat, I wouldn't have to go through with this. The palace guards interrogated me three times and each time, I showed them your letter from the queen! One suspicious and unpleasant officer told me to leave because I waited for an hour. I left then came back, only to go through another round of interrogations!"

Mei replied, "We were interrogated too. The palace guards searched our bags carefully, then the security people, even the servants. The queen became frustrated with the waiting and interrupted the servants. The phone that Haro gave us was a perfect disguise. I am sure the queen is reading the message from the Brotherhood now."

Ladya urged them into the car, "Let's go!"

☞ ☞ ☞

And above the palace, Griop watched gleefully with another minion named Screep. They caused much havoc in the royal household, starting with the bomb threat of the previous day. None of the troubles had reached past the door of the queen's private room while she entertained her guests. The servants were fighting with each other, the chef almost burned the dinner, the dogs were constantly barking and driving people crazy because of the fight, and the security was so overdone. Everyone was so stressed that a few people snapped, even the usually reserved butler. And the royal family was too busy sorting out the problems with their household that they never paid attention to the queen. The fiasco continued well into the night. That night changed the destiny of Indigor.

The minions realized their mistakes and didn't want to

face Locitan until Sarotten found them and forcibly threw them at his feet. Again.

The battle between the angels and Locitan's army finally ended. The Elders received visions of the accomplished mission. The next day, when the people clicked on the daily world news, the Good News appeared instead. They learned about Indigor's genuine history and the Holy Writings.

The Biters could not find the source of the information to remove it. That same day, the king made a public announcement about the new edict to all the people of Indigor, proclaiming from this day forth that the Holy Writings would be freely available to all. The king's speech became famous for years to come.

From that day, the Indigans could access the Holy Writings on their devices, and discovered that they were not the only humans in the galaxy. They had hope where there was none. For many days to come, it was all they could talk about.

Haro, Jamik, Ladya, and Mei continued to get together to give thanks to the Creator. And the floating village went back to its rightful home on Kristalis.

CHAPTER THIRTEEN

SWEET FELLOWSHIP

But it is you, my equal,
my companion and friend.
Together, we shared sweet fellowship.
We walked with the crowd of worshippers
in the house of Yehovah.
~The Complete Psalms

KRISTALIS, LAST DAY OF SEMESTER

The Aliyah Academy had flown back to planet Kristalis after the victorious spiritual battle. For the next weeks, Daleah continued her classes. On the last day of the semester, she wrote the last entry in her academy journal.

19314.12.30
Tomorrow we are all going home! I will miss the
Academy and my friends. It was a wonderful
spiritual adventure! We began walking together in

*the barren wilderness and arrived at a place
teeming with life. Our victory has restored the Holy
Writings to the people of Indigor. They are aware of
the Creator and other life in the galaxy. We have
accomplished our mission. We are having a special
gathering today at the ancient place that I visited
two years ago.*

Hundreds of Academy students were flying together with their professors on their Lipicans. They appeared like swiftly shifting clouds in the azure sky. The young Seraphies flew amidst the students, their wings well suited for the serene weather of Kristalis. Shanielle and Elizon were in the lead. Daleah flew on her favorite Lipican, Liberty. She laughed as Rory caught up with her, grinning with his sharp teeth, his mane flattened by the current. They flew over rainbows dancing in the mist of the geysers. They landed smoothly at their destination, a curious place with moss-covered ruins. As they dismounted, the Lipicans seemed curiously drawn to Rory and the other Seraphies, being used to humans and Elders.

Daleah remarked to Rory, "Strange how Liberty and the other Lipicans are drawn to you and your friends. She didn't act like this the first time I met her. Lipicans will shy away from new humans. Not so with you!"

Rory replied, surrounded by the Lipicans. "They are telling me they missed me, even though I only met them today." He patted Liberty's neck with his paws, grinning in delight.

"So you can definitely talk to them telepathically, like the Elders?" Daleah asked.

Professor Elizon overheard the conversation and said, "Their behavior has something to do with an ancient memory. I will explain later." He let Blazer go, freeing him from his strap. "All right, students, please gather here! Let's sit on the grass." Everyone sat down except

Elizon. He stood up, stepping onto a large block of rock covered in moss.

"You see these rocks here? See how they still keep the shape of round pillars and square blocks? This place used to be an ancient Seraphi civilization. Now, these buildings are all that's left before the Seraphies moved en masse to Serfaretz. I would like to invite Rory to tell us about this place."

Rory stood up to speak as Elizon stepped down from the moss-covered rock. "When the Elders first discovered these ruins, they contacted us. We had to research the history behind this place because it is far older than my father or grandfather. What you see is the remains of the Seraphi civilization, much like your cities. We dismantled most of it, but we did not have enough time to finish before Lucifer came to search for us. According to my ancestors who have long memories of this place, these ruins belonged to the residences of the Seraphi royal guards, responsible for protecting the families of the first ruling councilors. These guards were the last Seraphies to leave the planet."

Elizon spoke, "Thank you Rory for this brief explanation. Now, you had some questions about the Lipicans' reactions to the Seraphies. Can you tell us more about that?"

"When the Seraphies moved to Serfaretz, we had to leave our friends behind. We had a symbiotic relationship with the creatures here, especially all the flying species. This was the one thing that we missed. We didn't call them Lipicans. The reason they are drawn to us is that they still remember us. They are delighted that we are back here!" He ended with a grin, sharp teeth showing, and his whiskers fluttering in delight.

Then Elizon announced, "Let's worship our Creator!" Moralee lifted the guitar she had been carrying on her back. She began strumming a lilting melody, singing with an exquisite voice that carried throughout the forest. Elizon joined her and sung in a joyful baritone voice. And everyone else joined in, clapped, and danced in a large circle with joyful steps.

> *All of heaven worship you and all earth sing*
> *   praises to you.*
> *The mountains and the hills burst into songs to*
> *   their Creator.*
> *Halleluyah!*
> *Every creature on earth and under the sea sing*
> *   praises to you.*
> *All the trees of the field clap their hands to your*
> *   name most high.*
> *Halleluyah!*
> *All the nations bow down and worship Him who*
> *   sits on the throne.*
> *The rivers roar and foam and the seas rise their*
> *   waves.*
> *Halleluyah!*
> *Adonai reigns forever!*
> *All of creation worship you!*
> *Halleluyah!*

KRISTALIS, A MONTH LATER

Daleah was lounging on her own bed at home, scribbling away in her journal. Lupel was laying next to her, his pointed ears twitching at the noise of her pen scratching on the paper. He missed the sound of her voice when she was transcribing into her tablet. His tail, however, told a different story. It was wagging because he was happy she was home.

19314.2.1

So much had happened since I said my farewells to my Academy friends. I hardly had time to sit down and write about my experience during the student exchange program! It has been an awesome privilege to get to know Rory, Mona, Soraya, and Nataniel on Serfaretz. They seemed more relaxed and open in their environment. I got to see a side of that homeworld I have never seen. I used to think

Daleah couldn't help thinking, *Thank goodness the ceiling is high enough for my tall friends!* The first time Daleah's little quadruplet brothers saw the Seraphies, their eyes bulged, and they stared at them open-mouthed for a while. After warming up to them, the quads couldn't stop their inquisitiveness.

Rory and his three companions were bouncing the quads in their arms, and the quads wouldn't stop squealing with delight. The Seraphies were tireless, patient, and perfectly happy to indulge her little brothers. Daleah was happy to let them. She felt relaxed.

Isaiah, the oldest of the quads, with his big hazel eyes and chubby cheeks, asked Rory as he pointed at his two wings, "Why wing, wing?"

Ezekiel interrupted, "Rory is lion bird! Mona is cow bird!"

Hoshea added, "Soraya is real bird with feathers!"

Malachi questioned, "Nataniel is angel. Can you fly?"

Rory, Mona, Soraya, and Nataniel laughed at the adorable toddler talk. They let Rory answer the boys. "Yes, little humans, we can fly high with our wings!"

They squealed and jumped on the Seraphies' laps again. Isaiah asked, "You fly me!"

Ezekiel interrupted, going to Mona, the bovine Seraphi, "You fly me, too!"

Hoshea added, taking Soraya's feathery hand, "Fly, fly, fly up to Halo!" He pointed his little chubby finger at the Halo outside.

Malachi spoke while grabbing Nataniel's rugged hand, "Fly together!"

The Seraphies turned to look at Daleah. She shrugged her shoulders with hands palm up, "We have to ask my parents' permission to let them fly with you."

Rory said to Daleah, "Our parents used to take us flying when we were young, before we learned to fly. We were strapped to them, so it was safe. It's a pleasant experience for our young."

Daleah nodded and directed her gaze toward her little brothers, bending down to talk to them, "Isaiah, Ezekiel, Hoshea, Malachi, gather here." They obediently came to her. "Remember what I told you, when you want something, you must ask Mama and Papa first. They will be back soon. If you behave, maybe you will go flying with them."

The four of them nodded eagerly, "We be good!"

Later, Rory smiled, showing his sharp teeth, "Why don't we all go outside, and you can watch us fly?"

They went outside toward the children's playground, and the Seraphies flew together while the little boys watched in awe at their beautiful flying dance. It was the first time Daleah understood how harmoniously the Seraphies got along with each other.

When Daleah's parents got back, they discussed the matter. They had doubts at first, then gave their consent on one condition—that the boys be fastened to them safely. The parents permitted the young Seraphies to fly the little boys as high as the top of blue pine forest, but no further.

Daleah watched from the yard as the Seraphies flew with her little brothers strapped to their chests, facing forward, so they could view the lay of the land. They squealed with joy. Daleah captured the episode on her camera. Rory grinned widely as he accepted a copy of the tape. "Thank you, Daleah. We will show it to our parents!" And he cherished those moments as he viewed the recording at his home, time and time again. Daleah kept a copy for herself, watching the Seraphies' dance of wings.

Several days later, Daleah scribbled in her journal again. Lupel was laying next to her, his ears no longer twitching at the scribbling noise. He had gotten used to it.

19315.2.9

> *My family and I had such sweet fellowship with Rory and his companions, breaking bread together and chatting. The Creator has blessed us so abundantly! After the semester is over, the student exchange program will continue. The Seraphies will go to Ankatar, Kato's homeworld next. Then, they will go to Evanglar, Revelyn's homeworld afterward.*
>
> *After they left, the quads missed my Seraphi friends so much, asking for them for many days. Papa called the Academy to find out how to contact the Seraphies' homeworld. There wasn't much we could do. So, Papa took the matter into his own hands and make the first step in establishing satellite communication between our two worlds. We have a satellite stationed outside our solar system for contacting the other colonies, but the Queen has ordered a new satellite stationed within our solar system. Soon we will chat with Rory and his friends. It is another step toward closer relations between*

our races. Ancie Shanielle told me by phone how the Elders at the Academy are excited about the satellite, even though they don't need it for themselves. As Elders, the Spirit of the Holy One carries them anywhere in the universe. The satellite will be for us humans to connect with the Seraphies.

THE ROYAL PALACE, INDIGOR

Haro shifted uncomfortably in his stiff new suit. He was thinking, *How well Mei and Ladya must take pleasure in this! I must endure it. We need the support and blessing of the monarchy if we are to continue to keep our freedom to write.*

While Ladya was excited at the prospect of meeting the royal couple, Mei was in her element. Jamik, however, looked dour and uncomfortable having to listen to Mei's instructions on the proper etiquette for interacting with the royal family. It was driving him crazy. Haro leaned toward Jamik and elbowed him. Jamik grumbled but agreed. "Alright!" He mouthed silently to Haro.

They stood before Mei as she spoke to them, her demeanor confident, "Your formal dress is up to code, therefore you have passed inspection." She was signing and speaking simultaneously, for Ladya's benefit. They were all dressed in their finest semi-formals for the dinner with the royal couple. Haro and Jamik wore their three-piece suits that included a vest, their hair neatly combed and parted in the middle. Ladya and Mei wore their long evening dresses proudly. Their long hair up and expertly coiffed up in intricate knots, their necks adorned with necklaces of small sparkling jewels, with earrings to match.

"Next item on the agenda is how to greet the royal family. The proper address is, 'Your majesty' or 'Your royal highness.' And a good conversation starter is, 'How do you do?' You can't say these words, 'Pleased to meet you.' Don't ask me, as I really don't know." Jamik chuckled.

"Is it funny to you?" Mei stopped to glare at him.

"Not really," Jamik replied, "That's because not everyone is pleased to meet the royals. It feels like an obligation, so they don't say it."

Haro elbowed Jamik, who let out an oof at the jab. Haro said to Mei, "Don't mind him, Mei. Please continue. We need to use whatever time we have left for this lesson."

The room they were in was rich in decor, with lots of elaborate gold, mirrors, and sparkling chandeliers. They had a private suite with adjoining bedrooms.

Mei continued, "You are to refrain from any physical contact unless they offer it. So, no handshaking and definitely no hugging! I am the only one allowed to touch the queen because she is my cousin. Even then she must make the first move. It is proper for men to bend down a little and women to do a small curtsy. Like this." She showed the male bow with one hand behind the back and the other hand resting across her chest. Then she showed Ladya the female curtsy with one foot crossed behind the other, the other knee bending, and head bowed.

Ladya copied the female curtsy while giggling, enjoying herself. Mei looked at Haro and Jamik, waiting with her arms crossed and a haughty look, as if daring them.

Haro obliged and did the head bow. Jamik looked dour and stiff while doing it.

Mei smiled and spoke sweetly, hands on her hips, "Jamik, don't be so stiff and formal. We're supposed to enjoy being in the presence of the royals. They're human like us. We learned from the journal that the royals are symbolic of the Elders. The royals are curious about the Elders too."

Jamik restrained himself from making snide remarks and tried to smile while doing the greeting again.

"And finally," Mei seemed satisfied and smiled sweetly, "the last thing to keep in mind, don't do something unless the royals do it first. Eat only when they eat, stop only when they stop. Talk only when they talk. Rest only when they rest." She paused and signed, "It's done." Then voiced, "You have learned the proper protocol for meeting and greeting the royals. Let's go meet them!"

Haro and Jamik sighed with relief. Jamik leaned toward Haro and whispered to him, "Never would have imagined Mei as a hard taskmaster!"

The four of them walked from their suite through the large hallway of the royal palace. They passed numerous closed doors and arrived at the reception area. A servant bowed to them and said, "Miss Mei Herre, are you and your guests ready to meet the royals?"

"We are! Please show us the way." Mei smiled and answered gracefully, her hands clasped.

He bowed, "Very well, please follow me." And they followed him through another lengthy hallway, also with many closed doors. He let them in, then he left. They entered an ornate dining room with a round table set with the finest dinnerware and gold flatware, surrounded by six ornate chairs. The large crystal chandelier softly illuminated the room, and the tall draped windows were closed for privacy as the sun was setting.

The royal couple was standing beside the door, ready to greet their guests. The king was wearing his suit with a diagonal sash held on his left epaulette, with many shiny military medals pinned to it. To Jamik's surprise, he wasn't wearing his white wig and his hair color was dark blonde. Like many Indigor men, his hair was styled in the popular style of the time—parted in the middle, long sideburns, and a long curled mustache.

The queen was wearing an elegant lavender evening dress that brought out the lovely color of her platinum blonde hair. She spoke warmly, "Darling Mei, so good to see you again!" She took Mei's hand and gave her a peck on each cheek. "I am so glad you all arrived here safely. There are some angry people out there." She was referring to the peaceful protesters outside the palace who were challenging the BITE authority, demanding to stop the oppression. The entire world was in an uproar since the truth of Indigor's origins came out.

"Your royal highness," Mei replied graciously, "We arrived safely yesterday, without a hitch."

The queen turned to the king, her height matching his. "Darling, my cousin Mei, whom you met at our wedding. Mei, please introduce your friends to the King!"

"Good to see you again, Mei." The kind smiled pleasantly as Mei curtsied before him. He was not much for small talk.

Mei stepped close to Ladya and proudly introduced her, "This is my best friend Ladya Victoria Gallant. I wrote to you about her, a wonderful deaf woman who helps me with my schoolwork. Believe it or not, she is smarter than I am!"

Ladya who had been the quietest since they arrived at the palace, curtsied and signed with her hands. "Your royal highness! Me hard believe you look like Mei!"

"Ah," smiled the queen graciously, "so I've been told many times!"

"And," Then Mei pointed her hand at Haro, "this is her brother Haro Lametz Gallant. Haro is the hero who brought the Holy Writings to our people!" Haro bowed his head respectfully, as was the custom. Then Mei pointed at Jamik, "And this is Jamik Bond TaHaven, his best friend." Jamik beamed and bowed his head, first to the king and saying, "Your majesty." Then he bowed to the queen, "Your royal highness." He surprised Mei by transforming into a charming young man.

"Let's adjourn to the table." The king spoke as he welcomed his guests with his hand toward the table.

After they all sat down, the king continued, "I must tell you, it is more of an honor for me to be here with you, especially you, Mr. Gallant. We are eager to hear about your exploits and the exciting things you have learned about our forgotten ancestors. And I promised you, I will do all I can to protect you and your family. No one else knows you are here. I believe my beautiful wife came to me about your secret for such a time as this. The monarchy has always been at odds with the Biters and their goal. When my father was king, the monarch came close to being eradicated by its former leader, Contrero Hadebar, who destroyed many of the Holy Libraries. We can talk freely when the servants are not in the room."

The king pressed a communicator that chimed like a bell. Moments later, the servants brought out the savory food, each plate beautifully crafted, garnished on the side with green leaves, and the sauces drizzled in zigzag patterns. Then the servants left the room.

"This is our first course!" The queen announced with a flourish, "Bon appétit!" Then Haro shared with them what he learned from his father. Later, he reflected on how well the evening went on. Sharing about the Creator with the royals had been sweet fellowship.

KRISTALIS

Immediately after her morning routine, Daleah ran outside to the mailbox tree, her dark blond curly hair bouncing. Lupel was happily following her, his tail wagging. The postal doves had dropped two letters in the mailbox's slot. Daleah opened the mailbox and her heart skipped a beat as she read the return addresses on the envelopes. They were from her friends, Revelyn and Kato. She ran excitedly to her bedroom to get the letter opener, for she was planning on saving the envelopes and keeping the seal intact. After opening, she read Revelyn's letter.

19315.3.16

My dear friend Daleah,

I hope this letter reaches you in time. I enjoyed being at your house. I miss your little brothers and their funny, adorable comments! I miss your furry friends from that endless beautiful forest of blue pines and red maples. Your wolf Lupel is such a softy! I couldn't believe he would let the quads ride on him! Here on Evanglar, our animals have adapted to hide from the constant rain. I spot the occasional moose and bear through my bedroom window. One more month of the rainy season with the constant daily rain, then I will venture out to make some new furry friends!

I asked my parents if I could have siblings soon and I tried to tell them they didn't have to wait until I was twenty something. My suggestion shocked them! Pregnancy happens when it happens, that it's not something planned. If our Creator wills it, He can make it happen sooner. Our bodies are different from that of Old Earth's people, our lives are longer, and so are the length between births. The Creator planned it that way from the beginning. I accept that your family is special. Mama told me that there is no need to rush, that I will continue to live at home when my first sibling is born.

I have gotten used to being back on Evanglar. The sun hides almost every day under the thick cover of clouds. It feels strange to use my umbrella again. Believe it or not, I have so many umbrellas, one each to match the color of my raincoats and boots! This morning was a light rain, so I took my small umbrella. Tomorrow the forecast is for heavy rain and I have my big umbrella ready. We even have umbrella hats for people who have two busy hands!

I think of Kristalis and everything that shines so brightly, and I miss you and our friends. I can't wait for you to visit. There are so many places we can explore. Evanglar has a great variety of recreation and entertainment spots. Because of the constant rain, people have introduced many ways to have fun indoors. Each city in Evanglar has its own indoor "green parks" with a variety of animals, large aquariums, and playgrounds. We might be stuck indoors, but we are hardly bored!

I was busy with homeschooling, trying to catch up on what I missed while I was at the Academy. It's not as exciting as the stuff we learned together. I

*miss our professors. I admire their courage. I can't
wait for your visit. Let's keep in touch!*

    *Love and hugs, your roomie and loving friend,
Revelyn*

Then Daleah read Kato's letter. It was short and sweet and made her smile.

19315.2.30

Dear Freckles,

    *You know me. I am more of a talker than a
writer. My family is happy to have me back home. I
shared with them all that happened at the Academy,
about Kristalis, the Elders, the Seraphies, and about
my new friends. Enoch was here for a week, then
Revelyn came. They were pleasant visits. We enjoyed
the museums and all the "tourist traps" we went to.
Revelyn got a little sunburned, but nothing serious.
My family liked to fuss over her. They asked me why
I kept calling her Black Beauty. I told them it's
because of her beautiful silky raven hair, so unlike
our frizzy hair. Can't wait for your visit. Then Rory
and his companions will be next. Wondering if I
should I refrain from calling you Freckles around
my family?*

    Hugs, your friend Kato.

THE BROTHERHOOD, A YEAR LATER

Haro's training had been fruitful. He was writing his first journal entry with excitement, feeling his heart pounding, and the determination flowing from his heart to his hand.

19316.2.20

*School is over for the summer and I am hiding at
the Brotherhood, getting my first training in
handwriting and journaling. If Dad and Grandpa
were here, they would be proud of me. I will become*

more proficient as I keep writing. The brothers have been very welcoming and caring. I remember my dream about the Holy Writings dissolving into my hand, then into my whole being. It came true. I have absorbed them. I have come a long way since my father's funeral.

The Holy Writings are finally out on Indigor's network. I am learning how to celebrate the Holy Shabbat with the brothers. When I go back home, I plan to celebrate the Shabbat with my family, teaching them how to observe it. I asked the brothers why my father did not observe the Shabbat with the family and they could not provide me with a satisfactory answer. The brothers celebrate with their own families. I believe my father did not observe because of the extra burden of having unusual children, me with my special gift and my deaf sister. Brother Mateo said it should not have been burdensome, but it was. He could see that my sister and I were different and blessed.

One favorable thing came out of my search for the Brotherhood. Paper and pens are being produced and sold on the market since last year. And last month, Indigor has officially added postal mail to our home delivery services. I can finally send letters to my family. Everywhere I go, people are excited about writing on paper with their own hands. Artists are happy to be painting on paper. The king allowed the publication of books because reading is good for our souls and the economy. Since he dismantled the Bureau of Investigation for Technological Enforcement, they have stopped terrorizing the people. Prisoners have been released. The Creator has answered the Brotherhood's prayer—the biting terrors have disappeared!

I am so excited about this afternoon. I am eager for my first meeting with an Elder. And I finally figured out what the numbers at the top of the

Elizon was carried away in the Spirit to the Brotherhood in Indigor. He arrived facing the entrance door and knocked. Brother Mateo answered.

Elizon greeted Mateo cheerfully, "Greetings, Mateo!"

"Elder Elizon, good to see you again! Our new brother is here! And what's up with this door knocking again? You don't have to teleport outside our door."

Elizon spoke as he bent down to walk through a door that was much shorter than him, "I know, human customs are hard to shed. I am being polite. Will I not startled you if I suddenly teleported too close?"

"Nothing surprise me these days, my friend." Mateo answered. "Haro is excited about meeting you. Let me get him for you."

Mateo walked to the "quiet room" used for scribing. Haro looked up and immediately knew the Elder was here. He stood up to follow Mateo. He said, "Just a minute, Brother Mateo. How do you greet an Elder?"

Mateo looked perplexed. "What do you mean?"

Haro replied, "Last year, I met the king and queen and we had to follow some standard protocol for greeting and meeting them."

Mateo understood and chuckled, "No, Brother Haro, no need! Greet him as you would a friend and he will treat you the same way!"

As Haro walked into the reception room, he saw the tallest man he had ever seen, with long white hair tied at the back. His first thought was, *Wow! He hardly looks like an Elder. How is this man supposed to be thousands of years old? He looks to be in his twenties!*

Elizon knew what Haro was thinking. He was used to humans' initial reaction upon seeing an Elder for the first time. He smiled and extended his hand in greeting. They shook hands. Elizon's warm hand flowed toward his arm, toward his heart.

"Haro," Elizon spoke first, "I am glad you are here with the Brothers. They mentioned wonderful things about you! Let's go to the conversation room. Brother Mateo, please join us too." Haro had to crane his neck to look at the Elder. He seemed at a loss for words as Elizon shepherded him to the room, with a smiling Mateo in tow.

They sat down on the comfortable couch and chair. Elizon continued, "Haro, I must tell you the reason you have successfully arrived here—because our people have been praying hard for you, for your friends, and your family. Many unique people and circumstances have come together to make this happen. We had an Old Earth saying, 'Thing can happen with the right people, at the right time, and the right place.' That's how it was with you. There is so much I must tell you, even Brother Mateo has not heard yet."

Haro was quiet, slightly awed by the Elder. Elizon was patient. Finally Haro said, "You meant the Holy Writings are finally getting out to our people?"

"Yes, Haro, you understand perfectly. The Holy Writings are the precursor of many wonderful changes, of dreams to be realized, of hope to be fulfilled, and blessings to follow. Through the Writings, the people will get to know who the Creator is. Already, we are hearing their prayers. Many are asking for wisdom and understanding. Now, let me ask you a question, do you know who Locitan is?"

"I've heard, but I haven't studied about him in-depth yet."

And beginning with the oldest Holy Writings, Elder Elizon explained what the Holy Writings said concerning the Creator. Haro looked at the Elder with respect, for he repeated the Holy Writings, word-for-word, with perfect memory recall, without searching in a book. As he spoke of the Creator and his wonderful love for all creation, Elizon seemed to glow. Haro felt like he was taking a trip through time, seeing with the eyes of the

Elders. He felt a peacefulness descend on him, something he had never experienced in his young life. And before Elizon left, he proclaimed the Aaronic blessing over Haro.

> *Y'simeich Elohim k'Efrayim, v'che*
> *   Menasheh*
> *Y'varechecha Adonai v'yish'merecha*
> *Ya're Adonai panav eliecha vichuneka*
> *Yisa Adonai panav eliecha v'yasem l'cha*
> *   shalom*

> *May Elohim make you like Ephraim and*
> *   Manasseh.*
> *May Adonai bless you and guard you.*
> *May the light of Adonai shine on you.*
> *May Adonai be gracious to you.*
> *May the presence of Adonai be with you,*
> *And give you peace.*

THE VOID ABOVE INDIGOR

After his defeat, Locitan became enraged for weeks, his minions cowering and shamed before him, afraid to say anything to him that might set off another round of curses at them. After he calmed down, he called everyone together. Woevil, Vexid, and Griop and all his other minions were assembled. Thousands and thousands of them assembled in the void above Indigor.

"I have a plan. The Biters are passé and no longer useful. We will work through another group, those who are unhappy with the recent changes. From there, we will conquer through their fear and uncertainty. You will all go out and find individuals who have sin crouching at the door of their hearts, ready to wreck life. You will manipulate them and push them to the edge, then you will get them together to plan against our enemies. This is the first step. I will inform you at the next meeting how to implement the next strategies. Report back to me when you have accomplished this first step. Is that understood?"

His minions all responded with, "Aye, aye, chief!"

Woevil, Vexid, Griop, and Screep were happy to do his bidding for a change, instead of cowering before him.

As they left, Woevil remarked, "Finally, we have a new plan in place. I don't know what took so long!"

Vexid nodded in agreement, "Yeah! I hate the smell of desperation! It stinks! Let's get our work done." The negative emotions caused the minions' bodies to stink. While they stunk to high heaven, the prayers and praises of the righteous Elders and their students ascend like sweet smelling incense into the heavenly realm of the Father.

Griop added, "I have some idea where to start. Follow me!" And they all zoomed in toward the planet, pleased and ready to do their evil master's dirty work with glee.

THE LIGHTHOUSE, A MONTH LATER

The meeting had begun a while ago. Elder Elizon opened his report with excellent news. "I am overjoyed to report that the Indigans have reopened factories for producing pens and papers. The Holy Writings are finally available in books. In conclusion, there is a great revival across the land. The Biters are becoming a thing of the past." He paused.

"Recently, the Creator sent me a vision—of a purple sphere caught in a storm, and a visit from the messenger, Alaniel. He informed me that Locitan has visited our Supreme King for permission to stir up a new tempest, to prey on the souls of angry men who are lusting for power. I will receive more information on my next visit to Indigor. I ask for your prayers again."

The chief councilor Saludel replied, "We know this was inevitable. The prophecies were clear. The end of Locitan's reign is near. Our Supreme King will return to Indigor some day, to restore all things the people have lost, and the Elders will in charge once again."

And the council held an intense prayer meeting before the Spirit carried them back to their homes.

LET GO AND LET GOD

When writing, nothing is more essential
than to let go of the world,
And let the God of the Creation work through you.
~Elder Shanielle, The Guide to Journaling

KRISTALIS, 9 YEARS LATER

Daleah had finished packing her suitcases and carried her luggage out of her bedroom. Her four brothers, the Quads, had been waiting for her in the family room, along with her parents. Isaiah, Ezekiel, Hoshea, and Malachi were all grown up, smiling and serene. They looked perfectly identical, but the family had learned to tell them apart as they developed distinct personalities. Soon, it will be their turn to go begin their first spiritual studies at an Academy. As Daleah dragged her luggage, the Quads went up to her.

Isaiah was the first to speak, being the oldest, "Here, let us carry your luggage outside."

Out of the blue, a memory came to mind. Daleah stood there, unmoving and hesitant. She remembered a time when the Quads had messed up her suitcase.

Ezekiel was holding the handle of her other suitcase, but she wasn't letting it go. He looked in puzzlement at his brother Isaiah.

"Daleah? Did you forget to pack something?" Hoshea asked, observing that she wasn't moving or answering.

"Halo Daleah? Are you fully awake?" Malachi asked jokingly, waving his hand in front of her face.

Daleah shook her head, realized it was an old memory that had nothing to do with the present. She sighed and said, "I've not forgotten anything. I'm ready as ever. Let's go." Years of traveling to the Academy taught her to prepare well. Packing her suitcases had become easy as a breeze. She let go of her suitcases and let her brothers carry them.

The entire family stood in front, waiting for the hover shuttle to take Daleah to the Academy. Daleah looked at her brothers, amazed at how they turned out, so different from that time long ago when she swore that she would have a good time without them. They had outgrown the "terrible three" stage, or the "terrible three four," as their father jokingly said. They grew up and turned out to be well behaved. For the first time, she felt like she would miss them. She smiled as the hovering craft landed, ready for another spiritual adventure with her old friends, Revelyn, Kato, and Rory.

KRISTALIS, 4101 YEARS LATER

Inside the Aliyah Academy, an Elder sat at his desk in his office. He was passionately scribbling, dipping his feathered quill into an ornate bottle of ink. He finished jotting and laid the paper on the tall pile of handwritten papers. He picked up a blank paper from the shorter pile and scribbled again. The view of his window showed the glorious ring sparkling in the azure sky, but he paid no attention to it. His thick white wavy hair shadowed his youthful face as he kept scribbling away. He could not let go until it was done.

A female Elder walked into his open office, standing at the door, her white curly hair flowing down her shoulders and gold-striped mantle. He hadn't heard her come in. She stood there, tapping her foot a few times. He still didn't hear her. He was too absorbed in his writing. A slight frown appeared on her youthful face. She cleared her throat and made a slight noise, "Ahem." Still no response.

Finally, she interrupted him, knocking at his open door, "Professor Haro, I'm sorry to interrupt, but it's time to meet your new students. They will arrive soon."

Haro replied, not bothering to look up, "I am almost finished."

"What is so important that you have been writing so intensely all week? Do you realize it's the first day of the semester?"

"Professor Daleah, I do realize! What do you think I am writing about? A fantasy or a science fiction novel? Or the adventures of Haro the hero?" He replied, still consumed by his scribbling.

"What an amusing title! You certainly aren't writing a fantasy book here in this school! Our stories should be real."

Haro waved his unoccupied hand, not looking up. He replied, "I know, Daleah, I was jesting, but seriously, we do not need another Elder Chronicle! We have enough of these books to fill an entire planet!" Still scribbling, he said, "If you must know, it's the *Chronicles of Indigor*. Please go announce to the new students that I will be there soon."

Shaking her head, hands on her hips, Daleah realized Haro was not letting go of his work. "Humph!" She exclaimed and turned to head back toward the classroom, her long curly hair bouncing and swinging across her back, her white garment billowing. Her face didn't reflect annoyance. She was smiling widely, happy that Professor Haro was finally writing the book he had longed to write. She had long hoped he would, because she had played a big part of his story. It felt like yesterday but it was four millennia ago. She had seen the high pile of finished papers on his desk. They were ready to be folded, threaded, and bound into a book.

Haro wrote as fast as he could, feeling the Spirit of the Holy One pushing him to the brink of a breakthrough. Then he straightened and jotted down the dot at the end of the line with a flourish, the feather of his quill quivering in the air. His face changed and brightened to a radiant smile. He was finished. And thus, begins the story of Indigor, a lonely planet with a purple sky.

☞ GLOSSARY ☞

Adonai: The Hebrew word for Lord.

Aliyah: To go up, also the name of a floating village above Kristalis.

Ancie: An ancestress.

Ancit: An ancestor.

BITE: The Bureau of Investigation for Technological Enforcement.

Biters: Officers who work for BITE.

Clion: A small white lion with wings.

Crown City: Capital of Kristalis.

Descie: A female descendant.

Descit: A male descendant.

Elder: A person who was once human, who received a new body at the time of the resurrection. This term comes from the "twenty-four Elders of Revelation."

Elohim: Hebrew word for God.

Halo: The white ring of the planet Kristalis.

Indigans: The inhabitants of Indigor.

Indigor: The name of Haro's homeworld, named after the purple or indigo flower.

Indipolis: A city in Indigor.

Josephites: Descendants of the tribe of Joseph.

Judahites: Descendants of the tribe of Judah, also another word for Jews.

Kristalians: Inhabitants of Kristalis.

Kristalipolis: The name of the largest city on Kristalis

Kristalis: The first and oldest world in the Milky Way galaxy.

Lipican: A horse with wings, named after Lipizzans of Old Earth.

Mishkan: The Tabernacle.

New Earth: The new world after the old order passed away, after the Millennium.

Nova Zion: New Jerusalem.

Old Earth: Day one of the Creation until the end of the Messianic Millennium.

Ruach Kodesh: The Holy Spirit.

Seraphi: The inhabitants of Serfaretz, descendants of the mighty Seraphim.

Seraphies: Plural of Seraphi.

Seraphim: A classification of angelic beings.

Serfaretz: Another planet in the Kristalis solar system, inhabited by Seraphim.

Shul: Synagogue, also German for "school."

Tallit, tallitot, tzitzit: A white prayer shawl with corner fringes called tzitzit. Tallitot is plural for tallit.

Torah: The first five books of the Bible, the Writings of Moshe.

Yehovah: The name of the Creator.

Yeshua: The name of the Messiah and Savior.

Yochanan: Hebrew word for John.

☞ **THE STORY** ☞

Under the Purple Sky is a coming-of-age epic fantasy that spans the vast eternity of space and time, across millennia and worlds and generations. Daleah is a young disciple in her teens, an innocent child of the Light, who travels to a high place for her spiritual studies. She learns from the Elders, a race of ancients, one of whom is an ancestor, and encounters other teens like herself. Together, they embark on a spiritual adventure where they stumble into the unexpected. They see glimpses of an unusual world, of something unpleasant that has eluded their people. Will these glimpses be a hindrance to their quest for spiritual maturity? Or will they gain much sought after wisdom? In another faraway world, shrouded in darkness, lives another teenager. Haro faces an unexpected discovery and embarks with his friends on an adventure in their search for a hidden place. The perspective shifts between these two groups as they face the same challenges under different circumstances. And the ancient Oracles of Zion are their best link for holding on to the Spirit of the Holy One.

☞ THE AUTHOR ☞

V. C. Cheney grew up in a conservative Jewish family of Sephardic descent. At 19, she underwent a dramatic spiritual transformation when she accepted Yeshua HaMashiach (Jesus the Christ) as her Jewish Messiah. She graduated with a Bachelor of Social Work and worked in the social services for eight years. As a talented pyrography (wood-burning) artist and acrylic painter, her work appeared on *Switched at Birth,* an American teen drama television series on the ABC Family network. She founded Signs and Wonders, a ministry blog in 2010. She became an ordained minister under the Full Gospel Fellowship of Churches and Ministers in 2011. She currently teaches Torah to passionate Bible students and is the author of *Torah Study: His Story,* a workbook for the one-year online course from MYID, the Messianic Yeshiva Institute of the Deaf.

When she is not busy being a helpmate to her husband, she teaches and leads worship in American Sign Language to Deaf groups. Other times, she nurtures her passion for writing. She kicks off her shoes, drinks her favorite herbal tea, opens her laptop, and transforms into a raconteur who weaves Biblical truths into epic fantasy tales. She grew up in a Jewish family of storytellers and has a fascination with Jewish parables. Her vision is to write new parables with a modern literature slant to bring people closer to Yeshua HaMashiach. She lives with her husband in Sarasota, Florida, and has two older children.

Under the Purple Sky is her debut novel. In the works is a prequel, *Under the Halo: A Collection of Short Stories.*

Website: www.vccheney.com
Email: author@vccheney.com
Page: www.mewe.com/p/vccheney2
Profile: www.linkedin.com/in/v-c-cheney-8540b556/
Ministry site: www.signswondersministry.com

www.ingramcontent.com/pod-product-compliance
Lightning Source LLC
Chambersburg PA
CBHW071509110726
47908CB00003B/779